THE HOTEL

PAMELA KELLEY

Ebook ISBN 9781953060105

As always, a huge thank you to Cindy Tahse. Also to Jane and Taylor Barbagallo, Amy Petrowich, and Laura Horah.

A special thank you to Suzanne Matthews for answering my many questions and sharing her experience in hotel management.

CHAPTER 1

"Coconut shrimp?" The tuxedo-clad waiter held out the silver platter of plump shrimp that were lightly battered, coated with toasted coconut and fried to a golden crisp. Paula never said no to coconut shrimp. She took two and a paper napkin.

"Thank you, Tony."

The server nodded and wandered off to the next guest. Paula ate her shrimp and took a sip of chardonnay as she glanced around the event and back at the hotel itself. Everything was going beautifully, so far. About a hundred and twenty people were sipping cocktails and nibbling on passed hors d'oeuvres before heading into the hotel ballroom for the dinner part of the wine tasting.

It was a perfect night. A warm, early May evening with soft breezes coming off the shore. If Paula turned, she could watch the sun set over Nantucket Harbor. But her attention was focused on the people milling about. She thought, not for the first time, when they'd held events on the front lawn that it reminded her of The Great Gatsby. The rolling lawn was so expansive and green. The crowd attending the event was elegantly attired—the women in flowing dresses, the men in expensive suits and in the distance, there was a well-dressed family playing croquet.

This event was the most desired of the many events that happened during the Nantucket Wine Festival. All week, various dinners and wine-related events took place at restaurants all over Nantucket. That was in addition to the wine festival itself, which was a fun event, an afternoon or evening of roaming around and tasting hundreds of wines. Of all the wine dinners, the one at The Whitley Hotel, was the most expensive and sold out the fastest.

Paula glanced at the time on her phone. She was waiting for her grandfather to arrive. She'd offered to pick him up at the airport, but he wouldn't hear of it and insisted she send one of the hotel drivers. He knew she was knee-deep in financials as they were bringing in some kind of a consultant and he'd asked her to pull years of financial data to send to him. He hadn't explained what the consultant was going to do with the information, but that was fairly typical too. She knew he'd reveal his plans when he was ready to. Her grandfather always had a flair for drama. He'd texted her an hour ago that his plane had been delayed and again she offered to come get him, but he insisted that she stay and keep an eye on the event. She wasn't in charge of it, that wasn't her role at the hotel, but he trusted her to be there and to help out if needed.

Paula could see that the catering team had everything under control. She was surprised that her cousin Andrea who was the hotel's general manager, wasn't there—though, she supposed that's why her grandfather had insisted that she stay. Somehow, he always knew everything that was going on, even when he wasn't around. She guessed that he and Andrea had been in touch earlier.

Of all her many cousins, Andrea was her least favorite. She was much more assertive and bossier than Paula, who was reserved and content in her back-office role at the hotel. Her office was next to her grandfather's, and she handled all the accounting and financials for the hotel. But because they'd all grown up working there, she'd held just about every other role over the years too, from cleaning the rooms as a teenager to serving in the restaurant and working at the front desk, checking people in.

When she'd graduated from Amherst College with a business degree, she'd spent a few years working at a big hotel in Boston in their finance department, before returning to Nantucket. She'd wanted to work at the hotel right after graduating, but her grandfather had insisted that she work elsewhere for a few years, and experience living in Boston as a young person. She smiled, remembering how firm he'd been about it. She'd agreed, but she'd known even then that she'd return to Nantucket, and to The Whitley. How could she not?

Although she had to admit, as usual, that her grandfather had been right. It was a good experience working in Boston at one of the big hotel chains. Like The Whitley, the hotel she worked for there was focused on offering luxury and superior customer service. She learned a few things during her time there that they then implemented at The Whitley. And after three years of living and working in Boston, she was more than ready to go home.

Boston was fun, but it wasn't Nantucket. It was hard to explain to people who hadn't been to Nantucket, but Paula always breathed a sigh of relief when she drove over the Cape Cod canal, leaving Boston behind. And then again, when she boarded the ferry in Hyannis, and they set off to Nantucket. The air felt fresher, cleaner somehow on Nantucket and it was just home.

Her mother, of course, had been thrilled when Paula decided to move home and work at The Whitley. Both of her parents had worked there over the years. Her father was first, managing all the grounds. And it's where he met her mother, when she worked at the front desk one summer break while in college. It was love at first sight for her father, but her mother took a bit longer. But by the time she graduated from college though, she'd fallen madly in love too and they married a few months later.

Her mother returned to the hotel, working the front desk until she had Nick, the first of their three children. Paula was next, and then Lucy, the baby. That's when her father shocked everyone, especially her grandfather, by announcing that he was leaving The Whitley to open his own landscaping business. Her grandfather was upset at first, as he'd hoped his children would love the hotel as much as he did, but he quickly came around and understood that her father wanted more. He wanted to grow his own business. And he had. Whitley Landscaping was the biggest lawn company on Nantucket, and The Whitley was one of its key accounts.

Her brother and sister both worked at the hotel too. Nick was the assistant chef, under Roland, who'd been head chef since Paula was a small child. It was understood that someday, when Roland was ready to retire, Nick would take over. Nick was magically talented in the kitchen and he was the reason why Paula wasn't worried about this event at all. Lucy was a different story. She was a sweetheart and everyone loved her, but she was a bit flighty and even though she did a decent enough job working at the front desk, welcoming guests and checking them in, Paula sensed that to her, it was just a job.

Lucy was the artsy one in the family. She liked to paint and create things—jewelry, clothing, hand-painted wine glasses, and wood furniture—whatever struck her fancy. Paula had encouraged her to do something with it, to open a shop on Etsy or maybe put some of her creations with local shops, and until recently, Lucy had resisted. She'd said she wasn't ready, and it was all just for fun. But, Paula sensed that she was she was trying to come to a decision about something. And she wondered if Lucy was ready to treat her hobby like a business.

But then Paula told herself that she might be imagining things and over-analyzing as usual, though her grandfather considered that a strength. Paula loved analysis, to take in information, process it, and consider a solution or to dream about possibilities. She'd had a few ideas over the years that she'd tentatively presented to her grandfather, always wondering if she might be dreaming too big, and her ideas were too silly and far-fetched. But her grandfather had always listened and seriously considered them. He didn't take every suggestion, but he liked some of them and was impressed when they implemented her ideas and they were successful. And he always encouraged her to 'keep them coming'.

So, to Paula, she really had her dream job. She liked being invisible, behind the scenes, but still doing work that mattered. And even though her grandfather was almost eighty, he was still so smart and full of energy. In addition to The Whitley, he also had other related business holdings in Boston and New York. There was a company that made linens specifically for the hotel industry and another company that rented them. In addition, he owned office buildings in both Boston and New York and had many tenants in both cities. He'd built quite an empire—and over the years, Paula had taken on overseeing the financials for all of it. Not the day-to-day accounting, but each month, a detailed report was sent to her from each business and she analyzed and summarized it for her grandfather.

Still, as she looked around, Paula was surprised that Andrea wasn't there. She usually loved these kinds of events. She loved mingling with the guests and having everyone know that she was a

Whitley and as general manager, that she was in charge. She treated Paula somewhat dismissively as if she was just a back-office AP clerk and she herself was miles above her. Paula had never been impressed by titles and she'd never aspired to a role like Andrea's. It was too visible, and Paula had never craved the need to be 'in charge'. She was very happy in her role. So, she always wondered what Andrea's problem was.

But then she considered that Andrea had always liked to try and push Paula around. They were the same age and should have been best friends, but instead, Andrea was a bit of a bully at times. For some reason that Paula could never quite understand, she'd bounced back and forth from being a fun friend to seemingly jealous over an imagined slight. It grew to be exhausting and in high school, Paula finally had enough and pulled back from having much to do with Andrea aside from family gatherings where she had no choice.

But Paula had to admit that Andrea's aggressive qualities had helped her be mostly effective as general manager. Paula kept her distance, aside from their weekly leadership meetings where she distributed the financials to Andrea, Nick and her cousin Hallie who led the sales department. Her grandfather presided over those meetings and Paula usually just kept quiet and listened as Nick reported on the restaurant side of the business, Hallie reported on new meetings and events that were booked, and Andrea gave an overview on the front desk and general operations.

Paula enjoyed the meetings as it was interesting to listen to everyone's perspectives. Her own report generally consisted of a handout with the financials that no one except her grandfather and Hallie did more than glance at. Numbers were of no interest to Nick. Hallie liked seeing how sales impacted the bottom line and Andrea generally had little interest in the meticulous spreadsheets, graphs and detailed financial summaries that Paula prepared. Like Nick, she seemed bored by data.

But she liked to talk and to tell them all about her various successes no matter how small. Paula listened but often found herself drifting off as Andrea rambled on and on. Her grandfather often had to interject to keep things moving along. Now that she thought of it, Paula hadn't actually seen Andrea since yesterday morning, before her grandfather left for his overnight trip to his New York office. Maybe she had the day off? Though the timing seemed odd, with one of their biggest events happening. One that Andrea normally would never miss.

"Did you save me a coconut shrimp?" The familiar, teasing voice surprised Paula. Her grandfather had snuck up on her while she was sipping wine and staring out at the ocean, lost in her thoughts.

"You made it!" She pulled him in for a hug and a kiss on the cheek. "Do you want something to drink? I was just about to get another glass of wine."

He made a face. "You know I hate that stuff." Her grandfather rarely drank and never wine. But once in a while he indulged. "Although, I think I will have a Kahlua Sombrero as we have something to celebrate. When you come back, let's find somewhere to sit and chat."

He looked excited and Paula wondered what he was up to. His trips to the New York office were usually pretty uneventful. Paula went to the service bar that was set up on the lawn, specifically for this event, and ordered their drinks. When she returned, she found her grandfather seated at a small cocktail table, away from the crowd, happily eating a stuffed mushroom with several coconut shrimp waiting for him.

"Have a seat. Have another shrimp. I got extra. I know they're your favorite."

Paula reached for a shrimp and they chatted for about ten minutes as her grandfather brought her up to speed on his trip. There was nothing unusual about it. When he finished his summary, he waved a server over who had a platter of pate on baguette slices and took one for each of them. He took a bite and then shocked her with his news.

"I let Andrea go yesterday, before I left for New York. That's why I wanted you to be here."

"What happened?" The news was so unexpected. Andrea had been in the role for nine years. Paula and just about everyone, especially Andrea, assumed she'd be there forever.

"Lots of little things that added up to a problem that can't be fixed. It's who she is." He told Paula about the complaints from employees that had come in over the years. How he'd given her so many chances to change, and to do better.

"She's only gotten worse. And it's impacting the business in a negative way. Cassie came in yesterday morning and resigned and that was it, the last straw."

"Cassie quit?" Cassie had worked for The Whitley for close to twenty years. Everyone loved her. She had started as a server, then grew to service manager of the restaurant, and to director of catering. She oversaw all meetings and events.

"She tried to quit. I finally got her to admit that the reason was Andrea. She took a job in Boston, because of course there's no other comparative job here on Nantucket. But she was miserable about leaving. She said it was the hardest decision she'd over made, but she felt like she had no choice."

"Because of Andrea. How awful," Paula said.

"Unacceptable is what it is." Her grandfather looked stern and disappointed at the same time. "I asked her to please reconsider and I promised that she wouldn't have to worry about Andrea anymore. She was hesitant, but once I assured her that she would have no interaction with Andrea at all, she agreed to stay."

"She loves Nantucket. I can't see her being happy in Boston," Paula said.

"And she does a fabulous job here. I didn't want to lose her."

"How did Andrea take it?"

"Not well. She doesn't see it. And you have no idea how many chances I've given her. It's a shame. But it's done now. I did offer her something else of course. She can be charming, when she wants to be, and she loves Nantucket. I offered her the position of head of concierge services. If she decides to take it, it will work out perfectly as Harry put his notice in last week. He's moving home to Wellesley as his mother needs some help and his wife has never loved Nantucket. She's wanted to move for years."

"Is Andrea going to do it?" Paula also thought it could be a good role for her cousin, as the concierge was like an ambassador, answering questions about the island and suggesting restaurants and other places to visit. It was a social position, which played to her strengths. But Paula imagined Andrea might not be happy and would see it as a demotion.

"I don't know. I hope so. I told her I'd support whatever decision she makes. If she wants to go to Boston and stay in hotel management I'd help with a reference, but I also said I would be truthful on what I feel her strengths and weaknesses are. I hope she'll realize this will be better for her in the long run. I told her that I didn't think her future was in people management. I don't think she liked hearing that though."

"I can imagine. What will you do about the general manager role? Do you have anyone in mind or do we need to call Elaine?" Elaine Humphrey was the hotel industry headhunter they occasionally used for difficult-to-fill positions, when there was no one local who was qualified. Elaine always found them great candidates that were happy to relocate to Nantucket.

Her grandfather smiled and there was a mischievous twinkle in his eyes.

"I have someone in mind. I'd like to offer you the role."

Paula thought she must have heard wrong. "What did you just say?"

"I want you to be the next general manager. I think you're more ready for it than you realize."

"Me? But I'm not general manager material. I've never aspired to that role. I like being in the background, handing the financials."

"I know you do. But you're capable of more. You listen to everything in our meetings and you've had some very good ideas and as you well know, some have worked out well. You're also a lot nicer than your cousin. People like you and I think they will like working for you."

"But I've never done any kind of people management before," Paula protested. She was flattered by her grandfather's confidence in her, but this was way out of her comfort zone.

"Yes, I've thought of that too. I met with a consultant in New York. David Connolly was recommended to me. He's an expert advisor in hotel management and he agreed to come work with you."

"Work with me?" What did that mean? Paula felt a bit like Alice in Wonderland when she stepped through the looking glass and her whole world instantly shifted.

"He's a great guy, and he has family on Nantucket too, so he knows people here. You'll like him."

"When is he coming?" This was all happening too fast for Paula. She was not an impulsive person. She liked to process and digest information before making a decision. Especially a decision this big.

"He'll be here a week from Monday. He just has to wrap up his current engagement."

"Okay. When do you need a decision by? I need to think about this. Maybe you should call Elaine and give her a heads up, just in case."

Her grandfather patted her arm. "I know this seems sudden and maybe a bit overwhelming. But I have every confidence that you will do a marvelous job. But I figured you'd need to sleep on it. Today's Friday. Why don't you take the weekend, make your pros and cons list or whatever you do and then let's talk Monday morning. If you really don't want this, I'll call Elaine then. But I know you can do it."

"Thank you. I'm flattered that you have so much confidence in me. I wouldn't want to disappoint you."

Her grandfather lifted his glass and tapped it against hers. "I don't think that's possible. Unless you say no." He grinned. "I hope we'll have something to celebrate on Monday."

CHAPTER 2

Paula didn't stay for the whole wine dinner. She sat with her grandfather and, once the main meal was served, they were both ready to go. He was tired and she was eager to get home and spend the weekend trying to process what had just happened.

She walked home after saying goodbye to her grandfather. Her house was a small cottage on the outskirts of the hotel property. It was an area that was considered too far from the main property to be attractive to visitors, especially as it lacked the stunning views from the main hotel.

There were very distant views, especially from the second floor and all of the grandchildren had been granted a plot of land when they were young. He'd given all of his children land and it was understood that eventually, the hotel itself and all of his other properties would go to his children and grandchildren. Her grandfather occasionally wanted to talk about his will or even his funeral and Paula would never allow it.

"I don't want to think about a time when you're not here."

"Well, I don't plan on going any time soon, but I like to plan these things. To make sure everything is taken care of. I just told your father that no one will have to worry about my funeral."

"What do you mean?"

"I stopped by the funeral home today and paid for it, picked out my music and everything. There will be no crying at my funeral, no sad music. Just happy memories." He had looked very pleased with himself.

"That's a very thoughtful thing for you to do. But I really don't want to discuss your will or think about any of that."

Her grandfather had laughed. "I was like that at your age. When you get to be older, like me, you think about this stuff more. I just want to make sure it's all done right."

"I'm sure it will be."

Paula smiled at the memory as she reached her cottage. It was on a street with several similar cottages, owned by her brother, sister and her cousins, Andrea and Hallie. They all lived just a stone's throw from each other and within easy walking distance of the hotel, where they all worked. Most of the time, it was convenient to be so near to each other and to the hotel. But sometimes, it was a little too close for comfort. Especially as Andrea's house was just two doors down. Lucy was in the middle of them. Nick and Hallie were across the street.

And Paula worried about Andrea's reaction to her grandfather's decision. She tried to put herself in her cousin's shoes and imagined she was feeling angry, hurt and betrayed and not just by her grandfather. Paula suspected that Andrea might direct some of that frustration her way as well. Paula had considered refusing the job partly for that reason, but she also knew that her grandfather had made up his mind about Andrea. So, if Paula said no, he'd just call the general manager search out to Elaine. He would not reconsider giving Andrea another chance. He'd made that clear.

Paula flipped the light on as she walked through the door and into her small, all-white kitchen. She'd designed it herself and loved the sleek white cabinets, white subway tile backsplash and elegant Carrera marble countertops and island. She poured herself a glass of cold water and smiled as her slightly chubby, cream-colored cat, Chester, sauntered into the room and shot her a glare as he stopped by his empty dish.

"I'm sorry. I didn't intend on being home this late." Paula quickly filled his bowl with wet food and he attacked it like he hadn't been fed in days. She'd left him a bowl of dry food to snack on while she was gone, so she knew he was just being dramatic.

She flopped on her living room sofa, grabbed the remote and turned on the TV. She found a Hallmark movie that was just starting and half-watched it as she thought about how her life was about to change. Did she want it to go in this direction? Did she really have a choice? She knew if she turned the opportunity down that her grandfather would be disappointed in her. And she also knew now that it was in front of her, even though she'd never aspired to being the general manager, if she didn't give it a try, she would always wonder.

Chester hopped up next to her, walked around in a circle a few times then plopped down on her lap. As she petted him, she made her decision. She'd take the job. She didn't want any regrets on what might have been.

***

"Did any of you know that Grandfather was thinking of doing this?" Paula asked her family. They were all gathered at her parents' house for Sunday dinner. It was the one day of the week they usually had off and, whenever possible, everyone gathered to enjoy a meal together and catch up on their week. Her mother was a great cook and loved to have all of her children over.

Today's meal was 'company pot roast' with mashed potatoes and roasted root vegetables. It was an Ina Garten recipe that her mother had made so many times that Paula recognized the rich scent as soon as she'd walked in the door. She put her fork down and looked around the table, waiting for answers. They were oddly quiet, for her family.

Finally, Nick spoke. "Do you mean letting Andrea go? Or offering you the GM role?"

"Either one, but mostly I was curious about if you knew he was thinking about me for the role."

"Well, he didn't say a thing about letting Andrea go, but he did recently ask my opinion on if I thought you'd be interested."

"He did? What did you say?"

Nick grinned. "I told him you'd be terrified, but that you'd probably do a fantastic job. I think you should do it."

Her parents both nodded. "He mentioned it to me too," her

father said. "And I agree with your brother and told him the same thing."

Her mother smiled. "And your father of course told me, and I couldn't be happier for you, honey. It's a big job, but I think you're ready for it. You've done almost every job in the hotel and you have the advantage of knowing the business side better than just about anyone other than your grandfather."

"Thank you. I just truly never even thought about that job, though. I didn't think Andrea would ever leave."

"I don't think she would have," Nick agreed. "But Grandfather did the right thing. No one ever said anything to me directly, but I've overheard some of the kitchen staff muttering about her over the years. Andrea wasn't easy to work with."

"What do you think, honey? Now that you've thought about it, will you accept the promotion?" her mother asked.

Paula nodded. "How can I say no? It's an incredible opportunity. I just had to think about it and process what it would mean. It's going to be awkward with Andrea, though. I feel badly about that."

"Don't feel bad. It has nothing to do with you," her father said. "That's all on her. I agree with your grandfather that the concierge role is a much better fit. Hopefully she will see that too and accept it. It might be a little awkward at first, but it's not a role that has any people management, so she won't be at your weekly meetings anymore. You might be able to avoid her, for the most part."

Paula sighed. "That all sounds good, but I don't think Andrea is going to be easy to ignore. Knowing her, I suspect there might be a good amount of anger directed my way. She probably thinks I orchestrated this with Grandfather."

"She should know you better than that, honey," her mother said.

"She should, but I don't think she ever really has taken the time to know me. She's always seemed resentful for reasons I could never understand."

"Andrea's not a bad person. She's had her issues. Things weren't easy for her when she was younger. You know that," her mother said.

Her mother was referring to when Andrea's father disappeared for almost five years and her mother struggled as a single mother while he was gone. Andrea was in middle school then, around twelve or thirteen. Her grandfather wanted to help, but her mother wouldn't take any handouts and insisted on working long hours at the hotel front desk.

Looking back, that was the beginning of Andrea turning difficult. Paula didn't learn until many years later that Andrea's father had been incarcerated, sent to Cape Cod and sentenced to five years in the Barnstable County jail for possession of drugs with intention to distribute.

"I know. But Hallie is such a sweetheart, and she went through the same thing."

"Everyone is different with how they handle things like that. And as the oldest, Andrea was more aware of what was going on than the others. Tracy said she had a really hard time with it." Paula's Aunt Tracy was best friends with her mother. Paula had often wished that she and Andrea could have a similar close relationship, but it never happened. Hallie, on the other hand, was like a second sister.

"It really is funny how different two sisters can be," she said.

Her mother laughed. "It's true. Look at you and Lucy, the two of you are like night and day as well."

Paula glanced at her sister, who had recently colored the bottom half of her hair a deep purple, had a nose ring and was wearing paint-splattered overalls and a tie-dyed shirt. Paula meanwhile had more of the typical Nantucket preppy look with a clean, crisp light brown long bob and she wore a simple, light pink crew neck cashmere sweater and tan pants. Lucy wore her hair up and took the nose ring out though when she worked the front desk at The Whitley.

She and Lucy were very different, but they also were close. Both of them were laid back and easy-going. Of the three children, Nick was the one that was the most outgoing and energetic.

"She'll come around, I bet. My father is a pretty sharp guy. I think he knows that Andrea will ultimately be more effective and happier in this new role. If she gives it a chance," her father said.

―――――――

A FEW MILES AWAY, A VERY DIFFERENT CONVERSATION WAS happening.

"Did you know about this?" Andrea asked her sister. She and

Hallie were at their parents' house late Sunday afternoon, but no one was cooking. Her mother set out a container of French onion dip and rippled potato chips and poured red wine for Andrea, Hallie and herself, while they waited for Andrea's father to return with pizzas. Andrea hadn't talked to anyone yet about what had happened. She'd been in shock after the meeting with her grandfather and went home and sulked for the rest of the weekend and debated what she wanted to do.

Hallie looked uncomfortable. "No, I didn't have any idea. But I can't say that I'm surprised. Cassie confided that she was going to give notice and I knew Grandfather didn't want to lose her."

That stung. "You thought he'd rather keep her than me? Thanks."

"No! That's not what I meant at all. I just sensed that maybe changes might be coming. I didn't know what that would look like. And he does want to keep you or he wouldn't have offered you the other position. You loved the concierge role when you did it one summer during college."

"Sure, I did. But as you said, that was during college. It's a huge demotion, Hallie. You have to admit that." That's what hurt the most, that she'd be taking such a big step down.

But Hallie didn't see it that way. "I don't think you're right about that. Grandfather kept your salary the same, right?"

Andrea nodded. "As far as I know."

"He's not going to blindside you after the fact. My guess is he sees that role as an important one. It's like you are an ambassador for the business. It's a very visible role. And it's social. It could also be a lot of fun for you. No more pressure."

Andrea thought about that. There were some advantages to the role. Hallie was right about that. But to Andrea, what was most visible about it was the fact that she was no longer the general manager. Would the staff think less of her?

"Paula's behind this. She's always whispering in Grandfather's ear. She's his favorite," Andrea said bitterly.

"It really doesn't seem very fair," her mother agreed.

But Hallie would have none of it. "Paula had nothing to do with this. She doesn't even know if she's going to take the job. She was shocked. She was never after your job, Andrea."

"Well, she has it now. That actually makes me feel worse if it's true."

"I'm just saying, don't be mad at her. None of this is her fault. Grandfather just did what he felt was best for everyone."

"I don't know about that."

"Have you decided what you'll do?" her mother asked.

Andrea sighed. "I don't really have much of a choice, do I? I thought I'd ask Grandfather for a few weeks off before I start. Harry gave a month notice a week ago, so that would give me three weeks to take a break and start sending resumes out. I know the job so there's no training required."

Her mother looked concerned. "So, you'll try for another management job. Will you just focus on Nantucket or look off-island, too?"

"I don't think there's much available here on Nantucket, and everyone knows me as a Whitley. That might not be an easy transition, even if there is anything available. I think I might have to focus on the Boston area, maybe even New York."

"I think you should give the concierge role a real chance first. What if you love it?" her sister asked.

"I'm not ruling anything out. But I need to keep all my options open."

CHAPTER 3

"Lucky you, heading off to Nantucket. You get all the best assignments. Maybe you need an assistant? I just went on the bench, so I'm available."

David Connolly looked up from the computer screen he'd been glued to and saw Bethany, one of the junior consultants standing there, holding a file folder. He knew she was teasing, but he also knew she had a bit of a crush on him and would jump at the chance to be part of his team on Nantucket. Except that he didn't have a team for this assignment. It was just him and it wasn't likely to be a fun trip—though he was glad that the opportunity had come up, otherwise he would have had to use some vacation time to head home to Nantucket.

"No time on this assignment, I'm afraid," he said with a smile. Bethany was a good kid and a talented consultant. But she was barely twenty-three. He was almost thirty-six and preferred to date women closer to his own age. When he dated. That was one downside of the consultant lifestyle. It was hard to maintain a relationship when you traveled as much as he did.

"Oh well. Here's the data you asked for. Michelle asked me to give it to you." She handed him the folder. Bethany left and he flipped open the folder and gave it a quick look. Michelle was his assistant in the New York office and she'd printed out a bunch of research he'd gathered online, as well as the detailed documents and emails that Alvin Whitley had sent to him.

They'd had an interesting meeting when Alvin was in the city and the timing of what he was looking for was ideal for David. He'd agreed immediately and blocked his calendar for the next two months, which was the time period they'd discussed for him to consult with The Whitley and also for him to mentor Alvin's grand-daughter. He'd questioned Alvin hard about that decision.

At first, it didn't make sense that he'd promote someone from a back-office position—especially someone who expressed a desire to remain in the role. But Alvin was persuasive. And he also agreed to respect David's opinion after the two months were up. If David didn't think it was working out with Paula in the role, he wasn't going to hold back from recommending that Alvin go in a different direction. Alvin hadn't been fazed though.

"You haven't met Paula. I'm not worried about that."

DAVID FLEW HOME TO NANTUCKET ON SATURDAY. ALVIN WANTED him to start the following Tuesday. His father was at the airport waiting when his plane landed. It was good to see him, but he looked exhausted.

"Dad, are you feeling okay?"

His father smiled. "I'm fine, now that you're here. It's been a long week. Your mother had a couple of rough days. She knows you're coming though, and she's been better."

"She didn't want to come with you?" His parents almost always came together to pick him up. He didn't care, but it made him worry that things might be worse than his father had let on.

His father hesitated before saying, "She probably would have loved to, but it was easier for me to just run out and to be honest, I needed the break."

"Oh, okay. How is she doing?"

"You'll see soon enough." He sighed. "She's good. She's excited to see you and she's thrilled that you're staying a while."

They arrived home fifteen minutes later. It was a good-sized house with four bedrooms and distant water views. His parents had lived there for as long as David could remember. He'd been born there and had gone to the Nantucket public schools. He tried to picture Paula but couldn't remember her well. She'd been a freshman when he was a senior and even though the high school was small, she'd been younger and they didn't share the same circle of friends.

His father pulled into the garage, and David grabbed his suitcase and followed his father inside. He was surprised that his mother wasn't at the door to greet them. He heard the sound of the television and walked into the living room. He found her there in her recliner, watching a sit-com. She got up when she saw them.

"David! It's so good to see you! Did you have a good flight?" She looked and sounded perfectly fine. It was a relief to see her familiar, friendly face. He pulled her in for a hug and a kiss hello.

"You look great, Mom!"

"Well, thank you. But I think I probably look the same as ever. Are you hungry?"

"I could eat." He hadn't had anything other than a banana since lunch. And it was nearly eight.

"Let me fix you a plate. We had roasted chicken with mashed potatoes earlier. You love that."

"I do." He followed his mother into the kitchen and she quickly made him a plate of food, then put it in the microwave and heated it up for two minutes. When the buzzer went off, she opened the oven and looked confused when the food wasn't there.

"Check the microwave honey," his father said.

She did and pulled the plate of food out. "How silly of me! Here you go." She set the plate in front of David and he ate seated at the island while his parents chatted with him. Other than the mix-up with the oven, his mother seemed really good, better than he'd expected.

THE NEXT MORNING AFTER A GREAT NIGHT'S SLEEP, HE WOKE around eight, feeling energized and hungry. It was a beautiful day and he'd brought his running shoes. A run down to the beach and back after he ate a light breakfast seemed like a good plan. He dressed and went down to the kitchen where his mother was sitting at the kitchen island, reading the paper and drinking a cup of coffee. She looked up and smiled. "Hi, honey. There's coffee made if you want to help yourself. I could make you an omelet if you like. Your usual tomato and onion?"

David smiled. That was his father's usual breakfast. "No thanks. I thought I'd have a quick bowl of oatmeal and some coffee before I go out for a run."

"But you can't run, honey. What about your knee? You know the doctor said that wasn't a good idea since you had the surgery."

David just stared at his mother in confusion. His knees were fine. But ten years ago, his father had both knees replaced. What should he do? Should he correct her? Before he could say anything, his father walked into the room, saw David's face and glanced at his mother. "How's everyone doing this morning?"

A pained look crossed his mother's face for a moment before she smiled and glanced at David. "You look like you're dressed for a run. That's a great idea. It looks lovely outside today."

LATER THAT AFTERNOON, WHILE HIS MOTHER WAS TAKING A NAP, David sat down in the kitchen with his father. He'd never known his mother to nap. She was only in her late sixties.

"What do the doctors say?" David asked.

"We just had a battery of tests done at Mass General. We flew into Boston and spent the night there the day before. Had a lovely dinner in the North End and then met with her doctors the next day. It's officially Alzheimer's."

His mother had Alzheimer's.

"What exactly does that mean? Are there different degrees of it? And does she know?"

"She knows. Sort of. She was right there with me when the doctors went over everything. I'm not sure she's really processed it though. But I think on some level, she knows something is wrong. Sometimes when she forgets something a look crosses her face that is heartbreaking. She looks afraid. Imagine knowing that your mind is going? How do you deal with that?"

"How are you dealing with it?" David asked. He was worried for his father as well as his mother. He'd never seen his father so stressed.

"I'm not going to lie to you. It's been hard. Really hard. I think we might have some difficult decisions to make soon."

"What are you thinking?"

His father stood and started pacing the room. "Well, there are a few options. We could put her in an assisted living—Alzheimer's unit, which I am not ready to do. She's not that bad yet. We could both move to an assisted living place and then she'd have access to services if she needed them. Or I could hire someone to come here." He stopped pacing and sat down again and looked at David.

"She's at the point where she really can't be left alone for long. If I just run out to the store, it's fine, but longer than an hour and it's potentially unsafe. She left the stove on the other day and luckily, I was home. The smoke alarm went off and everything was fine. But if I hadn't been here…"

"How have you been managing? What do you do when you go to work?" David's father worked as an attorney and had an office downtown, near Main Street and the waterfront.

"I've been working from home for the past few months, except for when I need to meet in person with a client, and then I run into town and back as quickly as possible."

No wonder his father looked so exhausted.

"What do you want to do?" David asked.

"I want things to stay as normal as possible. I don't think I'm ready to move to an assisted living place, not yet. I think if I can get someone to come in here maybe every afternoon during the week, then I could go into the office."

"That sounds like a good plan. I can help you find someone."

His father looked grateful. "I was hoping you'd say that."

***

PAULA'S GRANDFATHER DIDN'T BELIEVE IN WASTING ANY TIME. WHEN she told him first thing Monday morning that she was accepting the general manager position, he'd been pleased but then surprised her by saying, "Good, because David Connolly, that consultant I mentioned to you? He starts tomorrow, and so do you."

So, the next morning they all gathered in the conference room around a big oval table, for the weekly managers' meeting. Paula sat next to Hallie and across from Nick.

"How's Andrea doing?" she asked her cousin. Paula still felt somewhat guilty that she was taking over Andrea's job.

"She's ok. Disappointed of course and pissed off. I saw her on Sunday for pizza with the family."

"Did she say what she is going to do?"

"She's not ready to give up on a GM role somewhere. She has a few weeks before she is coming back, so I guess she'll feel the market out."

They all looked up as her grandfather stepped into the room and was followed by a tall, blondish man who looked vaguely familiar. Paula had done her research on David Connolly and she remembered him from high school. He'd been on the basketball team and he'd always had a quiet confidence about him. She didn't know him back then, but she could picture him walking the hallways surrounded by his friends or his girlfriend, Missy. She was a cheerleader, and they were together all of senior year. Paula knew they'd broken up soon after, because Missy married a local Nantucket boy a few years later. Paula also thought she'd heard recently that they'd gotten divorced.

Her grandfather made the introductions all around, then he and David took their chairs. Her grandfather led the meeting, as usual and everyone gave their weekly updates. Paula handed out her copies of the numbers. She went through them quickly, giving brief summaries so that she didn't bore anyone. Everyone nodded and she expected that to be the end of the meeting.

But then David opened his briefcase, pulled out a manila folder and flipped through it until he found a spreadsheet. He glanced at it and looked back at Paula's handout.

"It looks like you're down about ten percent from this time last year. Any idea why that might be?"

Paula glanced at her grandfather before speaking as she wasn't sure if he'd want to answer. He nodded at her to go ahead.

"We are down some, just over ten percent for the year. It varies by month. It started when a new hotel opened two years ago. Nantucket Grand is right downtown and a lot of people like that. Do you think we should lower our prices? We haven't done it yet."

David shook his head. "No, I don't think you should lower your prices. I think you should raise them." Everyone at the table looked confused.

"You think we should raise them? We're already one of the most expensive on the island," her grandfather said.

"Yes. You don't want to be one of them. You want to be the most expensive, most luxurious, most sought-after hotel on Nantucket. The people that come here can afford it. If they are looking for less expensive accommodations, there are plenty of options. There are many people that equate being the most expensive with being the best."

"You really think we should raise all of our prices?" Paula wasn't sure about that.

"Yes. But on the regular rooms don't raise by much. We can research the prices and just go a hair above the rest. But on the suites and villas, those can go up by 10 to 20%. I'm guessing they stay booked pretty steadily?"

Paula nodded. "Yes. We don't have as many of those rooms and they always go quickly."

"Good. So that's the first step. We'll also look at what you're doing for marketing and see if we can make some tweaks there. And over the next few months, I'll be assessing everything to see how we can be more efficient and more profitable."

"Excellent, we welcome your input," her grandfather said.

David turned his attention to Paula. "Have you told the staff yet that you've taken over the general manager role?"

"No, not yet." She smiled. "I only just accepted the role yesterday."

"Well, we should do that as soon as possible. We'll walk around the property today. You can introduce me, and yourself as the new general manager, at the same time."

"How do you suggest we present this?" her grandfather asked.

"Matter of fact. Andrea has accepted the concierge role?"

"Yes, she starts in three weeks," her grandfather confirmed.

"Okay, so we just say that. There's been a management shift. Andrea is going to be heading up concierge services and Paula is moving out of the back office and into the GM role. That's all we have to say."

"Good. I agree, let's do that today." Her grandfather stood. "Okay, great meeting everyone. Paula, do you want to show David around the property?"

"Of course."

Paula had opted to stay in her current office. It was the same size as the one Andrea was using which was right across the hall. It made sense to have David use Andrea's old office while he was going to be with them. Paula showed him his office first and he dropped off his briefcase before they headed out for their tour.

"It's a beautiful property," David said as they walked into the main lobby first which had soaring ceilings and white Carrera marble everywhere. Square-cut crystal vases filled with fresh flowers gave the room a lovely scent and welcoming feel.

Paula introduced David to the reception team and explained that she was taking over the general manager role. She was a little nervous about telling them, but as soon as she did, they were all smiles, and she breathed a sigh of relief.

"That's fabulous news, Paula. I know you'll do a great job." Maeve was close to her mother's age and had worked the front desk for as long as Paula could remember.

As they walked away, David gave her a curious look. "You seemed surprised that they were enthusiastic about the promotion. They seemed happy for you."

"They did. I just wasn't sure what people would think."

"You mean if you're ready for it? You were in a very different role for a long time."

"Yes. And I enjoyed it too. As you know, my cousin Andrea was the GM. It's a little awkward."

"It's not your fault that it didn't work out with Andrea. Your grandfather did the right thing in moving her to a role that better suits her."

"I know. It's just a big change, and sudden." She didn't add that she wasn't totally sure she was ready for it.

David looked at her closely. "It is a big change. Very different from what you were doing. You could hide in your office, do your thing with numbers. This is a very visible job. Are you sure that you're up for it?"

Was she? It was one thing for her to have doubts, but it irritated her to hear him voice them.

"My grandfather thinks that I am," she said stiffly.

He laughed and she saw the warmth in his eyes. "Yes, I know. He thinks very highly of you. So, let's do this. You have me for two months. Let's work together to get you up to speed and comfortable in the new role and see what we can do to get that ten percent back."

"Sounds good. So, let's head to the kitchen next. You can meet Roland the head chef and my brother, Nick, is his right hand."

They spent the rest of the morning making the rounds and talking to everyone in every department. Paula was relieved that everyone seemed supportive of the changes. They had lunch with her grandfather in the dining room and David seemed impressed with the menu and the food.

"I noticed that you do a fair number of weddings, but not very many corporate functions," he said.

"You mean like conferences and meetings?" Paula asked.

"Yes. That could be a huge growth area for you. This is the kind of place that companies would love for corporate outings or conferences. There are a lot of companies with deep pockets—hedge funds, investment firms, and we could tap into more of that market. The profits are as big, if not bigger, than a wedding—without the headaches."

Paula laughed. "No diva brides. We certainly get our share of those."

"It can be recurring income, too. A lot of these corporate events happen every year."

"That's a great suggestion," her grandfather said. "You can work with Paula to develop that?"

"We can. Oh, and another thing. You get a lot of celebrities that come here, but you could increase that too and overall awareness by using influencers on social media. We could choose a couple of highly connected Instagrammers and invite them for a complimentary weekend, with the understanding that they say nice things and post pictures. That can create some buzz fast."

Her grandfather laughed. "That's all Greek to me. Maybe Paula knows what you are talking about. The two of you can go after those influencers or whatever you called them. You have free rein to do whatever you think best."

Paula knew what influencers were and her head was spinning with all the possibilities. She'd known David was going to help her acclimate to the GM role. She didn't realize he'd have expertise in these other areas, too. She was excited to see what they could do.

CHAPTER 4

Bella was thrilled to discover how easy it was to hide in plain sight. All she had to do was turn her instantly recognizable long platinum blond hair into a deep brunette, chin-length bob. To be safe, though, she also added sunglasses and a pink Red Sox cap. Her jeans were baggy, and she wore several bulky sweaters. No one looked at her twice. It was wonderful.

She flew first class from LA to New York, then on to Nantucket and slept most of the way. When she landed and got her luggage, there was a white Range Rover parked out front and a driver holding a card with her name on it.

His name was Johnny, and he was very enthusiastic about the hotel he was bringing her to.

"Have you been to The Whitley before?" he asked, once her luggage was in the back and they were on their way.

"No, never. It looks lovely online, though. I'm looking forward to it."

"Oh, you'll love it. It's a special place. Everyone loves it there. Where are you from?"

Bella thought about that for a moment. Where was she from? She wasn't sure anymore. "I've been living in Los Angeles for the past five years. I grew up in Vermont, though. A really small town."

"No beaches in Vermont. I've never been to Los Angeles. You ever see any movie stars there?"

"No," she lied. "Some of my friends have, though." That was true.

"Oh, too bad."

Johnny was quiet for the rest of the drive and Bella stared out the window as they drove. It was still light out and the island was even prettier than she'd imagined. There was sand along the side of the roads and pink roses everywhere. Johnny turned off the main road and onto a long winding driveway. When he came around the final bend, Bella saw The Whitley straight ahead. It had a long, sprawling main building overlooking Nantucket Sound with individual cottages closer to the beach. The lawn was lush and perfectly maintained.

Johnny pulled up to the main entrance and jumped out to get Bella's luggage. She didn't have much with her, just one big suitcase and a carryon. Not a lot considering she was going to be staying for several months. But she'd wanted to travel light. She figured she could go into town and shop a bit and get whatever else she might need.

"I hope you enjoy your stay."

She pressed a generous tip into his hand. "Thank you, Johnny. Enjoy your night." She smiled big at him, the smile she was so famous for and it flustered him. He was adorable, like an enthusiastic puppy.

"Th-Thank you!"

***

BELLA WAS STILL SMILING AS A BELLMAN CAME RUSHING OVER TO help with her luggage. She handed it off to him and stepped inside the lobby, stopping for a moment to admire its beauty. The cool, white marble and gorgeous flowers had an instant calming effect. And calm was good. Bella had been in the eye of the storm for so long, she welcomed the serenity. She made her way to the reception desk and a woman who looked to be about her age, thirty, smiled when Bella walked up.

"Welcome to The Whitley. I'm Lucy. How can I assist?"

"Bella Bryant. I'm checking in."

Lucy looked her up in the system and Bella saw the surprise flash across her face. Just for an instant. She could tell Lucy was far too professional to react more than that. Bella gave her credit card, the one with her real last name, and Lucy ran the card then handed it back, along with her room keys.

"You're in the Siasconset Rose suite. It's on the second floor and is an end unit, so it's extra quiet. I think you'll love it. There are complimentary pastries and coffee in the lobby in the morning and you have a Nespresso machine in your room, and room service of course if you wish to order anything. Our restaurant is open until ten, as well."

"Thank you, Lucy."

Bella took the elevator up one floor, then walked down a long hallway and around a corner until she came to her room. She opened the door, stepped inside and breathed a sigh of relief. The room was perfect. It had two bedrooms, a living room, kitchen, two bathrooms, and a small deck with a stunning view of the ocean. She could drink her coffee there in the morning. The bedrooms were all white, with puffy comforters and bathrobes and matching slippers. She was tempted to fall into the bed. But she knew if she did, she'd fall fast asleep and wake in the middle of the night.

So, she decided to take a hot shower to wash off the travel grime and maybe order some room service for dinner. The hot water felt wonderful, both relaxing and reviving her. A half hour later, she was dressed and sipping a cup of hot tea on her deck and enjoying the feel of the warm breeze across her face and the crisp, clean air tinged slightly with the salty scent of the sea. From where she sat, she could see two families below, playing croquet on the lawn with their children. In the distance, several small sailboats sailed together close to the shore. She knew that the hotel had several catboats available for the guests to use. She'd never sailed before, but it looked like fun.

She was feeling relaxed, for the first time in weeks, until her phone rang, and she instantly tensed up when she saw her agent's number on the caller ID. She thought about letting it go to voicemail but decided to just see what her agent wanted, and then hopefully not talk to her again for a good long while.

"Hi, Jean, what's up?" Jean McIntyre had been her agent since the beginning of Bella's career. She liked her, most of the time. Jean was aggressive and a mover and shaker in the industry. She'd brokered some good deals for Bella. But she was also relentless when she thought Bella should do something. Even now. Bella knew she meant well, but she wasn't sure that their goals were the same anymore. Jean wanted more, more, more for Bella and Bella wanted less, so much less. She'd almost walked away completely.

"Just checking in. Wanted to make sure you made it there safely and to see if you're settled in and feeling relaxed yet?"

Bella laughed. "I've only been here for about an hour. But it's lovely. I think it's exactly what I need. I don't want to think about anything for the next few months. I just want to read books and relax on the beach."

Jean was quiet for a moment. "Well, there's another reason I'm calling, too. I know you said you don't want to hear about anything new for a while, but something just came in that is a once in a life-time opportunity. I think you should take a look at it."

Bella instantly felt her chest tighten and a headache begin to form. The stress was already building at the mere mention of a new project.

"Jean. I told you. I can't do it right now. I can't do anything. Any stress causes my Lyme to flare and the last flareup was the worst yet. I need to avoid all stress and just calm myself down. Just thinking about a new project has me feeling twitchy."

"Okay. I can probably put them off for a few weeks. You're their top choice, though. I'll keep you posted. I wouldn't be able to forgive myself if you lost out on the chance to consider this one. It's that good, Bella."

In spite of herself, and the creeping stress that was building, Bella was a little curious. "What is it?"

"I really think it could launch you to the next level—Oscar contention. It's an adaptation of a Peggy Marlow Book Club pick, and her production company, Blue Moon, is casting now. This was a breakout book by a debut author, and it stayed on the charts for over a year. It's a strong woman's story set in the south, with dark family secrets and a mystery that spans several generations. It's big."

"Is there a script yet?"

"No, it's in development. I can overnight the book to you, though. You can read it on the beach."

Bella sighed. Jean had won this round. "Okay, I do need some beach reading. Go ahead and send it. I'm not committing to anything, though, until I've read it and even then, I'm not available for several months. I'm not cutting my stay here short. It's too important to my recovery." Bella had been working non-stop for five years, without a real break. Even between films, she had all kinds of pressure and demands on her time.

"It's on the way. Will go out in the mail today. I'll let you go rest now…"

As soon as she put the phone down it rang again, but this time Bella was happy to talk to the caller. It was her sister, Julia. They spoke just about every day, even if it was just for a few minutes. And it had been Julia's idea for Bella to insist on a several month break, and to spend it at The Whitley.

"So, what do you think? Do you love it there?" Julia asked. She was just a year older than Bella. They were alike in so many ways, but Julia's life was so different. She was a librarian in the small Vermont town they'd grown up in and was happily married to her high school sweetheart, Jim, who was a firefighter. They didn't have any kids yet, but they were trying their best, and going through infertility treatments. In the meantime, they had a collection of pets, two dogs and two cats. Julia called it her menagerie.

"I do love it, so far. It's beautiful. When are you coming to visit?" Bella didn't really need two bedrooms, but she wanted plenty of room for her sister to come and spend a week or two.

"I can't wait to get back there. It's been ten years, but I still remember the weekend I spent at The Whitley for Candace's wedding. I checked with work and I can't take two weeks, but I can do a week, two weeks from now, if that works for you."

"Of course, anytime. Will Jim come with you?" Bella was a big fan of Julia's husband. He was easy-going, and fun.

"No, he can't get the time off. So, it will just be me. We'll have a girls' week."

"That will be fun. We haven't done that in forever." It had been over a year since Bella had seen her sister. She was supposed to spend the holidays with them, but then the film she'd been shooting in Ireland ran into delays and she had to go right from that film set to another in Italy that had already started filming. It was a whirl-wind and it was exhausting. She couldn't wait to see her sister and just play tourists, like normal people.

"How are you feeling?" Julia asked.

"I'm good. It's very calm here, and quiet. But then Jean called."

"What did she want?" Julia was not a fan of Bella's agent. She thought she was pushy. And she wasn't wrong about that.

Bella told her about the conversation. And Julia was not happy about it.

"She couldn't even give you a day. One day before she started bothering you."

Bella sighed. "I know. But she is the best and it is what I pay her for. I told her that's it though. I'll read the book, but no promises and I'm not leaving here early. If anything, I might want to stay longer."

Julia laughed. "You should. You're not going to want to leave."

They chatted for a few more minutes until there was a knock on the door.

"That must be room service."

"I'll let you go. I'll book my flights and touch base with you tomorrow."

Bella opened the door and let the room service attendant wheel in a tray with her dinner. She'd ordered a house special, day-boat fresh haddock, broiled with a lemon butter sauce, grilled asparagus and mashed potatoes. Pure comfort food. She ate on her deck, staring out at the ocean and felt the tension ease away. By the time she finished eating, she was already yawning. The bed was calling her name again.

She crawled under the covers, with a romance novel she'd picked up at the airport and read for a bit. The bed was so soft and comfortable, and her eyes quickly grew heavy as she slipped into a dreamless sleep. Her last thought before she drifted off was that she couldn't wait to go exploring the next day, as a normal person. It had been so long since she'd been able to do that.

CHAPTER 5

"Y ou're a Whitley and the general manager at your family's resort, the top hotel on Nantucket. Why would you consider leaving?" The interview had been going so well, until the inevitable question.

Andrea was in Boston at the Lennon Hotel, a luxurious boutique hotel in the Back Bay. It seemed like an ideal fit for her background. She had flown in the night before and stayed at the hotel. Elaine Humphrey, the hotel industry headhunter her grandfather had used for years, set up the meeting.

Andrea walked down Boylston Street the night before and had a delicious dinner and a glass of really good red wine at Abe and Louie's, her favorite Boston steakhouse. She'd gone to bed feeling full and relaxed and excited about the interview today. But now, she had a sudden, sinking feeling that it could easily slip away if she didn't answer this well. She took a deep breath.

"It's been a wonderful experience working there. But, as you said, it is a family business and sometimes family dynamics can be, well, challenging. I thought it might be a good idea to spread my wings and broaden my experience by working at another property. And I've always loved Boston."

The interviewer, who was also the owner of the hotel, was an older gentleman about her grandfather's age. He smiled. "That's understandable. Everything about your background seems to line up very well with what we are looking for. We have a few other candidates we are considering, but we will have a decision this week. I'll be in touch with Elaine as soon as we have an update."

Andrea flew home after the interview and spent the rest of the week anxiously waiting for word. Elaine had also set up two other interviews at Boston hotels but they'd both been canceled abruptly. She said they'd both moved forward hiring other candidates so didn't need to see Andrea, but it made her wonder. They'd both been presented to her as being at the very early stages and then suddenly, both opportunities disappeared.

She suspected that both places likely did backdoor references to gather information. It was a common thing, when companies asked around to see if anyone in their network knew anything about a candidate. Many employees over the years had gone to Boston hotels after working at The Whitley. And Andrea knew that some of those employees hadn't liked working for her. She could be demanding, but she had always thought that was a good thing, to get the most out of people. But not everyone agreed.

She'd left her reference sheet with Human Resources. All the names on it were family—her grandfather, her cousin Nick and sister Hallie. She did not include her cousin Paula. There was no way she was going to ask the person taking her job for a reference. She was worried though about what her grandfather would say. She knew Nick and Hallie would focus on her strengths. But her grandfather had told her he'd be brutally honest about both her strengths and her weaknesses.

There was nothing available anywhere on Nantucket that was appropriate. General manager roles were few and far between and were usually filled internally, by referral or through a headhunter like Elaine. And she'd said there was nothing that she was aware of currently on the island. Boston was Andrea's first choice after Nantucket as it was still close by and it was a very walkable city and much smaller than New York, which was just so big. Still, she told Elaine she'd consider something there too, but at the moment, Elaine had nothing.

And in a little over a week, she would have to start in the concierge role. She was dreading it, sure that everyone would be whispering about her. Hopefully it wouldn't be too awful, at least until she found something else. And she had no intention of going to those deadly boring weekly manager meetings.

She couldn't sit through that now, especially with Paula and her spreadsheets lording it over her in her new role. Andrea planned to have as little to do with Paula as possible. Hopefully they could stay out of each other's way. She didn't want to be continually reminded of the job her cousin stole from her by running into her all the time. She had no need for an office anymore and could just go right to work in the concierge kiosk.

The call came Friday afternoon at five minutes of five. Elaine kept it brief, delivering the news succinctly. "I'm sorry, hon. They went with one of the other candidates. They said you were great though. Enjoyed meeting with you. Sounds like it was close. I'll be in touch when something new comes in."

"Okay. Thanks, Elaine. Did they check references, do you know?"

There was an uncomfortable silence on the other end. "I'm really not sure. I sent them over, in case they needed them."

"Okay. I appreciate it. Please do keep me in mind."

"You got it, hon. Have a great weekend."

Andrea ended the call and stared out the window in frustration. She'd thought she had a good shot at that role. She needed to blow off some steam. See if she could round up anyone to go have a drink with her. It was time for happy hour, even if she wasn't feeling particularly happy.

NONE OF HER FRIENDS WERE AROUND, BUT SHE KNEW HER SISTER Hallie would be just getting out of work.

"Meet me at The Club Car for a cocktail? It's been a crappy week and I could use a good, stiff margarita."

Hallie laughed. "I'm sorry you've had a rough week. It's been crazy here too. I'm definitely up for happy hour. I should be able to meet you there by six."

"Great, I'm going to head over now and get a seat at the bar. I'll try to save one for you, if I can."

Andrea changed into her favorite rose pink sweater and her jeans that were faded and distressed and fit her like a glove. She was down about five pounds due to stress, but as she twirled in the mirror, she saw that had its advantages. She was looking cute and for the first time all week, felt the beginning of a good mood. She hadn't gone to The Club Car in ages. It would be fun to relax with her sister and share an appetizer and a drink or two.

The bar was busy when she arrived as she knew it would be, but she lucked into an empty seat as two people were leaving as she walked up to the bar. She sat and put her purse on the other chair. She wouldn't be able to hold it for long, but she could try. The bartender came right over, and she ordered her margarita.

"I'd like it on the rocks please, with salt and a splash of Grand Marnier."

"That sounds good. Maybe I'll get the same. Is anyone sitting here?"

Andrea turned at the familiar voice. It was Marco, one of the many Brazilians that worked at the hotel. Marco had worked there for five years now and had his green card. He was a year or two younger than Andrea and also worked in concierge services. So, she would be his new boss. She wondered if he knew.

"You are." She lifted her purse and hung it on the back of her chair. "Hallie's on her way."

Marco settled into the chair and grinned. "Okay, then I'll keep it warm for her."

When the bartender delivered Andrea's drink, Marco ordered one of the same.

"How's everything at the hotel?" she asked.

"Good, busy. The new consultant started. Seems like a nice enough guy. He explained that you're going to be my new boss."

Andrea smiled. She had to be positive. "Yes, though we probably won't work together too often." Usually there was just one concierge on at a time, except on weekends.

"It's all good. I usually do work weekends though, so we might work together some. It will be fun." His easy smile made her relax. In her fury about everything, she'd forgotten that Marco worked in concierge services. He was a lot of fun, and always in a good mood. Sometimes when schedules aligned a bunch of them went for drinks and it was always a good time. But it had been a long while since they'd had a night out like that. Her cousin Nick was often the ringleader. The kitchen staff was always ready to go out after their shift. It was like they got a second wind after running around and needed to wind down and burn off some energy.

She chatted easily with Marco, getting caught up on everyone they knew and then out of the corner of her eye, Andrea saw Hallie walk in and waved her over. Marco immediately stood and pulled the chair out so Hallie could sit.

"Such a gentleman, thank you!" Hallie sat and ordered a margarita too.

Andrea had been hoping to vent to her sister about her unsuccessful search efforts but couldn't go there with Marco hanging out with them. She didn't mind so much though. He had already been a good boost to her mood. He'd kept her laughing with funny stories about various guest requests. At least if she was going to be stuck in concierge services, it might be more fun with Marco around.

After a while, he excused himself to use the rest room and as soon as he was out of earshot, Hallie asked for an update.

"I didn't get it. And the other two interviews I had lined up were both canceled at the last minute. There's nothing else out there, not right now. So, it looks like I will be going back to work at The Whitley after all."

"Oh, Andrea, I'm sorry. I thought the Lennon Hotel sounded great for you. Though I have to confess, I'm glad you're not going anywhere. I like having you around. And I still think you might find concierge is a pretty cool place to be. You'll get to work with Marco, too. You guys always got along great. It might actually be fun."

"It's been a long time since work was fun," Andrea admitted.

Hallie looked at her with compassion. "Work can be fun. I love what I do. I know you don't see it now…but this might be a blessing in disguise."

"Hmm. I don't know about that. So, tell me about the new guy."

"David Connolly?"

Andrea nodded. "Yes. I vaguely remember him from high school. I was a sophomore when he was a senior. He was tall, blond, and went out with that cheerleader, Missy whatever her name was."

"Right. I don't remember her last name either, but I know who you mean. He seems nice enough. And smart. He had some great suggestions at his first meeting with us. I think he'll be good for Paula. She was nervous about stepping into the role."

"I bet she was," Andrea said bitterly. She still partly blamed Paula for her grandfather's decision.

"It's not her fault," Hallie reminded her.

"Whatever. So, what is this David's status? Is he single? Just passing through Nantucket or is he here to stay? His family is still here?"

"I have no idea if he's single. It didn't come up. I know he has family here, but I think this is just a temporary assignment. He lives in New York City."

"Of course, he does. There are no eligible men on Nantucket," she sulked.

Hallie shot her a look. "That's ridiculous. There are so many eligible men that come to Nantucket. Figawi weekend is coming up and the island will be overflowing with them." The famous sailing race took place every Memorial Day weekend when hundreds of huge sailboats with experienced crews raced from Hyannis to Nantucket and then back on Memorial Day. It was one of the busiest weekends of the year on Nantucket.

"You know what I mean. Men that live here, year-round. Maybe I should move to New York. Elaine is looking there, too."

Hallie didn't look happy about that. "New York is so far away and so big."

"It's just a short plane ride away. Plenty of direct flights to New York." There were many wealthy people that owned second homes on Nantucket and commuted back and forth on the weekends. Many of them had private planes and during the summer months, there were dozens of them parked at the Nantucket airport at any given time. However, although she'd told Elaine she was open to New York, Andrea really wasn't excited about it. She hoped something might eventually turn up in Boston.

As Marco returned to the bar, a seat opened up and he sat next to Andrea. His phone buzzed and he glanced at a text message and shook his head.

"My brother was supposed to meet me here. He just said he had a chance to pick up some overtime and is working instead."

"Why don't you stay with us? We were going to get some appetizers," Hallie said.

Marco happily agreed and they spent the next two hours eating, laughing and chatting. Around eight thirty, Hallie suddenly couldn't stop yawning.

"You guys, I know it's early, but I think I need to head home. This was a long day and it's caught up to me."

Andrea had switched to wine and was about to order another glass. She wasn't ready to go home yet.

"It's so early. Are you sure you don't want to stay for one more?"

Hallie tried to prevent a yawn and failed. She laughed. "Yes, I'm sure. You and Marco should stay, though."

"I'll gladly stay," Marco said.

Hallie smiled. "Great! Andrea, I'll talk to you tomorrow. Good-night, Marco."

Marco was good company. Andrea was glad to be out and, for the first time since losing her job, she wasn't stressing so much about her job search. She realized that she didn't know much about him, though, other than that he was from Brazil.

"Tell me about your brother. Is it just you and him here?"

"My sister Alana is here, too. We all rent a house together."

"Your parents are still in Brazil?"

He smiled. "Just my mother. We lost my father four years ago. We've been trying to get her to come here, at least for a visit. They both came a year before he passed. She said maybe this summer. We're going to hold her to it."

"I hope she comes. What do your brother and sister do here?"

"Sergio is the oldest. He works for a roofing company. He likes to be outside. Alana is the baby of the family. She works as a server at a restaurant downtown, Mimi's Place. She loves it there. Nice people."

Andrea nodded. "They are. I met the girls that took it over, Mandy, Emma and Jill. They had an open house a year or so ago when they reopened."

Marco grinned. "I send a lot of guests there." One of the most common questions for the concierge desk was what restaurants they would recommend.

"What do you like to do on your time off? Do you like to fish?" Andrea was curious to learn more about Marco. He was so easy to talk to, and she loved his accent. She'd never really noticed before how dark his eyes were—a deep, warm brown that lit up when he talked. They were almost as dark as his hair, which was thick and wavy, and she liked that it wasn't too short. She'd always had a preference for hair that was on the longish side. Not that she was thinking of Marco that way. She never had before and given that she was going to be his boss, it was not a good time for any thoughts like that.

"I'm not much on fishing. I've tried it a few times. I prefer surfing."

"You know how to surf?" Andrea was impressed. "I've always wanted to try that."

"You should. There are a couple of surf schools on the island. I took lessons when I first moved here, and I get out whenever I can. I like the South Shore beaches, Cisco or Surfside usually."

"I've lived here all my life and haven't gotten around to it yet. Someday."

"So, what do you like to do, then?"

Andrea thought for a minute. "This. I love to go out to dinner or drinks. And when the weather is nice, I like to just be at the beach. I did try paddle boarding last summer. That was fun."

"If you can do that, you can surf."

"Maybe you can give me a lesson," she teased.

But he took her seriously. "Anytime. Just say the word."

"Another round?" The bartender noticed that their glasses were almost empty.

"What do you think?" Marco asked.

"Sure, why not?" Andrea found herself saying. She didn't really want the night to end just yet. Didn't want to go home alone to her small cottage and get depressed again thinking about her job search. She wanted to keep forgetting everything for just a little while longer.

She and Marco lingered over their drinks, chatting and laughing. They learned that they liked a lot of the same TV shows and were both baseball fans. Andrea loved going to Boston for a night or two and taking in a Red Sox game.

Marco insisted on paying even when she tried to give the bartender her credit card. "But there were two of us." She had owed Hallie so was planning on treating tonight.

"Well, I did crash your night with your sister. Let's consider it a celebration for your promotion."

"My promotion?" She was a little fuzzy from the last glass of wine and was about to correct him and say 'demotion'. But he spoke first.

"Yes, in my opinion this is a much better job. General manager just seems stressful. Can you honestly say that job was fun?"

Andrea laughed. "Fun? No."

"See? Work should be fun."

"My sister said that earlier, too. Thank you, Marco."

"She's a smart girl." Marco signed the charge slip and they headed toward the door.

When they stepped outside, Andrea tripped and almost went down, but Marco caught her.

"Thank you, again."

Marco looked at her and hesitated for a moment. "Why don't you let me drive you home? You can get your car in the morning?"

"That's way out of your way." Andrea lived by The Whitley which was a good fifteen to twenty minutes away. Marco was less than a mile down the road.

"I don't mind. Let's go."

He led her to his truck and helped her into the passenger side. As they rode in comfortable silence, Andrea felt her eyes growing heavy and knew she'd be out as soon as her head hit the pillow.

When they reached her cottage, Marco walked her to her door. And she automatically invited him in.

"Would you like to come in? I could make coffee."

He smiled. "I'd love to, but I'd better not. You need your sleep."

"Okay. Goodnight, Marco and thanks so much, for dinner and driving all the way out here." She hugged him and he seemed surprised at first, then hugged her back and dropped a kiss on her forehead.

"Sleep well, Andrea. It was a fun night."

CHAPTER 6

P aula wasn't sure what she thought about David Connolly. He certainly knew what he was doing. He was as gifted with a spreadsheet as she was, and he knew the hotel industry inside and out. She asked him one morning over coffee how he'd become such an expert.

"I went through the Four Seasons management training program right out of college and worked in several different properties. Then I went back to school for my MBA and went into consulting. With the hotel background, they put me into that niche and sent me out on the road with some of the senior consultants. Our typical assignments are two to three months and we see the same issues come up over and over."

"You travel so much. Do you ever get sick of it?" Paula couldn't imagine living that lifestyle. She knew most consultants flew out on Sunday and home on Friday. She wouldn't want to do that short term, let alone all the time. But she'd always been a homebody. She liked being at home, and close to her family.

"Sometimes. It's okay most of the time. The work is interesting." And then he'd changed the subject. And that's why she wasn't sure about him. One minute he was reasonably friendly and the next he was distant and almost cold. Sometimes he looked a million miles away. She wondered if The Whitley was boring to him, too small to be a challenge.

"We must be small compared to the size hotels you usually deal with."

"Yes, it's on the smaller side. But we deal with hotels of all sizes." He smiled. "It was nice to come here. To come home to Nantucket. I don't see my parents often enough. And they are getting older."

"How are they? I think you mentioned your father still works as a lawyer?"

He nodded. "He does. He has an office downtown and he works from home some."

"And your mother?"

"She's fine. She doesn't work." He stood, signaling that the coffee break was over.

Later that afternoon, they had a meeting with her grandfather to go over David's recommendations for where they could make some cuts. He had a list of suggestions and most of them made good sense. He'd pointed out areas that they could streamline and improve how they ordered to take advantage of discounts on larger orders. But then he made a recommendation that Paula hadn't seen coming. It was one that she disagreed with completely. Before she said anything, she glanced at her grandfather, but his face was hard to read. He never gave much away in a business meeting. He'd told her years ago that success in business was like playing cards. You never let them see you sweat, and you keep your cards close to your vest.

Her grandfather nodded at her. "What do you think about those recommendations, Paula?"

"Well, I think there are some great suggestions. Things we can implement right away, like the ordering. But I have to say I don't like the idea of cutting staff. That seems drastic."

"It would make us more efficient and more profitable," David insisted.

"It's up to Paula," her grandfather said.

She looked at him in surprise. "What do you think?"

He grinned. "I think you know. Do what you think is right."

She took a deep breath and looked at David. "No one loses their job. We can make the other suggestions and continue to try to grow profits other ways."

David didn't look pleased, but he nodded. "Okay."

His phone rang and when he glanced at the number, he stood and excused himself.

"I'm sorry, but I need to take this."

"No problem. We're all done here," her grandfather said.

David stepped away and returned a moment later, looking a bit pale.

"I need to take the rest of the afternoon off. My mother fell and my father just called from the hospital."

"Of course," her grandfather said.

"I'm so sorry. I hope she's okay," Paula added.

"Thanks. I'll see you both tomorrow."

After he left the room, Paula turned to her grandfather.

"Was that what you would have done? Did I make the right decision?"

"Yes, it's what I would have done. Profits are important but people are, too. I've never had a layoff here and I don't intend to start now. If we were to cut people, something else would fall short. People are what make The Whitley what it is."

"Good. That's what I thought. It's what you've always taught me. And I think it's what sets us apart, what keeps people coming back."

"Right. So, fill me in on what's new. Do we have anyone especially interesting or famous with us this week?"

Paula laughed. Her grandfather loved to be up on all the gossip.

"We do, actually. Cami Carmichael arrived last week. And she's staying for two months."

"Cami Carmichael? She's that pretty blonde girl, the one in all the romantic comedies, with the big smile?"

"Yes, that's her."

"I like her smile. She's everywhere lately. I saw her picture on the cover of People magazine yesterday and they keep playing the commercial for some new movie she has coming out. I hope she's not being bothered too much?"

"She's kind of here incognito. Changed her hair. It's short and dark brown now and she's going by a different name. Bella, I think.

Lucy checked her in and said she didn't recognize her at all. The hair made her look so different."

"Good. If she's staying here for two months, she obviously needs to get away. I hope she has a relaxing and peaceful stay."

WHEN DAVID ARRIVED AT THE NANTUCKET HOSPITAL, HE CHECKED in at the emergency desk and they directed him to his mother's room. She was propped up in bed, with one leg resting on a pillow. His father was sitting in a chair next to her, holding her hand.

"Hi, honey!" His mother seemed unusually cheerful, given the circumstances. His father looked nervous and exhausted.

David gave his mother a gentle hug and sat next to his father.

"What happened?"

"Your mother went out to get the mail. She forgot there was a step, and she went down hard. Luckily, I was home when it happened."

"Did she break anything?"

"We're not sure yet. The doctor should be back soon. They ran a bunch of tests and took x-rays."

"How are you feeling, Mom?"

"Pretty silly. I can't believe I missed that step. I just wasn't paying attention. It doesn't hurt too bad. Hopefully we can go home soon." She sounded good, clear and upbeat.

"I think I'm going to go get a coffee. David, do you want to take a quick walk with me? Barbara, we'll be right back. Would you like a coffee or anything?"

"No, thank you. I'm feeling kind of tired. I might just close my eyes for a minute."

David followed his father out of the room, and they walked the short distance to the cafeteria. They both got a coffee, and on the way back, his father updated David on the search for an assistant. "I think we found someone. Her name is Meghan. She goes by Meg and she can start on Monday. She'll work afternoons Monday through Friday and she said she could be flexible if we ever need her on a weekend."

"That sounds good. What is she like?"

"She's in her early sixties, a retired teacher looking to work part-time. I think your mother might like her company."

"Good, then you can have a break. You look tired, Dad."

"I'm fine. As long as someone is here with her, then I can relax a bit. I do miss being at the office."

When they walked back into his mother's room, the doctor was there and was wrapping his mother's ankle. He looked up when he saw David and his father.

"So, I have some good news. We took a bunch of pictures and nothing is broken. But Barbara does have a nasty sprained ankle. I'm going to wrap it up and then you can take her home, but she's going to have to keep her weight off the leg and use crutches until her ankle heals. I'd give it a good six weeks."

"That is good news," his mother said.

An hour later, his mother was discharged, and they all went home. It took his mother a few tries to get used to the crutches, and a long while to slowly make her way to the car, but she managed.

When they arrived home, David's father helped get his mother settled in her favorite chair, a recliner in the living room, while David ordered a pizza to be delivered.

Once she was comfortable, they joined her and chatted while waiting for the pizza.

"How are you liking working at The Whitley? Such a fancy place. Your father took me there on our anniversary a few years ago. We did the tasting menu, and it was heavenly."

"It was kind of fancy for me. I didn't know what half of the things were. They did taste pretty good though," his father said. David smiled at that. His father's tastes were simple. One of his favorite meals was hot dogs and baked beans. His mother had more refined tastes and she'd told him before about that dinner. She'd loved it.

"It's good. There's a lot to do there. It was a nice chance to come home, and see you guys, too."

"We don't see you often enough," his mother said sadly. "Will you always have to travel this much?"

"David has a good job, and a life in New York City. There's nothing on Nantucket for him," his father said.

His father was right. Professional opportunities were limited on Nantucket.

"There's family. His family is here," his mother said.

David could sense a mood change with his mother. They were becoming more frequent. She grew agitated unless they were able to redirect her. The doorbell rang and he breathed a sigh of relief.

"Mom, the pizza's here. I ordered your favorite—the one with eggplant, feta and spinach."

His mother's eyes lit up. "You did? Oh, good. My girlfriends and I love that one the best. I haven't had it in so long." They'd had it delivered a few days ago, too.

His father stood. "If you get the paper plates and napkins, David, I'll get the pizza."

A few minutes later they were all happily eating in the living room. They laughed and chatted like everything was perfectly normal and his mother stayed clear-minded for the rest of the night. It gave David hope that they could manage this, that it might not be so bad.

CHAPTER 7

"Table nine wants their filet butterflied and well done. What does that mean?" Caitlin was one of their newer servers, a college student who had spent the last two years bussing tables and they were giving her a shot at serving. She'd been through extensive training, but butterflying was something they hadn't covered.

Nick groaned. "It should be outlawed. Doesn't happen often, thankfully. But that means they want the filet split in half so it will cook faster and absolutely ruin an otherwise perfect piece of meat. But that's how they want it."

Caitlin made a face. "That doesn't sound very good to me, either. When I grew up, I thought I hated beef because my mother always cooked it well done. When I went out to dinner with some college friends, they talked me into trying prime rib medium rare and it was an entirely different experience. There's a reason they call it red meat."

Nick laughed. "You're right about that." He took the order, hacked the beautiful piece of filet mignon in half and tossed it under the broiler.

It was Saturday night, and the kitchen was hopping. The hotel was full, and the restaurant was busy with both hotel guests and the general public. The restaurant's reputation had grown in recent years, and more and more visitors were making the trip to the other side of the island to dine at The Whitley's restaurant. Nick liked to think he had something to do with that.

He'd been working there forever, it seemed. He'd started as a dishwasher when he turned sixteen and worked after school and on weekends. He'd moved into other roles after that during college breaks, working every station in the kitchen. After graduating with a business degree, he realized he wanted to keep going as a chef. He worked at a few restaurants in Boston, gained some good experience, and then returned to Nantucket and into his current role about five years ago.

He liked working for Roland, the head chef. He'd learned a lot from him and in the past few years he'd gained the confidence to experiment a bit and do more of his own creations. So, when someone ordered well-done, butterflied meat, it just made him cringe. But as long as the customer was happy, he'd gladly make it.

The kitchen officially closed at ten, and it was a little after eleven when Nick was able to call it a day. Usually, on a Saturday night he grabbed an after-work drink with one of the guys in the kitchen. As long as they changed out of their work clothes, they could have a drink or two on the property at any of the bars or restaurants. But tonight, no one was able to join him. Usually if no one was available, he just went home. But Nick was feeling energized after running around all night and he wanted to go out.

He decided to have a drink at the outside bar that overlooked the ocean. It was the most casual of the hotel's bars. It was a beautiful night, and he loved that view.

There was one open seat at the bar, which was u-shaped and held about thirty people. The seat was on the end, next to the cocktail station where the servers waited for the bartender to make their drinks. That's why it was open. Nick didn't care, though. He knew all the servers, so at least he'd have a few people to chat with when they came to the bar.

He slid into the seat and Frank, the bartender, came right over. Frank was in his mid-fifties and had worked at The Whitley for as long as Nick could remember.

"Hey, Nick, what are you having?"

It was a warm, sticky night, hot for late May, and a beer seemed like a good idea. "I'll have a Whale's Tail draft. Thanks, Frank."

When it arrived, Nick took his first sip and relaxed as he looked around the bar. It was mostly couples. He was sitting next to a woman, but she hadn't turned his way and all he could see was that she had almost black, chin length hair. He figured she must be with the guy sitting next to her.

He sipped his beer and chatted with Sue and Jamie when they came to pick up drinks. They were busy still with scattered tables on the big patio. There was entertainment, too, two guys on guitars playing easy listening music like Jimmy Buffett and James Taylor. The crowd loved it.

He was almost finished with his beer and was going to ask for his tab when the woman sitting next to him turned his way, smiled and his whole world shifted. There was something about that smile. It lit up her whole face and it was directed at him. So much warmth. Her eyes were pretty, too—they were a blueish gray and stood out against her dark hair.

"I'm so sorry. That's rude of me to have my back to you like that. I thought the seat was empty." Nick noticed the guy that had been sitting next to her was gone.

"Oh, no worries. I snuck in a few minutes ago. I'm Nick."

She smiled again. "Bella. Are you staying at the hotel?"

"No. I work here, actually. In the kitchen."

"You do? Did you by any chance cook a piece of marinated grilled salmon an hour or so ago? I requested it on the rare side."

He liked her already. Almost no one ordered salmon cooked rare unless they were a true foodie.

"I did. It's the only way to eat it. I hope it was all right?"

"It was the best piece of salmon I've ever had. Cooked to perfection. Thank you."

He grinned. "My pleasure. So, are you staying here?"

"I am. I'm here for a while, an extended vacation."

"Nice. Where are you from?"

She hesitated for a moment he noticed, then smiled again. "Los Angeles, but I don't really consider it home, you know? It's just where I live."

"I know what you mean. That's how I felt when I lived in Boston for a few years. I liked it well enough, but it wasn't home."

"You're from Nantucket?" She sounded surprised.

He nodded. "Born here thirty-six years ago. My sisters work

here, too. Lucy is at the front desk and Paula is the new general manager."

"I met Lucy. She checked me in."

"Is this your first time on Nantucket?"

"Yes. My sister came for a wedding a few years ago and insisted that I come here. She loved it. She's coming to visit soon."

"That will be fun for you. Have you had a chance to play tourist yet?"

"A little bit. I took the shuttle into town yesterday and did some shopping. I figured I would wait until my sister gets here and then we can explore together."

"That sounds like a good plan."

Bella's phone buzzed with a text message. She glanced at it and immediately looked irritated. She shut the phone off and tossed it in her purse.

"That's one annoying thing about people on the west coast. They don't always stop and consider that it's three hours later here, and who wants to get a business text this time of night?" She sighed and took a sip of her drink.

"What do you do for work?" Nick was intrigued and wanted to know more about Bella.

She hesitated and chewed her bottom lip for a moment before answering.

"At the moment, I'm unemployed and that was someone with a lead for a job. Which is nice, but I don't want to think about work right now. Let's change the subject. What do you do for fun, when you're not working?"

Nick grinned and held up his beer. "This. Usually with friends, but no one wanted to come out and play tonight. If you mean hobbies—well, I love to fish. It's almost like meditation. My job is so hectic all the time, and I love that, but when I fish, I can spend hours soaking up the silence, enjoying the calm by the ocean. That probably sounds kind of goofy?"

Bella smiled, though. "Not at all. I used to love to go fishing, too, with my dad up in the mountains of Vermont. It's been a lot of years, though."

"Well, if you ever feel like going again, you're welcome to join me. Sundays are the day I usually go if I don't have other plans. I

pack a lunch, maybe a few beers, and a radio and make an afternoon of it."

Bella grabbed a pen from the bar and jotted her cell phone
number on a cardboard coaster and handed it to him. "Please let
me know when you go next. Like I said, I'm here for a few months,
so I'd be grateful for something to do. And I was actually hoping I
might get to fish."

Nick took the coaster and put it in his pocket. "Will do. We have
a family thing this Sunday but let's tentatively plan on the one
after."

Bella tried to stifle a yawn and failed. "I'm sorry. The day finally
caught up with me. I think I'm going to head up to my room. It's
been nice chatting with you, though. Definitely count me in for that
Sunday."

"You got it. Sleep well, Bella."

He watched her go and was already looking forward to their
afternoon adventure. She was a pretty girl and easy to talk to. And
there was something so familiar about her. But that didn't make
sense. He'd definitely never met her before.

CHAPTER 8

Monday morning arrived and Paula felt a sense of dread as she headed into work. It was Andrea's first day back in her new role as head of the concierge team. She hoped that Andrea wouldn't be too furious with her. Paula knew it wasn't her fault, but she still felt a sense of guilt as she did take her cousin's job. Her grandfather assured her that he would have let Andrea go regardless and just called the search out. But Paula knew Andrea often held a grudge—especially, for some reason, with her.

She didn't run into her cousin until mid-afternoon when she had to go to the front desk to help with a computer issue. Andrea was at the concierge desk by herself and was chatting with an older couple. Paula gave her a wave as she walked by, but Andrea just glared coldly at her before turning her attention back to the guests. Paula sighed. It was pretty much what she'd expected.

She handled the computer situation then went back to her office to hide for a bit and look over the weekly numbers. She still was most comfortable by herself in her office, but she knew she had to get over that and make a real effort to be out and about, visible with both staff and guests. But she did have some reporting to do, so was happy to spend the next few hours surrounded by numbers. She was just finishing up for the day when David poked his head in her office.

"Am I interrupting?" They'd only seen each other in passing so far that day. He was working on a project for her grandfather and Paula had been making her rounds earlier.

"Not at all. I just finished up what I was working on. What are you up to?"

"I just met your cousin. I thought she was quite charming, and we chatted for about ten minutes or so. But then I brought up your name, and well, I saw a different side of her. She's not too happy with you at the moment."

Paula sighed. "I know. She blames me for her losing her job. She probably thinks I manipulated Grandfather into doing it. She should know me better than that, but she doesn't take the time to really see things as they are."

"I tried to explain to her that you had nothing to do with it. That your grandfather had reached out to me and I suggested he do the same thing. Not that he choose you, necessarily, as I didn't know you, but just that it seemed time for Andrea to move to a different role."

"How'd she take that?"

David chuckled. "Well, she stopped flirting with me pretty quick."

Paula laughed. "That's Andrea for you. I do hope she likes the new job, though."

"She seemed to be. She was chatting away with an older couple and gave them some good restaurant suggestions. She can be quite engaging."

"When she wants to be, yes. She's probably the most social of all of us. She's always up for going out."

"And you're not?"

"Oh, I like to go out, sometimes. I am kind of a homebody, though. After a long day, I love to relax and unwind at home usually. What about you?"

"Kind of in the middle, I guess. I like to grab a drink after work occasionally. Do people do that much here? Other than Andrea?" He raised his eyebrows and Paula laughed again.

"My brother Nick is always up for going out after work. You should go with them sometimes. More often than not, they get a drink here. Outside if the weather is nice. That's my favorite bar here, too. We have some good entertainment on the patio Thursday through Sunday nights."

"I'll have to check that out. We should all do after work drinks one of these days."

"We should," she agreed. "How is your mother doing? Is she managing okay on the crutches?"

David was quiet for a moment before answering. "Yes and no. She can get around fine on them, but she was recently diagnosed with Alzheimer's. We worry about her forgetting that she needs them and falling again."

Paula's heart went out to him. The worry was etched across his face. "I'm so sorry. That sounds stressful, for all of you."

He nodded. "It is. For my father, especially. But we'll figure it out."

"There you both are. Could we go into my office for a moment? I have an idea I want to discuss." Paula's grandfather looked excited about his idea, whatever it was.

"Of course." Paula set her pen down, stood and followed her grandfather to his office. David was right behind her.

"Have a seat, please." They sat in the two chairs facing her grandfather's massive dark wood desk. He took his seat behind it, leaned forward and looked at them both.

"I want to do a Taste of the Town event on our front lawn. Invite a bunch of the area restaurants to participate as well as have a wine tasting. Paula, can you call Peter at Bradford's Liquors and see if he wants to help? He can arrange for all the wine vendors and then take orders if people want to buy wine."

"You mean like what they do at the Nantucket Wine Festival?"

"No, not like that. They mostly focus on wine with a few fancy snacks. This will be as much about the food as the wine. It's a chance for local restaurants to showcase their signature dishes. We can give out awards, too, like best chowder/soup, best appetizer and best entree. The restaurants can use that for marketing."

"I like it," David said. "It sounds like a great way to deepen your relationships with area restaurants. They may be more apt to refer people your way."

Her grandfather's eyes lit up. "Yes! That's exactly what I was thinking."

"When would you want to do it?" Paula knew they'd need some time to pull something this big together.

"I was thinking the week after the fourth of July. That's one of the busiest weeks here and if we do it on Monday, it will be easier on the restaurants and the people are here looking for something to do."

His excitement was contagious. Paula smiled. "I think it's a great idea, too."

"Okay, good. I'll let the two of you take this on. We'll need tents, of course, and ones that can be zipped shut if it rains. Lots of details to manage. But that's what you're good at." He stood. "Okay, we're done here. Get started tomorrow and make it happen!"

CHAPTER 9

The day that the book arrived for Bella, the weather chose not to cooperate. It was not a beach day. And she didn't feel like staying in her room all day, so she decided to venture out and go downtown. She put on her 'keep away' outfit—the baggy jeans, oversized Nantucket sweatshirt, jean jacket, sunglasses and the pink Red Sox baseball cap. No one would look at her twice in that ensemble. The thought made her happy. She stuffed the thick paperback her agent had sent into a tote bag, grabbed her wallet and room key and went off to find a ride into town.

A quick stop at the concierge desk helped her to arrange a ride.

"Head outside, and Johnny should be up in a few minutes. Look for the white Range Rover," Andrea told her.

"Thank you."

A moment after Bella walked outside, Johnny pulled up and seemed happy to see her.

She climbed into the back seat and they were on their way. The ride into town took about fifteen minutes or so and Johnny chatted most of the way.

"Are you enjoying your visit so far?" he asked.

"I am. It's wonderful and relaxing. Exactly what I'd hoped for."

"Good. Less busy than Los Angeles, right?"

She was impressed that he remembered. "Yes, so much nicer."

"Are you off to do some shopping?"

"I think so. I might find a coffee shop first and read for a bit. The rain made me stir crazy. I didn't want to just sit in my room."

"I get that. A coffee shop that's near the wharf is The Corner Table. And if you get hungry later and feel like pizza, down at the Wharf there's a takeout place, Oath, that is very good. If you want something sweet, stop by the chocolate shop, Sweet Inspirations. People go crazy for the dark chocolate covered cranberries."

"Really? Have you had them? That sounds kind of strange, to be honest."

Johnny laughed. "Yes, I've had them. They will give you a free sample and you'll be hooked. You'll see."

"Okay, now you've intrigued me. I will go try them."

"I can drop you right at that coffee shop, if you like?"

"That's perfect."

A few minutes later, Johnny pulled up to The Corner Table. Bella gave him a generous tip and headed into the coffee shop. It was busy, but she didn't mind the line. It gave her a chance to check out the menu and decide what she wanted. When it was her turn to order, she decided on a caramel latte and a banana nut muffin and once she had both, settled into a comfy armchair. She people-watched out the window as she ate her muffin and sipped her coffee. And then she opened the book and read the first page.

Two hours later, what was left of her coffee was ice cold and she felt the thrill that she often got when she discovered a great new book and didn't want to stop reading. She hated to admit it, but her agent was right. The story was incredible, and it would be an opportunity that could make her career. She was excited and nervous at the same time. She knew she couldn't pass this one up or she'd regret it. But she didn't have to call her agent yet. She had some time. She wanted to finish the book and make sure she still felt the same way. But in her gut, she knew that she would. She could see why the book stayed on the list so long. It had crazy word of mouth. She couldn't wait to tell her sister about it.

But her legs were getting stiff and she needed to get up and walk around. The rain had stopped, and the sun was peeking out through the clouds. It was a little past eleven, perfect time to go do a little shopping.

She walked toward the wharf, where the ferries came in. There was one pulling in now, a giant catamaran from Hyannis called the Grey Lady III. Bella watched as the boat docked and people started streaming off, many of them with dogs of all shapes and sizes.

She browsed a few gift shops, filled with all kinds of tourist trinkets like sweatshirts, hats, flip flops, mugs and more. Bella was wearing the Nantucket sweatshirt she'd bought on her last shopping trip, so she didn't really need any more touristy stuff. A window display with a pretty, floaty dress caught her eye and she stepped into another store, Nantucket Threads.

The store was adorable with all kinds of cute clothes and shoes. The clothing was an eclectic mix of touristy sweatshirts, casual fun clothes and some really nice high-end stuff. She would definitely have to bring her sister here for some serious shopping. Bella wasn't intending to buy much on this trip, but then she saw the cowboy boots. They were a really soft brown leather with blue and pink embroidered flowers. They were gorgeous.

"Those just came in this week and have been popular. Would you like to try them on?"

Bella turned to see a woman who'd been behind the register ringing up a sale when she first walked in. She was petite, with long blonde hair that fell in beachy waves and she was wearing a similar pair of boots, jeans and a tank top that fell in soft layers. It was a very pretty look. Bella wondered if she owned the shop.

"Yes, please, I'd love to. I'm a size eight."

"Great, I'll be right back. I'm Izzy, by the way. Welcome to my shop!"

She returned a moment later with the boots for Bella to try on. They fit like a glove and Bella sighed with happiness as she looked at her reflection in the mirror and saw how cute they were.

"What do you think?" Izzy asked.

"I love them. I'll take them."

Izzy took the boots, rang them up and put them in a big bag and handed it to Bella.

"Are you on vacation?" Izzy asked as she handed Bella her charge slip.

"I am. For a few months. My sister is coming to visit next week, and I'll definitely be back then. I wasn't planning on buying anything today. But when we come back, I want to spend more time looking around. Your store is wonderful."

Izzy beamed. "Thank you. I look forward to seeing you again, and your sister, too."

Bella left the shop and walked around for another hour. Most of that time was in Mitchell's Book Corner, where she found two more books for her beach reading. By the time she left the store, she was hungry. She took Johnny's suggestion and headed over to Oath Pizza and stood in line for a custom-made gluten free pizza with one of the best gluten free crusts she'd ever had.

After she finished eating, she found a bench and opened her book again. The sun was now shining brightly, and the air had warmed up quite a bit. Perfect weather for outside reading. Bella read for about an hour and then decided it was time to head back to the hotel. She texted the concierge desk to let them know she was ready for a return shuttle, and fifteen minutes later, Johnny and his white Range Rover pulled up to The Corner Table.

"Did you have a good shopping day?" Johnny asked as he put her big bag with the boots in the back of the car.

"Yes. Great suggestions, by the way. You were right about Oath Pizza. I'll check out the chocolate shop when my sister comes to visit."

He looked pleased to hear it. "Great, glad you liked it."

They chatted easily and in no time at all, Bella was back at The Whitley and in her room. She was just about to open the book again and read for a while before dinner when her phone rang. She glanced at the caller ID, saw that it was her agent and debated whether or not to answer. Finally, curiosity won.

"Hi, Jean."

"Bella, how are you? Are you loving it there? Is it relaxing?"

"It was. Until you called," Bella teased her.

Jean laughed. "Very funny. Listen you know I'd only call if it was important. It's about the book I sent you."

"I just started reading it today. You're right. It's very good."

"I knew you'd love it!" Jean sounded triumphant. Which was not uncommon.

Bella waited for her to get to the reason for the call.

"So, that's why I'm calling. I know you wanted a few weeks to decide, but there's a bit of a wrinkle. There's another actress they are considering. Someone they didn't think they could get, but it turns out she's read the book, loves it and reached out to them."

Bella felt a wave of disappointment and realized she really wanted the chance to do this movie. "So, that's it then? They're going with her?"

"Well, not yet. You're still their top choice, but they don't feel comfortable letting this other possibility go without having a commitment from you. They're afraid if they wait, they risk losing you and offending her."

"So, they want a decision now? I say I'll do it and it's mine?"

"Yep. If you say you're in, they'll just tell her it's filled. But they need to know asap. By tomorrow—what do you think?"

Bella smiled. "Tell them I'm in. But I can't start until my two months are up. That's non-negotiable."

"Excellent. I'll tell them. Congratulations, Bella! This is going to be huge for you."

CHAPTER 10

The next morning, after dealing with a few pressing issues, Paula and David met in Paula's office to go over ideas for the Taste of the Town event.

"We can use the same tent people we use for our weddings, so that's easy enough," Paula said.

"And I like your grandfather's suggestion to reach out to that liquor store and have them handle the wine vendors. It will be worth their while with the sales it's likely to generate," David added.

"Peter's a nice guy, too. I'm happy to give him the business. He's run these types of things before."

"Do you have some restaurants in mind?" David asked.

Paula nodded. "I've been thinking about that. How many do you think we want to limit it to?"

"I'd say somewhere between twenty and thirty would be good. Not everyone will say yes. It is an expense for the restaurants in terms of food and staff to attend. But it's great advertising."

"Especially if they win one of the 'best of' awards. I don't think I've seen one of these done on Nantucket before. Closest thing is the wine festival."

"Do you think there will be interest from the local restaurants? Maybe they will feel like they are busy enough and don't need to do this in the summer?" David said.

"I think if we can lock down a restaurant or two before we approach the others it might help. I was thinking we could ask Mimi's Place first. They just reopened a year or so ago under new management and might still be interested in getting the word out."

"Do they serve lunch as well as dinner?"

"Yes, they serve lunch."

David smiled. "Let's go there now. We can have lunch and ask them in person. It's harder to say no to someone face to face. Especially if they know you."

Paula laughed. "Okay, let's go."

DAVID DROVE, AND THEY ARRIVED DOWNTOWN AT MIMI'S PLACE AT A quarter to twelve. Mandy, one of the owners of the restaurant, was at the front desk and smiled when she saw them.

"Hi, Paula. Nice to see you. Two for lunch?"

"Yes, thank you."

Mandy led them to a table for two that was by a window with a nice view of Main Street and people walking by. She handed them each a menu. "I heard about your promotion. Congratulations!"

Paula was surprised and pleased. "Thank you. How did you hear?"

"Mia was in over the weekend and mentioned it. She said she's been dealing with a difficult bride that is having her wedding at The Whitley."

Mia was a wedding coordinator that they often worked with and to say her current bride was difficult was an understatement. Davina was a nightmare.

Paula smiled. "She is. I think she's happy now. At least I hope so. This is David Connolly. He's a consultant who is with us for a few months."

"It's nice to meet you. Stacy will be over in a minute to tell you the specials."

"Thanks, Mandy. Do you have a minute? There's something we want to run by you," Paula said.

"Sure, what is it?"

"So, David and I are working on an event at the hotel for mid-July. We're putting together a Taste of the Town. It will be on a

Monday night. We're thinking twenty to thirty restaurants handing out samples of whatever they'd like to highlight—a signature dish, something new, chowder, or dessert. There will also be a wine tasting."

"That sounds intriguing."

"We're also doing awards," David added. "Attendees will vote and we're thinking top entree, soup or chowder and dessert. Restaurants can offer all three if they like, it's up to them."

"That could be good marketing, just being there and if you win, too," Paula added.

"Well, it sounds good to me. I'll have to talk to Emma and Paul, our chef. They're both in the kitchen so I'll go run it by them and let you know."

"Great, thank you, Mandy."

As soon as Mandy walked away, their waitress, Stacy, came over and told them about the specials.

"We have mushroom tortellini in a gorgonzola cream sauce with toasted walnuts and also grilled swordfish with mango salsa. We also have lobster chowder."

"I'll have the tortellini." Paula loved anything with cream sauce and walnuts.

"And I'll do the swordfish and a cup of the lobster chowder," David said.

A few minutes later, Stacy returned with a bread basket and David's chowder, and they both dove in. Paula loved the bread at Mimi's Place. They got it from a local bakery, and it was served warm with a crispy crust and soft inside. She was happily spreading butter on it when she looked up and saw David looking at her curiously.

"What?" she asked.

He smiled. "I've just never seen someone so enthusiastic about a piece of bread."

Paula laughed. "You haven't tried it yet." She took a bite and sighed. It was that good.

She waited for him to take a taste. "So?"

"You're right. It's pretty good."

"How long have you been living off-island?" Paula asked. She wondered if it was strange for him to be home, or if he was liking it.

"Oh, it's been years. I left after I graduated from college and moved to Manhattan."

"Do you miss it? Or were you anxious to get away?" A lot of kids she'd gone to school with couldn't wait to get off-island and get a job in the 'real world'. Nantucket was like a bubble, and for some of them, a stifling one.

"A little of both, I think. For what I wanted to do, there were no opportunities here so it wasn't ever really an option. But yeah, I miss my family. And I do love Nantucket. It's hard not to love it here. What about you? Have you ever wanted to live anywhere else?"

Paula shook her head. "No. Never. I went away to college, so I experienced what it was like to live away from Nantucket. After four years, I was more than ready to come home. But, still, I lived in Boston for a few years first. My grandfather thought that was important for me. To see what it was like working at another hotel and get some good experience and also to live somewhere else. And Boston wasn't that far. I still got home often."

"You weren't tempted to stay in Boston?"

"Not a bit. Boston was great. I had a good time there, but it's not Nantucket. This is where I want to be, and I'm lucky that there is a good work opportunity for me here."

"Maybe someday I'll come back, too. I do miss seeing my family. Especially with what's going on with my mother. It's hard being so far away."

"They must love having you here now?"

"I think they do. My dad especially needed some support. Now that he found someone to be with my mother during the week, I think it will get easier for him."

A few minutes later, their meals arrived, and they were quiet for a bit. The food was excellent, as usual. Paula's pasta was rich, and she only ate half of it and saved the rest to take home. David cleaned his plate.

Stacy came to check on them and asked if they wanted dessert.

"What do you think? Do you want anything?" David asked.

"I'd love dessert, but I'm too full. You should get something, though. The tiramisu here is amazing."

"Really? That's one of my favorites. If I get one, will you at least have a bite?"

Paula laughed. "Of course."

A few minutes later, Stacy returned with the dessert and two forks. Paula took two small bites and let David enjoy the rest. As he was finishing up, Mandy came over to their table.

"So, I talked with Emma and Paul and they both love the Taste of the Town idea. So, Mimi's Place is in!"

"Oh, thank you. That's great!" Paula was thrilled. Now they could mention that they already had Mimi's Place confirmed when they spoke to the other restaurants.

Stacy brought the check and David immediately reached for his wallet, but Paula stopped him and put down her American Express card. "This was a business lunch, so it's on The Whitley," she said.

David put his wallet back in his pocket. "All right, then. Thank you. I'd say it was a productive lunch. And a delicious one."

———

AS THEY DROVE BACK TO THE WHITLEY, PAULA'S PHONE BUZZED with a text message from her cousin, Hallie.

Where are you? Please come find me when you get back. Davina's here and I want to kill her right now.

"Ugh. Our bride from hell is displeased about something, again."

"The one you mentioned at lunch? Danielle?"

"Davina. Yes, that's the one. We get our share of diva brides, but she is high on the list."

"What's her issue?"

"I don't know. Hallie's dealing with her now and I'll go find out when we get back. She's pretty much had issues with everything so far."

David chuckled. "Have fun with that."

* * *

When they reached the hotel, Paula headed to Hallie's office. She and Mia were there with Davina and all three women looked miserable.

"Paula, come on in," Hallie said. "I was just telling Davina that you were on your way. Davina, Paula is our general manager."

Paula smiled. "Hi, Davina. I hear you're having your wedding with us."

"Well, I was planning on it. But I'm having second thoughts now. I just didn't think this would be so difficult."

"What's going on? How can I help?"

"Davina wants The Whitley to only rent rooms on the Saturday of her wedding to people in her wedding party," Mia said.

Sometimes that made sense, if the wedding was big enough. Paula couldn't recall the size of Davina's wedding, but she didn't think it was that big.

"How many are attending your wedding?"

"One hundred and fifty."

Well, that wasn't going to work. The Whitley had over two hundred rooms. Paula decided to take a different approach.

"We could certainly work with you on that. You are welcome to book all of the rooms. But that would probably be more rooms than you need. We have a total of two hundred and twenty rooms. Your party will fill more than half of them. We have had weddings that have bought out the hotel before. It's up to you. But we can do that if you like."

Davina looked confused and then did the mental math. "I'd have to pay for all the rooms, even if we didn't use them?"

"Well, yes. If you don't want us to rent them out."

"You couldn't just not rent them?"

"I'm sorry, no. If we did that then we'd be paying for those rooms and that's not a good business decision for us. I hope you can understand that."

"Well, maybe I'll take my business elsewhere!" Davina stood in a huff and glared at Paula. But Paula called her bluff.

"That's your choice, of course. We hope you'll decide to stay. Let Hallie and Mia know what you decide to do."

"Thanks, Paula," Hallie said.

Paula walked back to her office and tried not to smile. She knew that Davina wasn't going to cancel her wedding. There was nowhere else that she could get on such short notice. Instead, she would likely continue to terrorize them. But once it was over, they'd never have to see her again.

Hallie came up to her office twenty minutes later.

"What did Davina decide?"

Hallie smiled. "What do you think? She's not going anywhere.

She calmed down after you left. Said she thought about it and understood."

"Good. Has she had her tasting yet?" All brides were invited in for a formal tasting of the menu options. It was usually a really fun night for the bride and groom and usually the mother of the bride and maybe the maid of honor or best man.

Hallie made a face. "No. That's next Thursday night. Poor Nick."

Paula laughed. "It might not be that bad. Nick's food is amazing. Maybe she'll actually relax and enjoy herself."

"One can only hope," Hallie said.

CHAPTER 11

"Good morning, ladies. Where did you end up going last night for dinner?" The two older women had asked Andrea for restaurant recommendations the night before.

"We went to Mimi's Place, and you're right, it's wonderful," Beverly Higginbottom said.

"Best swordfish I've ever had," her sister, Jane, added. The two women were visiting for a week from upstate New York.

"I'm so glad you enjoyed it. How can I help you today?"

"We wanted to ask your advice about the Whaling Museum. Is it really worth seeing? We're heading into town for the afternoon and trying to plan our day."

Andrea smiled. "It's definitely worthwhile. It's one of the places I suggest that everyone visit when they come to Nantucket. Give yourself plenty of time to go through it all. There's a lot to see, and it's fascinating."

"Good. Thanks, Andrea."

As the two ladies walked off, a message popped up on the computer screen, from Paula.

"When you finish up today could you please pop by my office for a moment? David and I want your advice on a new project we are working on."

Andrea's first reaction was irritation. The last thing she felt like doing was helping Paula. But still, she was curious what she might possibly need to know. She typed back that she'd stop by.

And an hour later, when Marco came on to relieve her, Andrea made her way upstairs and stopped outside Paula's office. The door was ajar, and David was in there with her. They were deep in conversation, so Andrea didn't want to barge in. She knocked lightly. Paula looked up, saw her, and waved her in.

"Thanks for coming." Her cousin sounded nervous.

Andrea felt like snapping that it wasn't like she had a choice. But with David sitting there, she bit her tongue and instead said, "What's up?"

"So, Grandfather wants to do a Taste of the Town event. David and I have been working on that today. We had lunch at Mimi's Place, and they agreed to participate. I talked to Peter at Bradford's Liquors and he's going to handle the wine tasting. We're putting a list together of restaurants to invite and wanted to run it by you and see if you had any additional suggestions."

"Let me take a look at the list." Andrea thought it was a great idea and something she'd love to attend, but she wasn't about to admit that to Paula.

She looked over the list. It had all the usual suspects, well-known restaurants that they'd all been going to for years.

"These are all good, but let's add some of the new ones. There are some great new spots that you might not know of yet, but they're very good." She mentioned a few names and Paula jotted them down. "I'd also add Oath Pizza and the restaurant at the airport."

"Oh, I forgot about that one," Paula said.

"What do you think of the idea?" David asked. He looked genuinely curious about her opinion. Andrea had enjoyed chatting with David when he'd introduced himself to her, until he mentioned Paula. She sighed.

"It's a good idea. I'm sure it will be a huge hit. Good luck with it." She turned to leave.

"Andrea…"

She turned back to look at her cousin. "Was there anything else?"

"No. I just wanted to say thank you."

"You're welcome. Goodnight."

ANDREA WALKED HOME, CHANGED INTO HER SWEATS AND WENT FOR A run along the beach. Nothing else relieved stress better than a good run. She'd been having a relatively good day, until her cousin wanted to see her. It still burned her that her grandfather thought that Paula, mousy little Paula who liked to hide in her cave of an office, would be a better choice for general manager. She'd looked scared to even talk to her. Andrea ran faster, harder, and forty-five minutes later when she returned to her house, she was exhausted and feeling calmer. She'd feel even better after a hot shower. Maybe she'd see if Hallie felt like grabbing a bite to eat somewhere downtown. She wasn't in the mood to cook.

After a long shower, Andrea was relaxed and in a much better mood. She changed, dried her hair and made her way down to the kitchen. Her cell phone was on the counter and there was a notification that someone had called. She listened to the message and it was from Elaine Humphrey, the recruiter.

"Hi, Andrea. I've got a good one for you! Boutique hotel in Manhattan needs a new general manager, ASAP. Call me."

New York, not Boston. Andrea was a little disappointed but called Elaine anyway. She picked up on the first ring.

"Hi, Andrea. This one is right up your alley. The Alexandria hotel is uber luxurious, a small hotel in a great area. When can you meet with them?"

Andrea was startled. "They don't want to start with a phone interview?"

"Nope. They loved your resume and want to meet in person. How soon can you go?"

Andrea thought about her schedule. She had this coming Sunday and Monday off.

"I could do Monday."

"All right. Stay tuned. I'll put a call in and get back to you asap."

"Thanks, Elaine."

Andrea looked up the hotel online. The Alexandria really was exquisite. It was small, only one hundred rooms, and the location excellent, close to everything. She supposed it might be fun to go there and check it out, even if she didn't want to pursue it further after meeting with them. And maybe she'd fall in love with it. It wasn't like she'd have to stay in Manhattan forever. Maybe a year or two, and it would be a good resume builder.

Elaine called back just as Andrea was about to walk out the door. She had an interview at The Alexandria Hotel on Monday.

HALLIE AGREED TO GO TO MILLIE'S, THEIR FAVORITE SPOT WHEN they were in the mood for Mexican. It was right on the beach and the food was so good.

They sat upstairs where the views were better. Andrea ordered a margarita and Hallie went with chardonnay. They both ordered the same things—a scallop and bacon taco and a fish taco—and some guacamole and chips to share while they waited for their food.

"So, how was your day?" Hallie asked as she reached for a chip.

"It was fine until Paula wanted to speak to me. I had to report to her office before I left for the day."

"Why? Is everything all right?"

"It's fine. She wanted my opinion for the event they are working on. Do you know about that? The Taste of the Town in mid-July?"

Hallie looked surprised. "No, I hadn't heard about that. What is it?"

Andrea explained it to her. "So, Paula wanted my opinion on the list of restaurants they were thinking of inviting."

"That's what she wanted to talk to you about?"

Andrea nodded.

"Well, that's a good thing. She wanted your opinion. Maybe it was a way of breaking the ice with you. I know she hates that you're mad at her."

Andrea sighed. "I'm not really mad at her. It's just frustrating, you know?"

"I do know. I'm sorry."

"It's not your fault. I'll get over it, eventually. What do you think of the idea?"

"For a Taste of the Town? I think it's fantastic, actually. I bet it will bring a lot of people to the resort and get it on more people's radars. Involving the restaurants will help spread the word, too, and it seems like it could be great marketing for them. This was Grand-father's idea?"

"That's what Paula said, yeah."

"He really is pretty savvy. Especially for someone his age," Hallie said.

Andrea took a sip of her margarita and ignored that comment.

"So, I have some news. I'm flying to New York Sunday night. I have an interview there Monday morning."

"You do? For a GM role?"

Andrea nodded. "At The Alexandria Hotel. Have you heard of it?"

"I have, actually. It's really exclusive if I recall."

"It's a high-end luxury hotel," Andrea confirmed. "I looked it up online and it's gorgeous, same level of quality as The Whitley."

Hallie smiled. "Well, that's good! I suppose it doesn't hurt to check it out, right?"

"That's what I figured. I'll fly in Sunday night and stay at the hotel, get a feel for the place and zip home after the interview on Monday. No one will even notice that I've gone."

"I hope it goes well, but I hate the idea of you moving so far away," Hallie said as the server brought their tacos to the table.

"I'm honestly not sure how I feel about it, either. But I'm going to go and check it out. So, on a different note, how's it going with your bride from hell?"

Hallie laughed. "Davina really is the devil. I had to call Paula to come explain to her that we couldn't simply refuse to rent out the hotel the night of her wedding."

"She seriously asked for that? Wow."

"Yes, and threatened to leave. But Paula handled her well. She just said it wasn't possible. And of course, Davina didn't cancel. Where else would she go last minute?"

"Mia must have been horrified," Andrea said. Mia coordinated a lot of weddings with them, and Andrea didn't know how she put up with people like that.

"She wasn't happy with her. And she felt bad that we had to get Paula involved. But Davina didn't listen to either of us. It was crazy."

"Well, hopefully that's the last of your issues with her. Everything else is settled now, right?"

"Not quite. We still have the tasting coming up. But that should be fine. Everyone loves the food here."

For once, Andrea was glad not to be general manager so she wouldn't have to deal with nightmare clients like Davina. Pretty much everyone that came to the concierge desk was in a good mood and appreciative for the help they received.

"Good luck with that," Andrea said.

"Thanks. Hey, speaking of Mia, she mentioned that she and her sister, Izzy, are having a cookout Saturday night and that we should come. Sounds like there might be a good-sized crowd there."

"That sounds fun. I don't have any plans. They live right on the water, too, don't they? Those condos on the wharf?"

"Yes. It's Mia's condo but Izzy is staying with her for a while. She had a baby not too long ago and she's expanding her store, Nantucket Threads."

"I love her store. I bet she'll do well."

"Mia told me she's doing even better than they anticipated. She's been working with a consultant to build her online store and that's been really busy."

"I'm not surprised. Online sales are booming, and people love Nantucket. I've often thought that we could do more with that at The Whitley. We could sell the monogrammed bathrobes and slippers online as well as the sweatshirts we sell in the gift shop."

"That's a great idea. You should mention it to Paula," Hallie said.

"I'm not mentioning it to Paula!" Andrea snapped.

"Sorry, of course. Maybe to Grandfather, then. I bet he'd be interested. It's a great idea."

"Hm. Maybe I will. We'll see." Andrea wasn't feeling especially generous toward either her cousin or her grandfather at the moment. Her good idea could wait.

CHAPTER 12

"Let's go to Mia's cookout. We don't have to stay long. It's a gorgeous day and there should be quite a few people there that we know." Lucy was sitting in Paula's kitchen, drinking coffee and nibbling on a maple glazed donut. She'd popped over as she often did on Saturday morning to catch up with her sister.

"I don't know if I'm really in the mood for a big crowd," Paula said. She often felt intimidated in large gatherings.

"Don't be silly. What else are you going to do? Besides, I'll be there, so it's not like you won't know people."

"I know. I'm sure Andrea will be there, too. I'm just not sure I want to deal with that."

"I really wouldn't worry about Andrea. She's not going to pay you any attention. You know your cousin. She loves a party and will be flitting around talking to everyone."

"That's true." Paula glanced out the window. It really was a perfect day. The sun was shining and there wasn't a cloud in the sky. And it was warm.

"All right, I'll go. You're right. I'm sure it will be fun. We should probably bring something. What are you thinking?"

"I was going to make potato salad. People always like that at cookouts."

"Maybe I'll make some brownies."

"That sounds good. I'll swing by around six and we can head over."

PAULA RAN ERRANDS THE REST OF THE DAY, DID SOME LAUNDRY, MADE brownies, and around five thirty started getting ready to go to the cookout. She decided on jeans and a pretty floral top in shades of pink and blue. Lucy came by a few minutes before six and they headed out.

It was always challenging finding somewhere to park downtown, especially on the weekends. Lucy had to drive around for a while before she saw a space open up a few streets over. The downtown area was packed with people walking around shopping and heading to various restaurants or to the waterfront and the ferries. Lucy parked and they walked over to Mia's condo, which was right on the wharf. Paula had seen these condos from a distance and always thought they looked lovely, but she'd never been inside one before.

They could hear voices as they approached Mia's unit. Lucy knocked and a moment later, Mia's sister Izzy opened the door.

"Paula, Lucy! Come on in." She glanced at the food they were carrying. "Thanks for bringing that. You can set it down in the kitchen. Are those homemade brownies? They look amazing."

Paula smiled. "Yes, thanks. It's an Ina Garten recipe, lots of butter and chocolate."

"My favorite kind." Izzy led them to the kitchen, and they found room on the counter to set the potato salad and brownies down. "There's wine and beer, help yourself to whatever you'd like to drink. Will's outside on the grill so wander out to the deck whenever you get hungry. He's making his famous Juicy Lucy burgers and hot dogs."

"What's a Juicy Lucy burger?" Lucy asked.

Izzy grinned. "It's out of this world delicious. Seasoned meat with lots of cheese in the middle of the burger."

"I think I have to try one of those," Lucy said.

Paula and Lucy poured themselves glasses of chardonnay, made their way out to the deck and said hello to Mia. Hallie was there, too, and Marco. Paula looked around but didn't see any sign of Andrea.

"Is Nick here, too?" she asked her cousin.

Hallie shook her head. "No, he's working tonight. You know how busy Saturday nights are in the restaurant."

"That's true. I know he has someone that covers now and then."

"He does, but he tries to save it for something he really needs the time off for. He'd have fun here, but he doesn't really know Mia and Izzy like we do."

"Who is that tall guy talking to Mia?" He looked familiar to Paula, but she couldn't quite place him. He had dark hair and a smile that lit up his face.

"That's her next-door neighbor, Ben. He was at the hotel last year for his sister's wedding. It was one of the biggest I've ever done. They live in Manhattan, Upper East Side. It was a spare-no-expenses wedding."

"Right. That's why he looked familiar."

Mia looked up and saw them, and waved them over. She gave them both hugs and introduced them to Ben.

"Paula and Lucy both work at The Whitley where your sister was married," she said.

Ben smiled and shook both of their hands. "Great to meet you. My sister's wedding was something else. It's a beautiful spot."

Paula nodded. "Thank you."

"I'm also Mia's next-door neighbor—well, part of the year."

"You live in Manhattan, too?" Paula asked.

"I do, but I love it here. During the summer months I mostly work from here and only fly back occasionally if it's a meeting I can't get out of."

"What do you do?" Lucy asked.

"Real estate development, mostly. I have some buildings I've bought and rent out or bought and flipped. And I do educational training stuff. That I can do online, so it's what I focus on more when I'm here."

"You're here for the season now?" Lucy asked.

"I am. I'm going to do everything possible to avoid leaving this island for the next few months."

"Ben!" Someone hollered from the living room. "You gotta come see this!"

Mia laughed. "You're being summoned."

He grinned. "Sounds like I am. I'll be back." He left to go see what his friend wanted, and Lucy immediately turned to Mia.

"What's Ben's deal? Is he single?"

Mia looked delighted by the question. "He is. He recently ended things with a girlfriend in Manhattan. She wanted to get married and he said she wasn't keen on spending time here. So, he's very much available. He's a great guy. We've become really good friends."

Lucy smiled. "Good to know."

Paula was intrigued. Ben wasn't the type that Lucy usually went for. Her past boyfriends tended to be more artsy—musicians, writers, painters. Mia chatted with Paula for a bit about Davina's upcoming tasting and another wedding that she'd just booked. When Paula looked up, Lucy was gone.

"We must have bored Lucy with our shop talk," Paula said.

"Or she found someone more interesting to talk to," Mia said.

Paula followed her gaze and saw that Lucy was deep in conversation with Ben in the living room.

"What about you, Paula? Are you dating anyone these days?" Mia asked.

Paula hated that question, though she knew people meant well. She just grew tired of giving the same answer. "No one at the moment. I've just been busy with work. It hasn't really been a focus."

"Hm. You know, Izzy mentioned the other day that Jason, one of Will's friends, is available. He's not here yet, but he should be soon. Really nice guy. His girlfriend dumped him when she got a job offer in Boston."

"Really? Boston's not that far."

"She said she didn't want to do the long-distance relationship thing. And that getting the job was a sign that it was time to move on."

"That's kind of harsh. How did he take it?" Paula already felt bad for this guy and she hadn't even met him yet. She could relate, though. The one serious relationship she'd had ended two years ago for a similar reason. Ryan took a job in New York—his dream job— and felt it was time to move on from Nantucket and from her. He never even considered asking if she wanted to go with him. Paula wasn't sure that she would have but still, it would have been nice to be asked. Since then, it was just easier to avoid getting serious again and going through the same type of breakup.

"Will said it was hard for Jason at first, as it caught him by surprise. But he realized that he dodged a bullet. She wasn't the one."

"Is he from Nantucket?" If he was, Paula probably knew him.

Mia shook her head. "No. He's from Duxbury. He moved here with Will and one other friend after college. He runs a painting business and does pretty well, from what I've heard. He and Will refer each other business." Will was a contractor.

"That's great. How are things with you and Sam?" Paula thought Mia and her boyfriend Sam made a great couple. They'd recently started dating after meeting in a bereavement group. Mia had lost her fiancé to a motorcycle accident, and Sam had lost his wife to cancer. Their friendship slowly grew into a romantic one.

Mia smiled at the mention of Sam. "He should be here soon. He was having dinner at home with his girls and then he'll be over."

A few minutes later, Mandy and Emma walked over and said hello, and Paula chatted with them for a bit. She was pleasantly surprised by what a good time she was having. She knew more people than she'd expected. When her glass was almost empty, she stepped inside to go to the kitchen for a refill. After she filled her glass and was heading back outside, Mia got her attention and waved her over.

Mia was standing in the living room talking to a tall, thin man with dark blonde hair.

"Paula, have you met Jason? He's a friend of Will's." So, this was Jason. He smiled and held out his hand.

"Nice to meet you."

"You, too." Paula shook his hand.

"I was just telling Jason that I've been doing a lot of weddings lately at The Whitley and that you work there, too," Mia said.

"What do you do there?" Jason asked.

Paula hesitated for a second. "I'm the general manager. I've only been in the role for a few weeks, so I'm not used to saying that yet."

Jason grinned. "Congrats on the promotion."

"Can you two excuse me for a moment? I see someone I have to go say hello to," Mia said and swiftly walked away, leaving the two of them together to chat. Paula suddenly felt a little nervous. She always worried that she would run out of things to talk about, which is why parties like this were sometimes stressful.

She scrambled for something to say. "Mia mentioned that you have a painting business?"

"Yeah, Nantucket Paint. It keeps me busy," he said modestly.

"Have you eaten anything yet? I was thinking of trying one of Will's burgers." That way if he didn't feel like talking to her anymore, he had an easy escape and she really was getting hungry. She noticed that Lucy was still deep in conversation with Ben, who looked like he was hanging on her every word.

"No. Will's burgers are legendary. Lead the way."

Paula went out to the deck and Jason followed. Will was just taking several burgers off the grill and set them on a platter next to an array of condiments. They helped themselves to burgers and some of the potato salad Lucy made which someone, Mia probably, had brought outside as well. Once they had their plates, they sat at a small table on the deck. The burger with the hot cheese oozing out of its middle really was delicious. Her face must have shown her enthusiasm as Jason laughed. "See, I told you they were good."

They chatted a bit as they ate, and it turned out they knew some of the same people. That didn't surprise Paula, though, as Nantucket was a small town. She found her nerves melting away as Jason was easy to talk to. He had a good sense of humor, too, and made her laugh as he told her about one of his particularly difficult customers. "I suppose you have your share at the hotel, too," he said.

She thought of Davina and smiled. "Yes, you could say that. Especially with weddings. Some of the brides can be…challenging."

"These burgers really do look great." Lucy sat down at the table with them and Paula introduced her to Jason.

"I'll be right back," Paula said as she went inside to use the restroom. On her way out, she ran into Ben.

"Did your sister leave?" he asked.

"No, she's on the deck eating a burger."

He looked relieved. "Okay, good. I had to run next door to my condo for a minute and when I came back, I thought she might have left. Is she single, by any chance?"

Paula smiled. "She is." She sensed someone looking her way, and saw that Andrea was looking at her and Ben with interest.

"I want to make sure I get her number before she leaves."

"I can help with that." Paula pulled a pen out of her purse and jotted her sister's number on a scrap of paper and handed it to him. She noticed that Andrea looked decidedly displeased.

"Thank you. You're sure she won't mind?"

She nodded. "I'm sure. But she's outside, so you can chat with her more."

"All right. I'll do that. How about you? Are you having a good time?"

"I am. So far, it's been a really fun night. I'll see you outside. We're sitting at a table."

"I'll be out in a few minutes. I see someone I need to chat with first."

ANDREA WATCHED THE EXCHANGE WITH HER COUSIN PAULA AND Mia's hot neighbor, Ben, and felt her blood boil. Was she giving him her number? How could he be interested in Paula? Ben was like the one hot guy at the party and Andrea hadn't really had a chance to talk to him yet. He seemed to know everyone and was constantly in conversation with someone.

But after Paula walked outside, he was alone for a moment, and Andrea pounced. She was across the room in two seconds and held her hand out.

"Hi, I'm Andrea. I don't think we've met yet."

He shook her hand, and she liked the feel of his firm handshake.

"Ben. Mia's next-door neighbor. How do you know Mia? You look a bit familiar."

"From The Whitley Hotel. I work there in concierge services. You probably saw me there at your sister's wedding. It was quite an event."

He laughed. "It certainly was. My sister doesn't do anything halfway. Mia did a fantastic job."

"She did," Andrea agreed. "Do you live here year-round?" She thought that she'd heard it was just a summer place for him.

"I wish. Not yet. I split my time between here and Manhattan."

"No kidding? Do you love living there? I always have fun when I visit, but it's so different from Nantucket."

He laughed. "Manhattan is the concrete jungle. It's great, but I don't miss it when I'm here. When I'm there, I'm almost counting the days until I can get back here."

Andrea looked at him curiously. "If you like it here that much, could you live here year-round?"

"I've tried to think of a way to make that work. But I'm in real estate and I physically need to be there for a lot of the work that I do. But I might be able to shift to spending more time here. That's the goal anyway."

Andrea smiled. "And what do you like to do here?"

"Well, I golf a lot. My family has a membership at the new club. But I like to go downtown to all the usual places, Club Car, The Gaslight."

"I like those places, too. I've never golfed. It's something I've often thought about learning."

Ben's face lit up. "Oh, you should. It's a sport you can play for years. My parents both play and there's a social aspect to it as well."

"I'd definitely like that." She leaned toward him and looked him in the eye and flirtatiously said, "I don't suppose you'd want to give me a lesson sometime?"

Something flickered in his eyes that she couldn't quite read. But then he laughed. "Of course. Anytime. I gave Mia some pointers last year and she loves the game now."

"How does Tuesday afternoon look for you?"

"This Tuesday?"

Andrea nodded.

"Sure. I can do that. Why don't you meet me at the driving range around three, and we can hit some balls?"

"That's perfect." She pulled one of her business cards out of her pocket and handed it to him. "That has my cell on it, in case you need to get in touch."

He tucked the card into his pocket. "Great, that will be fun."

"I was just going to head outside for a minute," Andrea said.

"I'm going that way, too."

Andrea walked outside and saw her cousin Hallie chatting with Paula, Lucy and some guy that she didn't recognize. They were sitting around a table on the deck. She wandered over to them, and Ben followed her.

"There you are. I was just thinking we should head out soon. Are you ready to go?" Hallie asked.

"Sure, I'm ready." Andrea glanced at Ben and then back at Paula and smiled, "Ben's going to give me a golf lesson next week, isn't that fun? I've always wanted to learn."

Andrea saw the look of surprise on Paula's face as she exchanged glances with Lucy. Finally, she managed to take something away from Paula for a change.

"I didn't know you were interested in golfing," Hallie said.

"I've always been curious about it. Ben said he golfs all the time and taught Mia how to golf."

Ben nodded. "It's true, I did. Mia's a good golfer now."

"I think I need another glass of wine." Lucy stood and headed inside to refill her glass.

"All right, we're heading out. Bye, everyone," Hallie said.

"Goodnight, all." Andrea glanced around the table and met Paula's gaze for a moment before heading inside. Paula looked annoyed, which made Andrea happy. She knew it was petty, but still, it made her feel better.

She followed Hallie inside and was heading toward the door when she ran into Marco coming out of the kitchen.

"Leaving already?"

"We've been here a while. Hallie's ready to go home."

"Did you have fun? You have that look, like you're up to something."

Andrea laughed. "Who, me? I don't know what you are talking about. And yes, I had a very good time. See you later, Marco."

When Lucy went inside and Hallie and Andrea went home, that left just Paula and Jason at the table. Paula hoped Lucy was okay. She'd looked annoyed when she went inside.

"I should probably head inside and talk to some people when your sister gets back," Jason said.

"Oh, you don't have to wait." Paula felt bad that he didn't think he could leave her alone.

He smiled. "Don't be silly. I'd rather just stay out here and talk to you, but that would be sort of rude. But I'm glad we have a few minutes to ourselves because it gives me a chance to ask for your number—if you might want to go out sometime?" He seemed a little nervous asking and the question took Paula by surprise. She'd enjoyed talking to him, too, but didn't expect that it was going anywhere.

"Sure, I'd be happy to go out sometime."

Jason pulled out his phone. "Okay, shoot…"

Paula rattled off her number and he plugged it into his phone and sent her a text message that said 'test'.

"Now, you have mine, too. I'll check in with you this week and maybe we can do dinner or something next weekend?"

Paula smiled. "That sounds great."

Lucy returned to the table a moment later, looking somewhat less annoyed, but she didn't sit down. "Are you ready to head home? I think I'm peopled out."

That was usually what Paula said when they went somewhere. "I'm ready."

Lucy glance at Jason. "It was nice to meet you."

He stood as well. "You, too, Lucy. Have a good night."

They said their goodbyes to Mia and Izzy and headed out to the car. Lucy was driving and as soon as they to the car and pulled out of their spot, Paula spoke. "So, that was fun. Did you have a good time?"

Lucy shot her a look. "I did. Until Andrea got her claws into Ben. A golf lesson? Really?"

Paula chuckled. "Yeah, that was a bit much. But it seemed like you and Ben were hitting it off. He asked me if you were single and I gave him your phone number."

"You did? Thank you. We were hitting it off. That's why I was so annoyed with Andrea, though I don't think she saw us chatting earlier. Maybe she was out on the deck. Ben explained that she asked him for a golf lesson and kind of put him on the spot. He asked me out to dinner, for Thursday night. But I wasn't sure what to think. If he was some kind of player. I don't want to be dating the same guy as Andrea."

"I would believe him. That sounds like something Andrea would do. She's not shy."

"No, she's not," Lucy agreed.

Suddenly Paula realized something. "I have a feeling I know

what might have happened. Andrea saw me talking to Ben and when I gave him your phone number, I bet she thought I was the one interested. So, her competitive nature kicked in. If she'd known it was you, I doubt she would have done that."

"You're probably right. But still, he is going to give her a golf lesson. And she is outgoing and so is he. They might get along well." Lucy sounded miserable at the thought of it.

"I wouldn't get ahead of yourself. He asked you to dinner. Go and have fun and get to know him better. He's not your usual type, either."

"No, he's not. I usually go for guys like the one you were talking to. Jason, right?"

"Yes, Jason. He actually asked me to dinner," Paula admitted.

"He did? That's great! Are you excited? He's cute."

"I don't know if excited is the word I'd use. He's nice. I think it will be fun to go to dinner and see how it goes."

"Well, all in all it was a pretty good night. We both met someone and have dates lined up. I think that's a first, both of us in the same night. Maybe it's a good sign?" Lucy always saw signs in everything. But this time, Paula was inclined to agree with her.

"Maybe it is."

CHAPTER 13

Nick took extra care Sunday morning when he showered, changed and splashed on a hint of cologne. He normally didn't wear cologne when he went fishing, but today was different. He'd texted Bella the night before to confirm that she was still up for fishing on Sunday. He hadn't seen her since the night he met her at the outside bar, so he wasn't sure if in the light of day, she'd still be interested. But she was and agreed to meet him just outside the main entrance at noon.

He loaded up his truck with everything they'd need—fishing poles, lures, a bucket for the fish, if they caught any, and a cooler full of snacks he'd made that morning. He also packed a portable radio, a bottle of wine and a few beers. He wasn't sure what she liked to drink, if anything. He usually had a beer or two when he fished as he was out there for most of the afternoon.

He was glad to see that the weather was cooperating. The skies were clear, and it was warm enough that he didn't need a jacket. He had a sweatshirt with him anyway just in case. The temperatures often dropped at the beach unexpectedly.

Nick smiled when he saw Bella waiting outside the front door and he was glad to see she was dressed appropriately in knee-length shorts, sneakers and a long sleeve tee-shirt. She also had a tote bag with her, and he guessed that she had a sweatshirt or jacket as well.

He waved as he pulled up and she came over to the truck and hopped in.

"Good morning!" Bella said cheerfully as she buckled herself in and put her bag on the floor.

"Did you bring a sweatshirt, just in case?" he asked.

She grinned. "I did. I brought my lucky lure, too."

"Did I hear you right?" He knew she'd said she liked to fish, but she had a favorite lure? He might be in love.

She laughed. "I told you I liked to fish. I was hoping to fish at some point while I was here. I haven't used it in ages, since I lived in Vermont actually, but I brought it with me just in case."

"Did you bring your own fishing rod, too?"

"No, that's too clunky. I figured I could just rent or borrow one. The lure is small."

"Well, let's hope it brings us both luck!"

"So, where are we off to?"

"I like Eel Point. It's usually less crowded and I've found the fishing there to be the best. It's also a gorgeous beach and if you like to collect sea shells, that's the best beach on the island for it."

"It sounds lovely."

"Are you hungry? I packed us some stuff to snack on."

"I'm starving, actually. I was hoping you'd say that. I brought some cheese and crackers, too, and some of that beer you said you like."

"Thanks! Are you a beer drinker, too?"

"Not usually. I'm more into wine."

"Good, because I brought a bottle of chardonnay. Bread and Butter. My sisters like that one."

"I do, too. I brought a thermos of coffee for now. Are you a coffee drinker?"

"Always. I had one cup this morning, but I could go for another. You don't have to be back at any particular time, do you?"

Bella shook her head. "No. I'm all yours for the day. I'm in no hurry."

Nick grinned. "Good, because I usually stay out there all afternoon. It's a great way to spend a Sunday and if I catch anything, that's a bonus."

"Well, I intend to catch something," Bella declared.

"Good! I hope you do. If we catch anything, I'll cook it up for dinner."

"I look forward to that."

Nick looked forward to it, too. He really hoped one of them would catch something. If not, he was pretty sure he had some frozen fish in his freezer he could defrost and throw on the grill if they both struck out. Hopefully, it wouldn't come to that.

"I've had pretty good luck the last few times I've been out here," Nick said as he pulled into the beach parking lot. He grabbed the cooler and fishing gear from the back of the truck, as well as two chairs and the radio. Bella grabbed one of the chairs, and they made their way down to the beach and set up the chairs by the shoreline.

Nick handed Bella one of the fishing rods and watched in admiration as she pulled her lucky lure from her bag and attached it to the rod. Once she was set, they walked a few steps to the shore's edge and cast their lines into the water. They stood there for a few minutes. Bella kicked off her shoes and dipped her toes in the water and pulled them out two seconds later.

"This is much colder than California waters."

"Yes, but the fishing is better."

Bella laughed. "That remains to be seen."

Nick moved everything up a bit to where they were standing, and they settled into the two chairs he'd brought. Nick opened the cooler and pulled out several containers of food.

"Do you like guacamole?"

"Of course. Did you make it?"

"I did. I made a pimento cheese dip, too. We can have that with crackers for now."

"I brought some cheese, too, just cheddar and Swiss slices. We can have those, too."

"Sure, let's do it." Nick set everything on top of the cooler and they helped themselves. Bella poured a cup of hot coffee for each of them.

"I've never had pimento cheese before." Bella spread some of it on a cracker. He waited anxiously for her reaction. This was his most-requested dip and it had just the right amount of spice and creamy mayonnaise binding the cheese and peppers together. Before she said anything, Bella was already going for seconds. After she ate her second one, she looked his way.

"That stuff is amazing!"

He grinned and felt a wave of happiness rush over him. Such a simple thing when someone said they liked his food, but it meant so much.

"I'm glad you like it."

Bella raved about the guac, too, which he expected. He knew he made a good guac and was glad she liked it.

"I once dated a girl that hated guacamole."

Bella laughed. "Obviously that relationship was doomed."

"Yep, I think there may have been a second date. That's when she actually told me that she didn't care much about food at all. How's that even possible?"

"Some people really don't. My roommate in California was like that. Super picky and just didn't really enjoy anything. I can't imagine."

"No. Neither can I. I love making people happy with my food. Really everything we do revolves around it. Family gatherings, celebrations, dates."

Bella nodded. "You love your job. Did you always know you wanted to be a chef?"

He thought about that for a moment. "I think I did, though I didn't always realize it. I worked in the kitchen doing everything, and then went off to college for a business degree. But when I graduated, the thought of working in an office wasn't appealing. I couldn't wait to get back to the kitchen. I've been at it ever since. What about you? I don't think you mentioned what you do?"

Bella looked uncomfortable for a moment and hesitated for so long that he wondered if he'd blown it and said the wrong thing. She clearly didn't want to talk about work.

"Listen, never mind. We don't have to talk about work stuff. Besides, you're on vacation. Work is probably the last thing you want to talk about."

"Thank you. Yeah, it's been a stressful year. I've had some health challenges. Nothing too serious. Are you familiar with Lyme disease?"

"When you get bit by a tick?"

She nodded. "Yes. Sometimes when you get bit there's a bullseye pattern rash and if you see the doctor right away, it's not an issue. You take medicine and it clears right up. But not everyone notices a rash. I didn't even know I'd been bitten and had no idea how long ago it was, but suddenly I was sick and couldn't figure out what it was. After lots of testing, they determined it was Lyme and I've been off and on treatment for the past year. It clears up, but then any kind of stress can trigger a flare-up and it's been a stressful year, so I finally put my foot down and decided to take two months off totally and just relax."

"That sounds hard. Will you be able to avoid stress after the two months are up?" He wondered what was so stressful and figured it tied into her job, whatever that was. He was starting to understand why she didn't want to talk about it, if it made her that stressed.

"I'm going to try. I'm making changes in how I work and hopefully that will help."

"I hope so, too. I hate to think of you feeling sick. You look so happy and relaxed right now."

Bella smiled. "I am happy and relaxed. I am loving Nantucket so far. It's just beautiful here and everyone is so friendly."

"We try! I think most of us, in my family anyway, feel lucky to have grown up here and to be able to work and live here year-round. A lot of my friends ended up moving off-island after college. Opportunities can be more limited here."

Bella smiled. "Unless you work in hospitality or retail?"

"Right. There are professions, too, just not on a scale of what's available off-island."

"I wish I could stay here year-round," Bella said wistfully. "It must feel like you're on vacation all the time."

Nick laughed. "It does. When I'm not working, that is."

The conversation slowed to a comfortable silence and Nick appreciated that Bella didn't feel she had to rush in to fill the silence with idle chatter. One of the things he always appreciated about fishing was the solitude, just being one with the beach, watching the tide come in and go out and feeling the breeze across his face and the warm sunlight. It was a good time for reflection, or for not thinking at all and letting go.

They sipped their coffee and watched people walking along the beach. Dogs racing into the surf. Other people getting ready to fish, as well.

Bella suddenly jumped up and Nick saw a tug on her line.

"I might have something!" She slowly reeled the line in and they both laughed when they saw what she'd caught—a seaweed-covered sneaker. She pulled the lure out of it and cast her line into the water again before settling back into her seat.

"False alarm! I was so excited there for a minute. I thought I had our dinner."

Nick chuckled. "It's early still. Plenty of time."

"Tell me about your family. You have two sisters, right? Paula and Lucy?"

He nodded. "Yes, I'm the oldest. Paula is in the middle. She's probably the most serious one. She's super organized and great with numbers. The GM role is new for her. I think she'll be great at it, but it's definitely out of her comfort zone. She's on the shy side and has to be around people more in this job."

"Sounds like it might be good for her," Bella commented.

"I think it will. Lucy's the baby. She's the most creative of all of us. She works the front desk but it's not really her passion."

"What is?"

"She likes to paint things."

"You mean like pictures? Artwork?"

"Sort of. She likes to repurpose things. So, she'll go to a yard sale, find an old desk or chair, or maybe an end table. Bring it home, sand it, paint it and decorate with a custom design. She paints flowers, or ocean scenes right onto the wood."

"That sounds kind of cool."

"She does nice work. Sometimes she shows her stuff at art festivals. People walk around, see her work and she almost always sells out. She told me she just set up a way to sell some of it online, too, through an Etsy store, whatever that is."

"Etsy is awesome. It's like an online arts and craft festival. I've bought some gorgeous things there. I'll have to look up Lucy's shop. Do you know what it's called?"

Nick thought for a moment. He knew she'd told him. What the heck was it called. Finally, it came to him. "Lucy's Looks."

"Cute. That's easy enough to remember."

"What about you? Do you just have the one sister?" He remembered she'd mentioned at the bar that her sister was coming to visit soon.

"Yes, it's just me and Julia. She's a year older than me. She's a librarian and is happily married to her childhood sweetheart. They live in the same small town we grew up in. We're pretty tight. She's only a year older but she likes to mother hen me. But, since she insisted I come here I have to say I don't mind that so much."

"And she's coming to visit soon?"

"Yes! Tomorrow and staying through the weekend. I can't wait."

"Do you have anything special planned?"

"Just all the usual touristy things. Shopping, we'll hit the Whaling Museum as she didn't get a chance to see that when she was here before and of course go to a bunch of different restaurants. We're both foodies."

"You'll have to be sure to come into The Whitley restaurant while she's here, too, and let me know when you come. I'll do a special tasting menu for you both."

"Really? That would be wonderful. She'd love that. I would, too."

Another hour passed before Bella felt another tug on her line and a moment later, Nick did, too. They both stood up and pulled their fish in. They were both striped bass and Nick did a quick measure. They needed to be at least twenty-eight inches to keep. Nick's was only twenty-six, so he threw it back. But Bella's was almost thirty inches, so it was a keeper and he put it in the bucket he'd brought along with some water.

"Looks like you're cooking tonight!" Bella said happily.

Nick was pretty happy about that, too. "Yep. You want to keep going for a while? See if we can get a few more?"

"Sure!" They cast their lines out again and sat down.

"Are you ready for a lobster roll?" Nick asked.

"Yes, please."

Nick reached into the cooler and brought out the lobster rolls he'd made earlier. They had big chunks of fresh, sweet lobster, tossed with just a bit of lemon and mayonnaise and piled onto a soft roll. He handed one to Bella and opened a bag of rippled chips and set it between them.

"I think I'm ready for a beer, too. Do you want a glass of wine?"

"I'd love one, thanks."

Nick opened the wine and poured Bella a glass in a big plastic cup. He opened a beer for himself, one of the ones Bella brought, and they enjoyed their lobster rolls.

"This is so good. We just don't have lobster rolls like this in California," Bella said.

"I've never been to California. What's it like there?"

Bella was quiet for a moment. "It's different. It's beautiful in its own way. Malibu has some gorgeous beaches. It's just a different lifestyle."

"Are you going back there?" It didn't sound like Bella was all that crazy about the place.

She nodded. "Probably. It's where the work is mostly for me. But maybe I can spend less time there. That would be ideal. I'm looking into how to make that happen."

"That sounds like a good compromise. Do what makes you happy. That's my motto."

Bella smiled. "That's a good way to look at things. I'll keep that in mind."

They stayed for another hour or so. Bella caught another fish, but it was too small to keep. Nick got one too that was just long enough, so he added it to the bucket, and they packed up and headed out.

When they reached the hotel, Nick pulled up to the front door.

"Are you still up for dinner tonight? We have a pile of fish to cook up."

"Yes, absolutely. Can I do anything to help?"

It was nice that she offered. "Just bring your appetite. I can come by for you around six, if that works? And then we can walk to my cottage. It's not far from here."

"Perfect. I'll be outside at six sharp."

CHAPTER 14

Bella took a long, hot shower when she got back to her room. It was just about four, so she had plenty of time to relax before she had to meet Nick. She untangled her wet hair and sprawled out on her bed in the snuggly Whitley Hotel bathrobe. She felt relaxed and a little sleepy from spending several hours in the sun and from having a glass of wine. She decided to set her phone for twenty-five minutes so she could close her eyes for a short nap.

As she drifted off, she thought about what a perfect afternoon it had been. She'd enjoyed her time with Nick more than she'd expected to. She was glad to have made a new friend, since she was going to be at the hotel for another month and a half. Truth be told, she couldn't help but wonder what it would be like to be more than friends with Nick. She found herself even more attracted to him after getting to know him better. And she'd totally fallen in love with his food. He had serious talents as a chef. And he was easy on the eyes, too.

She fell into a lovely dream world where she and Nick were dancing at the beach bar where they'd met, swaying to the soft music. She loved the feel of his arms around her. When their eyes met, she caught her breath and waited in anticipation as his lips came toward hers. But before their lips met, he faded away and the sound of her cell phone alarm grew louder as it pulled her out of her dream. She hit the snooze button and tried to get back to that happy place, but it was gone.

So, she swung her legs off the bed, got up and dried her hair. She changed into a comfy baby blue sundress and a pair of new leather sandals she'd bought at one of the shops downtown. She still had some time to kill, so she picked up her book and stepped out onto her deck to read for a bit.

The weather was still gorgeous. Warm with a soft breeze. Bella could see people below coming up from the beach, a family playing Bocce ball and an older couple walking along hand in hand. She tried to read a little but couldn't concentrate, and instead resumed her people-watching. And smiled when she saw a familiar face— Nick, striding across the lawn, looking so handsome in a Hawaiian print shirt and tan shorts. His hair looked damp and wavy like he'd just taken a shower. He went into the building and she checked the time. It was ten of six. She needed to get a move on.

She ran a brush through her hair, so it fell into place. She thought she'd miss her signature long blonde hair, but the shorter style was really growing on her. It made her eyes stand out and that was her best feature. She added a slick of peachy pink lipstick and a squirt of Yves St. Laurent, her favorite perfume.

Bella made her way down to the lobby at five of six and noticed quite a few elegantly dressed guests heading toward the restaurant for dinner. She looked forward to joining them when her sister arrived. She made her way outside and Nick was there, chatting with one of the bellmen. She noticed Nick was holding a plastic bag filled with something green, a vegetable or an herb, maybe.

He looked up as she approached and smiled. It was the same big smile she'd seen in her dream and it took her breath away. She quickly recovered and smiled back. "What's that?" she asked, glancing at the bag in his hands.

He grinned. "I ran into the kitchen to grab some fresh dill for our fish. Are you ready to go?"

"I'm ready!"

He led the way down the road about half a mile to a small neighborhood of similar white cottages.

"My sisters and cousins all have cottages here. The whole neighborhood is filled with Whitleys."

"That's pretty cool. And you can walk to work."

He laughed. "Yes, I think that was part of the attraction for my grandfather in giving us all these cottages, since we all work for the hotel in one capacity or another."

He walked past the first two cottages and stopped at the third. They all had farmer's porches out front. "This is mine."

He opened the front door and they stepped inside. It had a strong beachy feel with light, wide hardwood floors, and lots of white and navy blue everywhere. The sofa in the living room was a deep navy with yellow and white pillows and it looked very comfortable. There was also a well-worn brown leather recliner facing the television. Bella guessed that was Nick's usual spot.

She followed him through the living room and into the kitchen, which was bright and airy and opened into an eating nook that faced the ocean. It was in the distance, but she could still make out a sliver of blue water. The kitchen had a commercial look to it, with lots of stainless steel and poured gray cement counter tops. The stove was the centerpiece of the room with six burners and a double oven.

Nick opened the sliding glass doors that led to his back patio where his grill was. There was also a round glass-topped table and four padded chairs that looked comfortable and well-used. She hoped they'd be eating there tonight.

"So, this is my house. There are two bedrooms and a bath upstairs. It's small, but it's all I need."

"I don't think it's small. It seems perfect to me." Bella loved the feel of the cottage. It was casual and relaxing and cozy all at once.

"I hope you're hungry. We have a lot of fish. I could freeze some of it, actually. But then you'd have to come back to help me eat it."

Bella laughed. "I'm very happy to do that. Can I help you do anything?"

Nick thought for a moment. "I could put you on salad duty. You can throw some lettuce in a bowl and cut up a few vegetables."

"I can do that."

They went back into the kitchen and Nick showed her where everything was. While she was working on the salad, he put the fish and some asparagus on the grill after adding the fresh dill to the marinade. Once the fish was cooking, he came back inside. "Are you ready for some wine? I'm going to have a beer." She nodded and he poured her a glass while she finished chopping vegetables for the salad.

When everything was ready, they ate outside, and Bella thought it might be the best fish she'd ever had. Nick smiled when he saw her expression after she took her first bite.

"The fish is okay?" he asked.

"It's amazing. There's nothing like eating fish you caught yourself, and what you did to it, so good." He looked pleased by the compliment.

When they finished, she helped him clean up and they went back outside to finish their drinks, but this time, they went to the front porch and sat in the two rockers that faced the ocean. They sipped their drinks and rocked as they watched the sunset, and Bella couldn't remember the last time she'd felt so relaxed and happy.

"You're so lucky to live here. This house, it's perfect. Do you sit out here all the time? I would, if I lived here."

"Not all the time, but often enough. If I'm up early, sometimes I'll go for a run and then have my coffee here on the porch."

"That sounds wonderful."

Nick looked at her thoughtfully. "Nantucket suits you. Maybe you should think about moving here. Get a cottage and porch of your own?"

"I wish I could. That sounds heavenly. Maybe someday."

"Well, until then you're welcome to visit whenever you want. I'd love the company. It's more fun to sit out here with someone else," Nick said.

Bella glanced at him. "I bet there's no shortage of people that would love to sit out here with you."

Nick looked suddenly serious. "I don't invite just anyone over. This is a special place to me. I'm tired of dating, to be honest."

Bella found that hard to believe. "Nick, you're handsome and charming. You must have plenty of women dying to go out with you."

"Oh, I've done my share of dating. I just want to find someone that I have more of a connection with."

"You mean you're ready to settle down?" she teased him.

But he didn't laugh. "Maybe. If I meet the right person. I wouldn't mind that at all."

It felt so natural sitting on Nick's front porch, rocking back and forth and just being with him. She wished she could be that special person, but she knew it was impossible. Their lives were too different. Her stay on the island was temporary. She wished, not for the first time, that she could put roots down somewhere other than L.A. But she didn't see how she could. Unless she gave up her career and as stressful as it was at times, she wasn't ready to do that yet.

They stayed out there until the sun set and the air grew cooler. Finally, Bella yawned and said the words she'd been putting off. "I should probably head back to the hotel."

Nick nodded and stood. "I'll walk you back."

"Oh, you don't have to. I know where I'm going now."

"It's getting dark. I'm walking you. I don't mind at all."

"All right."

Nick walked her back, and it didn't take long, ten minutes at the most. They chatted easily as they walked, and the time almost went by too fast. Before she knew it, she was at the front entrance of the hotel.

"Thank you so much for dinner. For all day, actually. I had a great time," Bella said.

Nick smiled—the easy smile that reached his eyes and made tiny laugh lines dance around them. "Thanks for spending it with me. If you want to do it again, just let me know."

"I will. Goodnight, Nick."

CHAPTER 15

"Look who's here!" Paula's mother said. Paula had just walked in the door of her parents' house for Sunday dinner. And sitting around the kitchen table were her parents, her sister and the surprise guest, her Aunt Vivian. Great. Paula hadn't seen her aunt in over six months. She wondered what kind of new drama had happened. Aunt Vivian was all about the drama. She and Uncle Freddy had been touring Europe, last Paula knew. Uncle Freddy was not at the table.

"Come give your aunt a hug!" Aunt Vivian exclaimed.

Paula did as requested, giving her aunt the briefest of hugs and wiggling away when she tried to pull her in tightly.

"It's nice to see you. How was Europe?" Paula noticed that everyone had a glass of wine in front of them. It wasn't quite five o'clock yet, but Paula decided to join them and poured herself a glass before sitting down at the table.

"I was just telling everyone what's going on. I've asked your uncle for a divorce!"

Paula sighed. Her aunt did this every few years and never went through with it.

"I'm sorry to hear that." She didn't ask what happened, because she knew her aunt well enough to know she was going to tell them, in great detail.

"So, I was just telling everyone what's going on. I've just had it with Freddy. He was slowing me down. I wanted to see everything, and he wanted to stay put everywhere we went. I just couldn't take it anymore. Especially when he told me I was being dramatic. Me! Dramatic. He's the dramatic one."

Paula couldn't even look her sister's way. She knew if she did, she'd break into laughter. Her aunt had no idea how ridiculous she was.

"Where's Uncle Freddy now?" Paula asked.

"He's still in Tuscany. Said he needed a break from me. How rude is that? Says he's coming home next week. I'm thinking about having the locks changed. That will show him."

"I'd wait on that. See if you calm down," her mother advised.

"Hm. I'm really done this time," her aunt insisted.

"We have some news," her mother began. Paula knew she was trying to change the subject. "Paula is the new general manager. She just started a few weeks ago."

Her aunt looked confused. "What about Andrea?"

"She's heading up concierge services now."

Her aunt processed that for a moment, then smiled. "Well, that sounds like a good thing. Congratulations, Paula!"

"Thank you."

"I'll be in my office there tomorrow. Let me know if I can be of any help," her aunt said. Paula immediately cringed at the thought.

Aunt Vivian had a small office at The Whitley and, while she didn't have an official title, she popped in from time to time and acted as though she was visiting royalty and had the answers to everyone's problems. She liked being recognized by the staff, and she attended the manager meetings. Even though she had no idea what was going on day-to-day at the hotel, she always offered her opinion. Usually, after a few weeks, she grew bored of it and took off again. But Paula dreaded the upcoming weeks—her aunt flitting about and butting in was an added stress that she really didn't need while she was trying to get used to the new role. She was, however, amused thinking of how David would react to her meddling aunt.

Paula smiled. "I'll do that," she lied.

"So, where's your brother? Is he working?" Aunt Vivian asked.

"No, today is his day off," Lucy said. "He said he was going to go fishing."

"Who did he go with today? I saw him when I was on my way home from the store," her mother said. "He was driving off with a pretty dark-haired girl."

"Long hair?" Paula asked. She tried to think of all the girls Nick knew. She wasn't aware that he was dating anyone at the moment.

"No, she had a chin length bob. She looked vaguely familiar, but I may have confused her with someone else."

"Oh." As soon as her mother described Bella's bob, Paula knew who she was talking about. "I think it's someone staying at the hotel."

Lucy's eyes widened and Paula knew she'd connected the same dots. She wondered if Nick knew who Bella really was. She, David and Lucy were the only ones that were aware of Bella's true identity. Grandfather, too, since she'd filled him in. They generally tried to limit who knew that kind of thing to ensure as much privacy as possible for their celebrity guests. Once word was out to the whole staff, some people couldn't help but talk to their families and the next thing they knew, they'd have press arriving. So far, that hadn't happened. And Paula noticed there had been much speculation in the paper on where Bella might have disappeared to.

"So, girls, tell me everything that's new in your lives. Any interesting new men?" Aunt Vivian asked.

Another question that Paula dreaded. She wasn't ready to share that Jason had asked her out. She was preparing to give her usual non-answer when Lucy beat her to it.

"I've actually just met someone. His name is Ben, and he seems like a really nice guy. We're going to dinner later this week."

"Oh, that's wonderful," her mother said.

Her aunt leaned forward and lifted her glass of wine. "Tell us all about him…"

ANDREA SIPPED A GLASS OF CHAMPAGNE ON THE PLANE RIDE TO NEW York and stared out the window, deep in thought. She had mixed feelings about this trip. On one hand, she was excited to go to Manhattan. It was always a fun place to visit. But could she see herself actually living there? Once the plane landed, she caught a cab to the hotel, settled into her room, then ventured out to a nearby restaurant for dinner.

There was almost a sense of excitement in the air when she stepped outside and walked along the busy sidewalk. People were rushing along on their way home from work or out to dinner and there was so much concrete everywhere, not a tree in sight. It was night and day different from Nantucket.

The hotel was a few blocks away from a restaurant she loved and had been to several times, Becco. It was on Restaurant Row in the theater district and Andrea was a big fan of the triple pasta special. Servers kept walking around offering three different kinds of pasta, all delicious, and they varied each night. The pasta was also unlimited, so one could have seconds, or even thirds.

She started her dinner with a simple green salad and a glass of Italian chianti. All around her, people were dressed to go to the theater. It was fun to people-watch while she sipped her wine. The pasta was as good as she remembered and after she ate her fill, she slowly walked back to the hotel.

She took another look at the lobby when she entered the hotel. It was a contrast in black and white, with black marble floors and plush white sofas. The walls were painted a rich black and the reception desk was white. The staff all wore white suits. The overall look was sophisticated and elegant.

There was a bar off to the left in the lobby, and it had sleek dark brown leather chairs. Andrea was tempted to have a second glass of wine but decided instead to head to her room and get a good night's sleep. Her interview was early in the morning, at nine sharp, and she planned to head straight to the airport after that.

She let herself into her room and happily kicked off her shoes. They were gorgeous black leather, but new and a little snug and her feet were protesting. The hotel room was an oasis of calm. The bedding was all white, with a fluffy down comforter and luxurious Frette sheets.

Andrea slept well and woke early the next day. She took care getting ready for the interview and wore a bit more makeup than she usually did. On a typical day, she often just wore lipstick and maybe mascara. But today she also applied a hint of eyeshadow, concealer, a sweep of blush and a dusting of powder to set it all. She wore her best navy suit, and blew her hair stick straight.

She felt confident as she walked downstairs to the corporate offices. She was meeting with Human Resources first and then with the president of the company. Both meetings went very well. She had a better feeling about this interview than she had at the Lennon. There were no awkward moments and the president, a distinguished man in his early sixties, was interesting to talk to and he seemed to understand her wish to join a hotel that was not owned by family.

"I am impressed with your background, Andrea. I think your experience at The Whitley could be a very good fit for us. We have a few other candidates we are seeing this week and then we'd like to bring two candidates back for a final interview with our board. That might not happen for a few weeks, as several of them are out of the country. Does that work with your timing?"

"That's fine." Andrea wasn't in a hurry. Not for a Manhattan-based role. That gave her a little more time to see if something might turn up in Boston.

"We'll be in touch early next week with our decision."

"Thank you."

Andrea checked out after the interview and caught a cab to the airport. There was a shuttle leaving in an hour for Nantucket, so she didn't have to wait long. She got herself a coffee and relaxed at the gate, waiting for her plane. She had a good feeling about this interview. She would be surprised if she didn't get a call back for a final interview. And she'd go and see what happened. Maybe living in New York for a few years could be a fun adventure.

CHAPTER 16

Paula made her rounds Monday morning, checking in with each area of the hotel and, as she walked down the hall between the catering offices and the lobby, she noticed a woman standing in her doorway holding a towel and looking around, as if she was waiting for someone and she looked irritated.

"Is there something I can help you with?" Paula offered.

"You work here?" The woman did not seem happy at all.

"Yes, I'm the general manager."

"Well. I've been standing here waiting for close to ten minutes for housekeeping to bring me more towels. I asked them yesterday to leave extra and instead they only left one!"

"I'm so sorry. I'll get you more towels myself. I'll be right back." Paula went down the hall, around the corner to the laundry room and grabbed four towels that were still warm from the dryer. She added a handful of chocolates, too, and walked back to the woman as fast as she could. She was still standing in the doorway, glaring at Paula as she approached.

"Here you go. Again, I'm so sorry for the delay." She handed over the towels and the woman's expression softened when she saw the chocolates.

"Thank you. And thank you for the chocolates, too. We've been coming here for years and nothing like this has ever happened before."

"I'll make sure it doesn't happen again. Please accept my apologies."

"It's fine. Thank you for taking care of it yourself."

Paula reached into her pocket and pulled out a coupon for two free drinks at the outside bar and gave it to the woman. "Please have a drink on us as well."

That brought a smile to her face. "Thank you very much."

Paula turned to go and almost bumped into David. She hadn't heard him walk up behind her. He stayed quiet until the woman shut her door and they were halfway down the hall.

"Housekeeping screwed up?"

"Apparently."

"So, what will you do about it?"

"I need to go talk to them, of course."

"Right. Mind if I tag along?"

"Of course not."

They walked down another hall and saw two housekeeping trolleys outside rooms. Paula knocked lightly on the doors and asked each cleaner to step into the hall for a moment. One woman, Marie, had been with the hotel for years. The other one, Michelle, was relatively new, and much younger.

"I was just walking down the hall and there was a woman in room 200 that was waiting for extra towels that never came. And she said her room was short on towels. Do either of you know what might have happened?"

"I'm sorry, I don't. I didn't have that room," Marie said.

"I did. I screwed up," Michelle said. "I was supposed to get her those towels and totally forgot. I'm sorry." She didn't sound sorry, though. She sounded disinterested.

"Okay, well, please be more careful. That's not supposed to happen in a place like this."

"Got it," she said.

Paula smiled at Marie. "I heard you just got a new grandchild?"

Marie's eyes lit up. "Yes!" She reached into her pocked and pulled out a photo of an adorable baby and handed it to Paula.

"So cute!" Paula handed it back. "Enjoy the rest of your day, ladies." Marie was still smiling as she put the photo back in her pocket, while Michelle just turned and went back into the room she'd been cleaning.

David was quiet as they walked back to their offices. When they reached them, he turned to Paula. "I suppose this is as good a time as any for our touch base meeting. Do you have a few minutes?"

"Sure." Paula wasn't sure what he wanted to touch base about, but she followed him into his office and took a seat across from his desk.

"So, I've been working with you for a few weeks now and your grandfather wanted me to give him an assessment when I finish as to how suitable I think you are for the job. I thought it might be good for us to check in and discuss how that's going and where I see some areas for improvement."

"Okay." Paula suddenly felt a bit nervous and on the defensive.

"Overall, considering you haven't been in this role before, I think you're doing a decent job. People like you and that's the piece that was missing with Andrea. But I've noticed that some of them seem to be taking advantage a little. They've sensed that you're nicer than Andrea and they can get away with more. That Michelle is a perfect example."

Paula felt like she'd just failed a test. And she never failed tests. It wasn't a good feeling. She also knew he was right. "So, how do I fix that?"

"You just need to take a firmer hand. Let them know what you expect and that you won't put up with anything less."

Paula felt sick to her stomach. She hated conflict. Maybe taking this job was a bad idea. Maybe it wasn't too late to go back to hiding in her office and just focusing on the numbers. Grandfather could call the headhunter and get someone in that had experience and wasn't a pushover, like her.

"Are you okay? You look miles away." David looked at her with concern.

"I'm fine. Was there anything else?"

"I think that's it for now. Just think about what I said."

"I will."

Paula went into her office and closed the door. She felt her eyes well up with tears which she immediately wiped away. She was not going to cry over this. She'd actually thought she was doing a pretty good job. So, to have David say she wasn't was disheartening. Especially when she saw the truth in what he said.

Andrea never had that problem, but she also had employees intimidated by her and turnover was high. People didn't like working for her cousin. There had to be a middle ground. But it would mean Paula had to step out of her comfort level. Could she do that? She sniffled and grabbed another tissue.

And then she called housekeeping and Maria answered.

"Can you please ask Michelle to come to my office for a moment?"

"Of course."

Five minutes later, Michelle knocked on her door, her expression a mix of surliness and guilt.

"You wanted to see me?"

"Yes, please come in and shut the door. Have a seat." Michelle sat in the chair across from her desk.

"Michelle, how long have you worked here?"

"About three months."

"Do you like it here?"

"It's okay."

Paula looked closely at her. Michelle was in her mid-twenties and Paula doubted that she was excited about a career as a housecleaner. It was just a job.

"Listen, I know that housecleaning isn't the most glamorous work. But it's a good job. And this is a good place to work. There will be other growth opportunities here, depending on what you want to do. People have moved into all different areas—the ones that do a great job and are hard workers." She was quiet for a moment and Michelle was, too.

"What happened this morning can never happen again. I'm not sure if I was clear about that earlier. Our guests expect a level of service here that wasn't met. Can you assure me that won't happen again? If it does, we won't have any choice but to terminate you. We can't take the risk of potentially losing clients because of poor service. I won't put up with it. Do you understand?" Paula spoke quietly but firmly.

Michelle nodded. "I'm sorry. I do understand. It won't happen again."

"Thank you, Michelle. I appreciate that. You can go now."

Michelle left and when Paula stood to close the door, David was just stepping out of his office. He saw Michelle walk by and then caught Paula's eye and smiled. She ignored him, shut her door and sat back down at her desk. She was shaking. It hadn't been easy for her to talk to Michelle like that. She hoped that her words had sunk in. She really didn't want to have to fire anyone, but she meant what she said.

BECAUSE HER GRANDFATHER HAD A MORNING MEETING DOWNTOWN, they held the Monday update meeting in the afternoon. A little after one, they all gathered in the conference room—Nick, Hallie, David, Paula, and her grandfather. Paula was about to start the meeting when the door flew open and her Aunt Vivian rushed in.

"I'm so sorry I'm late. Don't mind me." She settled into an empty seat and looked around the room until her eyes landed on David. She held out her hand and introduced herself. "I'm Vivian. I help out here when I'm in town."

David looked a bit confused as he shook her hand. Clearly, her grandfather forgot to mention that Aunt Vivian was back. "Nice to meet you," he said.

Paula started the meeting and handed out her usual spread-sheets with the weekly numbers.

"Hallie closed a new conference this week, which bumped our numbers quite a bit. Hallie, do you want to tell us about it?"

Hallie leaned forward in her chair. "Sure. It was actually thanks to a lead from David. A Manhattan hedge fund called to see if we could accommodate them for a company weekend conference in late September. They booked all of our suites, including the four presidential ones." The presidential suites were their nicest, biggest rooms at almost two thousand square feet. They had three bedrooms, a huge deck, full kitchen, dining area and a conference room.

Grandfather looked pleased. "That's fantastic. Nice work, Hallie. And thank you for the referral, David."

David smiled. "I'm glad it worked out."

Paula went through the rest of the agenda, finishing with an update on the Taste of the Town event.

"David and I had lunch at Mimi's Place and they were the first to agree. So, we were able to use that with the other restaurants we spoke to. So, far, twenty have agreed to come on board and we're still waiting to hear from a few and have a few more to talk to. I think we'll end up with between twenty-five and thirty total."

"Good job, Paula and David," her grandfather said.

"We're doing a Taste of the Town event? Will The Whitley's own restaurant be participating?" Aunt Vivian asked.

"I'm planning on it," Nick said.

"Are you sure that's a good idea?" Aunt Vivian clearly didn't think it was.

"Well, yes. We are hosting the event, after all," Paula said.

"Exactly. So, maybe we shouldn't be participating as well?" Aunt Vivian argued.

"I think it's an excellent idea for us to participate. I'm excited to do it," Nick said. "It will be great advertising for us—to get people to sample our food and want to come eat here."

"Hm. Well, people already know about us. I think there's a conflict of interest," Aunt Vivian insisted.

"Vivian, it was my idea to have this Taste of the Town event, and a main reason was to showcase the property—all of it, including our restaurant," Grandfather said.

"There shouldn't be any conflict," Paula explained. "Everyone that comes will get to vote on all of the restaurants. So, the winners will be their choice, and everyone has an equal chance."

"All right, then. I see I'm outvoted," Aunt Vivian said.

"There was no vote. We're all on the same page with this event," David said.

"That settles that. What's next on the agenda?" Grandfather asked.

Paula smiled. "That's it. We're done here."

———

"I take it your aunt is a Whitley?" David asked as he and Paula walked back to their offices. Her grandfather and Aunt Vivian had gone in the opposite direction.

Paula nodded. "Yes, that's my Aunt Vivian. She is a character.

She just returned from spending six months touring Europe with my uncle. He's still there. He needed a break from her."

David chuckled. "So, is she working here full-time now? And in what capacity?"

"No one knows exactly what she does, other than drive us all crazy. She has an office and when she feels like it, she comes around. Usually, she gets bored after a few weeks and then we don't see her again for months."

"Okay. So, she has no formal role, then?"

"No. She likes to 'help out' in all areas as her mood suits her. So, we never quite know what to expect. I just hope she doesn't meddle too much with the Taste of the Town event. She didn't seem all that enthused about it."

"There's not much she can do about it. It's happening," David said.

"Yes, I suppose that's true." But David didn't know her Aunt Vivian.

CHAPTER 17

They were halfway through Davina's tasting on Thursday night, before Paula finally relaxed a little. Davina had brought her mother, her best friend, who was also her maid of honor, and the groom. Hallie and Paula were seated at a separate table and were having a smaller tasting of the same items. They didn't normally do that at a tasting. It was actually Nick's idea, and given how difficult Davina had been so far, Paula thought it was a good one.

The first course was appetizers and Paula couldn't imagine they'd find any fault there. Nick personally made all of the appetizers and Paula loved all of them. There were tiny tuna tacos—buttery sushi grade tuna in a mango vinaigrette with an avocado cream sauce and fresh cilantro, scallop cakes, Lobster Newberg in phyllo cups, Oysters Rockefeller, short rib ravioli, dates stuffed with gorgonzola and wrapped in crispy bacon, and The Whitley's famous colossal shrimp cocktail.

Paula and Hallie went to Davina's table for feedback and they were all smiles after the appetizers. Davina especially.

"I want to have all of them at my wedding. Can I do that? Those Lobster Newberg cups were amazing," she gushed. Paula had never seen her so happy.

"Of course, you can," Paula assured her. She didn't add that it would likely double the cost for appetizers, but if that's what she wanted to do, it was all good.

For the main course, they were trying four items—marinated and grilled swordfish, poached lobster, filet mignon with a red wine reduction sauce, and a roasted chicken with wild mushroom risotto.

When they went to check with Davina after the entree course, she was less enthused.

"The lobster, filet and chicken were excellent. But I can't bring myself to try the swordfish. I've never had it before, and I can't imagine my guests will like it."

"It's one of our most popular menu items," Paula said.

"I told her she should have a fish option. Lots of people like fish," Davina's mother said.

"Do you like fish at all?" Hallie asked her.

"Sure. I like the white flaky fish, cod or haddock, even halibut."

"If you like all those, you might be surprised to find you like swordfish, too. It actually reminds me a little of chicken," Hallie said. "Nick was experimenting the other day and fried up some swordfish chunks in seasoned batter, and it was very chicken like, and delicious. I'd encourage you to at least try a bite, before deciding."

Davina looked dubious. "Tastes like chicken?"

Hallie laughed. "Well, not exactly. But it's not fishy, if that's what you are worried about."

"Just try a bite," her mother encouraged her.

"Fine." Davina cut a sliver of swordfish and popped it in her mouth. She looked like she wanted to hold her nose as she did it. But after a moment, her expression changed, and she took a bigger bite. And smiled.

"Okay, you're all right. It's nothing like I imagined. Why don't we offer the swordfish, the chicken—because there's always someone that wants chicken, and the lobster and filet together as a surf and turf?"

"That's perfect. We can do that," Hallie said.

Nick and Roland came out to meet Davina's party when the tasting was finished, and Paula had never seen Davina so gracious. There were no crazy demands, and no complaints.

After Davina and her party left, Hallie and Paula decided to have a glass of wine at the outside bar. It was a gorgeous night and they both wanted to relax and celebrate getting through Davina's tasting unscathed. Nick had come in just to help with the tasting, so he said he'd come and join them shortly as well.

The bar was busy, but there were several empty seats and Paula and Hallie slid into them. Frank, the bartender, didn't even ask them what they wanted. He just said hello and set two glasses of J. Lohr chardonnay in front of them, their usual order.

There was a woman sitting next to Paula who looked vaguely familiar. Paula didn't think she'd ever seen her before, though. She was very pretty, with fair skin and dark, almost black hair that was cut in a chin-length bob. She had an intriguing looking drink in front of her. It was creamy and blue.

"What is that?" Paula asked.

"It's a Blue Hawaiian. I haven't tried it yet. Frank said it's like a Pina Colada. I told him I wanted a vacation drink." She took a sip. "Oh, it's really good!" She smiled and Paula had that same feeling again that she knew her, somehow.

"Are you on vacation?" Paula asked.

"Yes, a nice long one. I'm actually here for two months. It's going by too fast. Are you on vacation, too?"

Paula smiled. "No, I work here, actually. I'm Paula Whitley, the general manager."

"You're Paula! I'm Bella and this is my sister, Julia. I went fishing with your brother on Sunday. We had so much fun."

So, that was why she looked so familiar. Paula glanced at Hallie and saw she was chatting with Frank, the bartender. But still she lowered her voice a little. "Has anyone recognized you? I wouldn't have known if you hadn't told me your name. No one else on staff knows, by the way, just me and my sister Lucy that checked you in."

"I wondered about that. You haven't told Nick?" Bella asked.

"No. You should be the one to tell him, if you wish."

"Thank you. It's kind of nice that he doesn't know, to be honest. Everything changes once people know." A hint of sadness filled her eyes for a moment.

"Nick should be along any minute, actually." Paula didn't think Nick would change how he acted if he knew Bella's true identity. But he might be disappointed that because of who she was, having a normal life and settling down somewhere outside of L.A. probably wasn't going to happen.

"Oh, good. I want my sister to meet him."

"Who do you want your sister to meet?" Nick said with a teasing tone. He'd walked up to the bar and neither of them had seen him coming.

"Nick, you're here! I wanted to introduce you to my sister, Julia. She's here for the week."

Julia smiled. "It's nice to meet you. Bella said you had fun fishing."

"We did. We had a good day and caught some stripers."

"Nick cooked it up for our dinner and it was so good," Bella added.

Paula got Frank's attention and Nick ordered a beer. When it came, he held it up and toasted Hallie and Paula. "To surviving Davina's tasting." They all clinked glasses.

"Who's Davina?" Bella asked.

"A bride that had her tasting tonight. She's been a little…challenging with her demands. So, we didn't know what to expect, but fortunately she liked everything," Nick said.

"I've actually never seen Davina in such a good mood. Turns out she's a foodie and she loved everything," Paula added.

Bella laughed. "How could she not? Nick's food is amazing."

"Thank you." Nick looked at both Bella and Julia. "You two should be sure and come in one night while your sister is here. I told Bella I'll do a special tasting menu for you. It will be fun."

Julia smiled. "Bella mentioned that, and I am really looking forward to it. I leave on Sunday, so we are thinking to do it on Saturday night."

The chair next to Hallie opened up, so she and Paula both moved over to let Nick sit next to Bella as he was deep in conversation with her and Julia. Paula could tell her brother was interested in Bella as more than a friend. She hoped he wasn't going to fall too fast and end up heartbroken when Bella's two months were up.

"They look cute together," Hallie said. "Where is she from? Any chance there could be a romance there?"

Paula shook her head. "Not anything long-term. She lives in California."

"Oh, that's too bad." Hallie took a sip of her wine. "How's it going with David? He seems nice."

"It's going okay. I thought it was going better than it was. David had a meeting with me earlier today and told me I'm too nice. That I need to be firmer, so people don't walk all over me."

Hallie was quiet for a moment. "And what did you think about that feedback?"

Paula sighed. "That he was probably right. I just didn't like to hear it."

"Well, there could be some truth to that. You're the total opposite of Andrea and the way she approached people. She was a little too blunt and direct."

"I don't like conflict," Paula admitted. "But I'm going to work on that and do better."

"You'll do great. People like you. So, what's David's deal? Is he single?"

"Why, are you interested?" Hallie dated but wasn't seeing anyone regularly and hadn't been serious with anyone in a long time.

"No, I don't think so. He's a little too corporate for me. He seems nice, though, and he's certainly good-looking."

"He is. I don't really know his status. It's never come up in conversation. He hasn't mentioned a girlfriend."

"I was just curious. So, when's your date with Jason? Are you excited?"

"We're going to dinner Saturday night. He mentioned The Gaslight. Said there's a good blues band there that night."

"That sounds fun. I love that place—good food and they always have interesting live music."

"I'm a little nervous, to be honest," Paula admitted. "It's been too long since I've dated anyone. I'm feeling a little rusty."

"I'm glad you're getting back out there. You'll be fine. Just think of it as dinner with a new friend. See where it goes. Don't put too many expectations on it."

"Thanks. That's really good advice."

Hallie grinned. "Just go and have fun. And enjoy a delicious dinner."

"I think I can do that."

CHAPTER 18

"Any fun plans for tonight?" It was five of two on Tuesday and Marco had arrived to relieve Andrea at the concierge desk.

Andrea grinned. "I'm off to learn golf."

"No kidding? You're taking lessons? I didn't know you golfed."

She laughed. "I've never picked up a club before. But I've been meaning to learn. A new friend is giving me a lesson."

Marco raised his eyebrows. "I see. So, you have a date!"

"I'm not sure about that. For now, it's a lesson and we'll see." She'd love for it to be an actual date, but she didn't think that was how Ben was thinking of it. He was just being nice. But maybe once they spent some time together…

"Well, have fun."

"I will, thanks. Do you golf?" She knew he liked to surf.

"I love golfing. My brother and I like to hit the links for a round when our schedules match up. Anytime you want to play, let me know."

Andrea knew playing golf with Marco would be fun.

"I will. Once I figure out what I'm doing."

ANDREA HEADED HOME TO SHOWER AND CHANGE. SHE WAS MEETING Ben at the driving range at three thirty. She'd already bought a set of starter clubs and loaded them in her car.

It was a warm day, so she went with a pale blue sleeveless golf shirt and tan shorts. She didn't have golf shoes and didn't think it really mattered for the driving range, so she just wore sneakers. She tied her hair back in a ponytail and added a hot pink visor to block the sun. A quick swipe of lip gloss and she was ready to go.

She arrived at the driving range right on time and Ben was already there. He waved as she drove in and she quickly parked, grabbed her clubs and walked over to him.

"I hope you weren't waiting long," she said.

Ben smiled the big, easy smile that had caught her interest at the cookout.

"I just got here a minute ago. You're right on time. Are you ready to go?"

He led the way, and they found a good spot to hit from.

"I'm surprised it's not more crowded," Andrea commented. There were only a few others there hitting balls.

"It's too nice of a day. People are out on the course. It's usually busier in the morning."

"Oh, that makes sense."

"Okay, so first thing. This is how to hold your club." Ben demonstrated the proper way to grip and hold the club. He checked Andrea's positioning and had her move her hands down a bit.

"So, you want to keep your arms straight, but not locked straight, if that makes sense." He showed her what he meant and then she tried to do the same.

"Good! Okay, now we try to hit the ball." He hit a few to show her the way to swing and then he had her try it.

"Remember head down, arms straight." She swung and missed and felt like an idiot.

"Don't worry about that. Everyone does it. Keep your feet flat. You came up on your toes that time. Did you feel it?"

She hit again and again and again. Just when she thought she had it, her next hit would be awful.

"This is a frustrating game," she said.

Ben laughed. "It can be. It's as much a mental game as a physical one. The more you hit, the more you play the game, the easier it will get and the better you'll play."

They hit balls for about an hour and by the end of it, Andrea was hitting much better. Her balls didn't go anywhere near as far as Ben's did, but they were going straighter, which he said was a good thing.

"Let's work on our short game now and our putting." Ben showed her how to hit with her different clubs and how to chip, pitch and putt. It was a lot, but Andrea had fun learning and Ben was encouraging.

When they finished up, Andrea got up her courage to ask if he wanted to grab a bite to eat. "On me, of course. I'd love to thank you for the lesson."

Ben hesitated for a moment before smiling and agreeing. "How can I say no to that. You did really great today. We're not far from the club I belong to. Want to go have a drink there?" he suggested.

"Sure." Andrea had driven by Nantucket's newest golf club a million times but had never been there. She'd always been curious about what it would be like. She knew it was very expensive to join, something crazy like a million-dollar initiation fee. Way out of her budget. She'd suggested to her grandfather once that he should join for the family and he laughed at the idea. He was a wealthy man but told her that was a ridiculous amount of money and he didn't like golfing, anyway.

Andrea followed Ben down the road to the club. They parked and he led the way into the restaurant/bar area. They sat outside on the patio because it was gorgeous out. When their waitress came, Andrea ordered a margarita and Ben got a draft beer. "What are you in the mood for?" Ben asked. "They have great nachos and club sandwiches here."

"Both sound good." They decided to share a platter of nachos and a turkey club sandwich. It was plenty of food. While they ate, they chatted about the people they both knew.

"Mia and Izzy are great neighbors. I had a crush on Mia when we first met, but I don't think she ever saw me that way. She'd also met Sam and they really hit it off."

"Are you dating anyone now?" Andrea asked. She was curious if he'd mention Paula.

"I just ended a relationship before I came back here for the season. I'm dating here and there, but nothing serious. What about you?"

"I was engaged until about a year ago. I'd dated Steve for six years and we got engaged because we were tired of people asking about it. It was the logical next step, but I don't think either of us really wanted to do it. He's a great guy. But we probably should have ended it way sooner. Sometimes it's just easier to coast along than to deal with a breakup."

Ben nodded. "I can see that. How far did you get with wedding planning?"

"Not far at all. I realized when I started making lists of everything I needed to do that I just wasn't excited about any of it. I see brides here all the time who are obsessed with every last detail of their weddings. And I just wasn't feeling it. I dreaded having to do it, to be honest. That's when I realized it would be a mistake to go on. I talked to Steve and he was surprised at first, but mostly relieved."

"Good you realized it before it was too late," Ben said.

"I know. Funny thing is Steve got married last month. He met someone a few months after we broke up and they got engaged six months later."

Ben grinned at that. "I think when you know, you know."

Andrea laughed. "Right. It shouldn't take six years to figure it out."

They chatted easily as they finished their drinks. Ben was funny and had her laughing with some of his stories. He was an adventurer and loved to travel and to sail.

"Last year, I rode on a friend's boat for the Figawi race. That was a blast. Have you ever done that?"

"Yes, once. Steve's boss raced in the Figawi every year and the first year we were dating, we both got to go. It was really something. Did you do it again this year?"

"No. He didn't race this year. I went to all the parties here, though. That was fun."

"I'm sure it was. It's always a fun weekend." That was another thing she liked about Ben. He was social and outgoing, like she was. She was glad she'd suggested the golf lesson. She couldn't get a read, though, on if Ben was attracted to her at all. He had the kind of personality where he was charming and flirtatious with all women in a fun way. But it made it harder to tell if he just thought of her as a friend.

When they finished up, and the waiter cleared their table, Andrea asked him for the check. He seemed startled by the request at first then glanced at Ben. "There is no check. Ben has a house account here."

"Oh, okay." When he walked away, Andrea turned to Ben, "I wanted to treat you."

He flashed her that smile. "Sorry. You're actually doing me a favor, though, by coming here. I have to spend a certain amount at the restaurant every month as part of my membership. So, it just went toward that."

"Okay. Well, thank you, then."

They walked out and when they reached their cars, Ben asked, "So, think you're up for an actual round on the golf course soon?"

"Do you think I'm ready for that?" Andrea was a little nervous and wondered if she needed more time on the driving range first.

"The best way to learn how to play golf is to play golf. I can take you through and give you some pointers as we go. If you're interested."

"Oh, I'm definitely interested!"

CHAPTER 19

David noticed that Paula had been a little cold towards him since their meeting where he gave her the feedback that she needed to be firmer with the people she managed. He could immediately tell that he'd upset her, and knew she was sensitive and had been worried about moving into the role to begin with. He thought he was helping, though, so she could try and improve and develop her management skills.

He'd been encouraged when he saw Michelle in her office not long after their chat and took it as a good sign that she was making an effort already to improve. He'd nodded and smiled but she'd simply turned and went back into her office. And since then, she'd been a little distant toward him. And he didn't like it.

He realized he'd enjoyed their interactions. Paula was smart, and they both enjoyed analyzing data and using it to guide their decisions. And they'd had fun working on the Taste of the Town event together. She'd made him laugh with her stories about nightmare brides and though he didn't talk about the situation with his mother much, when he did, Paula was a good listener.

So, he was determined to get back into her good graces. His opportunity came when he ran into her brother Nick in the kitchen. David had a question about logistics for the Taste of the Town event and Nick had the answer. He was also finishing up a day shift and had the night off.

"What are you doing tonight? A few of us are going out for drinks after work. You should come."

"That sounds good to me. Where and when?" David hadn't been out for after work drinks yet with anyone.

"We're meeting up at five thirty or so at the outside bar."

"I'll see you then. Maybe I'll see if I can get Paula to join us."

Nick laughed. "Great idea. Tell her it's been too long since she's come out with us."

"I will."

David went back to his office and finished up what he was working on. At a quarter past five, he knocked on Paula's door.

"Come on in."

He pushed the door open. Paula had a spreadsheet up on her computer screen, one pencil in her hand and another stuck in her hair. It was all twisted up into a knot and the pencil held it in place.

"Nice hair-do," he teased her. She didn't wear her hair like that outside of her office.

She laughed. "I know it probably looks ridiculous. But when I'm focusing on something, I don't even realize I do it— I twist my hair up and off my face and grab whatever is handy to secure it."

"It looks cute."

"Thanks. Did you want something?"

"Yeah. I ran into your brother a little while ago and he invited me out for drinks with him and a few others. He said you should come, too, and that it's been too long since you last went out with them."

Paula smiled. "He's right. It has been too long. I guess I could go for one drink. What time?"

"I'm heading down in fifteen minutes. I can come get you then."

"Perfect."

At five thirty sharp he knocked on Paula's door again. Her messy bun was gone, and her hair was down and straight and shiny. Her computer was already shutting down. She stood and grabbed her purse, and they made their way downstairs.

Nick was already at the bar, sitting next to Marco and Andrea. David sensed Paula hesitate when she saw Andrea. He made a point to sit next to Nick so when Paula sat, she'd be as far away from

Andrea as possible. Andrea simply nodded when she saw them and went back to talking to Marco.

David ordered a draft beer when Frank, the bartender, came over and Paula got a chardonnay.

"So, how did your day go?" Nick asked. "We were busy in the kitchen. Lunches have been slammed lately. Although today wasn't exactly a beach day, so that helps."

On better weather days, guests at the hotel sometimes got lunches to go, but usually were out and about, either on the beach or sightseeing and so lunch service usually wasn't all that busy. But on a cloudy or rainy day, it was different.

"We've been working on a few things. The Taste of the Town event is keeping us pretty busy. I think it will be a fun event and good for the hotel."

Nick nodded. "I'm excited for it, too. Roland is letting me handle it and decide what to offer. I've been tossing around a few ideas for appetizers. We'll do our seafood chowder, of course."

"Will you do an entree sample, too?" Paula asked.

"Yes. I'm leaning toward short ribs with rosemary mashed potatoes. And maybe some kind of seafood for the appetizer."

"That sounds like a good combination," David agreed. "Some people don't like seafood and just about everyone likes beef."

"It's one of our most popular dishes," Nick added.

"Bella's sister, Julia, seems nice. Are you going to do something special for their tasting? Paula asked.

"Her sister is great. We closed the bar last night. They're both fun to talk to."

"I chatted with Bella a bit before you got there. She seemed excited to see you again," Paula added.

David noticed that Nick seemed both embarrassed and pleased to hear it.

"Yeah, I was happy to run into her, too. I'm still working out what I'm going to make for them, but it will be impressive."

Paula laughed. "I know it will be. I wonder what they are up to tonight?"

"She said they were going into town today to do some shopping and eat tonight somewhere on the water. Maybe the Straight Wharf."

"Nick, what do you think about this?" Andrea asked.

Nick turned his attention to his cousin and Marco, and David turned to Paula, who was sipping her wine and looking around. The two guys that were the night's entertainment seemed like they were almost ready to start playing.

"Are they good?" David glanced at the two musicians.

"They are. It's vacation music, lots of Jimmy Buffett, that kind of thing."

"It really is a great spot. I almost feel like I'm on vacation, too, sitting outside here." He was glad to see that got a smile out of Paula.

"I know. I really feel lucky to live here year-round. It's such a beautiful spot."

"So, where do you go on vacation? Do you have anything fun planned?"

"I haven't gone anywhere in a while. Last year I just relaxed at home and caught up with friends I hadn't seen in a while. I've thought about going to Europe, though. I've never been there, and we have some relatives in London, so that might be fun."

"London's great. All of Europe, actually. I'd love to go back, especially to Italy. The food and wine there are so good."

"That sounds fun, too. Maybe I should do two weeks and fit more in."

"When are you planning this vacation?"

"Probably not until the fall. It starts to slow down here in October so that might be a good time. Until then, I'll just take some days here and there, and make long weekends. What about you?"

He hadn't given vacation a thought. Until Alvin offered this consulting role, David had thought he'd be using some of his vacation time to visit his family.

"I don't know. I like to ski so maybe later this year I'll do that somewhere."

"Paula? Is that you?" David and Paula both turned to see an older, elegantly-dressed woman with a silver-gray bob standing in front of them.

"Mrs. Ferguson? We missed you last year. It's so good to see you."

"It's good to be here. I had some pesky health issues last year but I'm fit as a fiddle now and so glad to be back." An older man joined her. He was holding a cardboard to-go box.

"Well, that's good to hear. Did you just have dinner?"

"Yes, and everything was just marvelous, as usual. I ran into your grandfather earlier today and he told us about your promotion. Congratulations, dear. We both think you'll do a fabulous job."

"Thank you, both. David, this is Mr. and Mrs. Ferguson. They've been coming to The Whitley every year for as long as I can remember. David is consulting with us."

"Lovely to meet you," Mrs. Ferguson said. "Well, we're on our way back to our room. I just saw you and wanted to say a quick hello."

"Thank you. It's so good to see you both."

They left and David smiled at Paula. "You have some fans there."

She laughed. "They are sweethearts and they have been coming here forever. I worried when we didn't see them last year."

"You know a lot of the guests?" David was impressed that she remembered them so well.

"Yes. That's one of the first things Grandfather taught me. We want to treat these people like they are all guests in our home. It's easy to do as most of them are like the Fergusons, just nice people. And so interesting. People come from all over the world to stay here."

"Little things like that, remembering people by name, makes such an impression," David said. "I think that's the key to success in any service business. When people feel valued and welcome, they want to come back and tell their friends."

"Exactly." Paula smiled and reached for her wine. "How's your mother doing?" she asked.

"She's doing better, both physically and mentally. My father hired a woman around her age to stay with her in the afternoons so he can go to the office. She likes the company and he really needs the break."

"It has to be hard for him, and for you and for her, too. I can't imagine," Paula said.

He nodded. It was so hard to see his mother like that and he felt awful for his father. He was glad, though, that since he'd been home, his father seemed less stressed and more optimistic about it all. David wished that he could be around more often, but in a little over a month, his assignment would be over and he'd be heading back to New York. Usually, he was eager to get home to his Manhattan apartment, but this time, he was in no hurry. Summer on Nantucket and spending time with his family was where he needed to be, for as long as possible.

He noticed that Paula's glass was just about empty. "Would you like another glass of wine?"

"No, thank you, though. One was perfect. I think I'm going to head home."

"Okay. See you tomorrow, then. I'm glad you came out with us." She seemed more relaxed and he would have liked to talk to her longer. He was just glad that she seemed to have thawed out towards him.

She smiled. "I'm glad I came out, too. See you tomorrow."

CHAPTER 20

Andrea was in a fantastic mood. Earlier that afternoon, she'd received a text message from Elaine the headhunter. She'd made the final cut for the two candidates the Alexandria Hotel wanted to invite in to meet the board. It wouldn't happen for three weeks because of some travel schedules but Andrea was totally fine with that. She still wasn't sure what her interest level was to actually move to Manhattan, but it was nice to be a step closer to having that option.

And while she wouldn't admit it to her grandfather or Paula, she was enjoying her new role. There were almost no management responsibilities other than scheduling people and passing along any company-wide updates, which were few and far between. As Marco had said when they met up at The Club Car a few weeks prior, it was a fun job. And Andrea was having fun, for the first time in a long time. The role really did play to her strengths. She loved Nantucket and loved sharing what she knew about restaurants and different sightseeing options on the island.

The weekend shifts when she and Marco often worked together were the most fun. He made her laugh, and they shared a similar sense of humor. He was quickly becoming a good friend. It didn't hurt, either, that he was quite good-looking with his dark hair and eyes and warm smile. He made everyone feel welcome and flirted with all the women, no matter their age, and they loved it.

She couldn't help but notice that the few times their hands accidentally touched as they both reached for something that there was an immediate buzz of electricity. So, yes, she was attracted to Marco and she sometimes ever so faintly picked up a similar vibe from him, but each time he quickly made a joke, and the moment was gone. She suspected that he felt, as she did, that it would be a huge mistake for them to do anything beyond friendly flirting. Her track record wasn't great, and the last thing she needed was an awkward breakup and then have to still work so closely together. Plus, she didn't want to lose their budding friendship. They'd gotten into the habit of having after work drinks once or twice a week and she looked forward to it.

She was surprised to see Paula join them at the outside bar. Miss goody-two-shoes rarely went for after work drinks. Even her brother seemed surprised to see her. She couldn't help but notice that Paula's hair looked more polished than usual and she was wearing lipstick, something she rarely did. And the consultant, David, was with her.

She wondered if Paula was interested in him? Maybe she didn't even realize that she was. That wouldn't surprise Andrea. Especially as she gave Ben her number. Andrea assumed if they hadn't already had a date that they'd be going out soon. Paula wasn't the type to date around. She wasn't surprised when Paula only had one drink before calling it a night. And she noticed with interest that David finished his beer and then left, too.

When she'd first met him, she found David attractive, but after that initial conversation when she realized he agreed with her grandfather's decision to replace her with Paula, she wrote him off as stuffy and boring. Maybe he and Paula would make a good match, after all.

"You're deep in thought. Should I be scared?" Marco teased her.

She laughed and turned her attention back to Marco and Nick. "Sorry, just spaced out for a moment. What are we talking about?"

"Nick was just saying that he's going fishing on Sunday and asked if I want to join him."

"I thought you didn't like to fish?" she asked.

"Good memory. I told Nick that but he's pretty persuasive."

"You should come, too, Andrea. When was the last time you fished?" her cousin asked.

"It has been a long while. I don't even remember."

"It's not about the fishing as much as it's just fun to hang out on the beach on a beautiful afternoon. It should be a good time. I was thinking of asking Bella to come again. She actually enjoys fishing and I know her sister leaves Sunday morning."

"Who is this Bella? Is this someone you're dating?" Andrea asked. She noticed that Nick flushed a little.

"I can't say that we're dating really. I took her fishing once. I enjoy her company, but she's a guest. I know she won't be here for long."

Andrea grinned. "But you like her. I can tell. I'll come. I'm curious now to meet her."

"Okay, we'll plan to head out around noon."

"YOU'RE RIGHT. I WAS SKEPTICAL BUT DARK CHOCOLATE COVERED cranberries really are delicious," Julia said. She and Bella had just tried candy samples at Sweet Inspirations, the chocolate shop that Johnny, the driver from The Whitley, had mentioned.

"You should bring a box home. I'm going to get one, too," Bella said.

"Good idea. I can't believe this is my last day. I'm a little envious that you get to stay for another month or so. I know you need it, though. I can tell it's helping."

"You can? That's good to hear. I wish I could stay longer."

"You seem more relaxed and for the first time in a long time, you seem happy instead of stressed. How are you feeling?"

"I'm good. I haven't had a Lyme flare-up since I got here and I'm actually feeling stronger every day. I wish you could stay longer, too. This week has flown by." And it had been a wonderful week. They'd managed to pack a lot into it, seeing the Whaling Museum, going on a walking ghost tour through one of Nantucket's oldest neighborhoods and eating at so many great restaurants.

They did quite a bit of shopping, too, and Bella made sure to bring her sister to Nantucket Threads. Julia fell in love with several cute tops and a gorgeous pair of leather sandals. It was all new stuff from the last time Bella was there. Izzy made sure to tell them about her online store, too, in case Julia wanted to order anything once she got to Vermont.

"I can't thank you enough for that Instagram post. My online sales blew up, especially for those boots." Bella had posted a pic of herself from the knee down, of her wearing the boots and had included a caption, "Surfing online and fell in love with these boots from Nantucket Threads. Gorgeous and comfy." She made sure to mention she got them online so people wouldn't connect the dots and think she was on Nantucket.

But the post made people curious about where she was. She'd been off all social media since she came to Nantucket—no Facebook, Twitter or Instagram. But a few days ago, she made that post and popped onto Facebook and immediately left after seeing post after post of people wondering where she was and who she was with, as if they knew her. She knew that was all part of being a celebrity, but still, it was a little unnerving.

The cashier, a young girl who looked about sixteen, rang them up and as she handed Bella her charge slip, she paused.

"You look so familiar. I was trying to figure out where I knew you from and it just hit me. Has anyone ever told you that you look like Cami Carmichael? It's the smile I think."

Bella nodded. "I get that now and then. She's much prettier, though, and has lighter hair."

"Right. Her hair is gorgeous. Anyway, thanks for coming in."

When they stepped outside, Julia whispered, "Well, that was close. Is that the first time someone has sort of recognized you?"

"Yes. I think she bought that it wasn't me, though."

"I think she did, but I'm not so sure about the people who were standing right behind us. I thought I got a glimpse of someone snapping a picture with their cellphone. It might not have been of you, though. It probably wasn't."

Bella felt a little sick to her stomach. She'd been thoroughly enjoying being an anonymous tourist and moving about the island freely without worrying about being recognized. "I hope not."

They called for a ride back to the hotel and relaxed for a bit in the room. They'd both picked up a few new books in the bookstore downtown and read for a while before showering and getting ready to head down to dinner.

It was Bella's first time actually eating in the restaurant, though she'd ordered room service many times. She'd never wanted to eat alone there and attract too much attention.

They had a reservation and were taken right to their table, which was by a window with a breathtaking view of the ocean.

"It's so close, I almost feel like we're on a cruise ship," Julia said as they sat down.

The room was beautifully elegant, with rich navy silk window treatments and gold and navy carpeting. Everything else was white —the linens, plates and flowers in square crystal vases.

Their server was an older man in his fifties, Bella guessed. His name was Ramon and he proudly told them that he'd just celebrated his twentieth year of working at The Whitley.

"And I understand that our chef, Nick, has a special tasting menu for you tonight. He's picked out matching wines as well for each course, if that suits you? Or you could order cocktails."

"The wines sound wonderful to me," Bella said, and her sister nodded in agreement.

"I'll be right back with the first one, a sparkling rosé."

When Ramon returned, he set down the flutes of pink bubbly wine and a small dish of some kind of paté and sliced baguettes. There were also a few small gherkin pickles, a grainy mustard and sweet pepper jelly.

"That's Nick's foie gras paté and assorted condiments. Enjoy!"

The next few hours were a blur of one delectable dish after another and an assortment of wine tastings that perfectly complemented each course—everything from spicy tuna tartare to a silky lobster bisque, duck confit and a sliced chateaubriand topped with orange-scented poached lobster. They finished with a crème brûlée that was a swirl of dark chocolate and coffee flavors.

When they were completely and totally finished, Nick walked up to the table.

"I hope you enjoyed the tasting?"

"It was amazing, incredible. Thank you so much," Julia said.

Bella smiled. "Insanely delicious. Truly the best food I've ever eaten. Thank you, Nick."

He grinned. "I'm so glad you both liked it. I had a lot of fun with the menu." He glanced at Julia. "I'm sorry you have to go home tomorrow."

"I really wish I could stay longer. But I'm heading out first thing in the morning."

"I'm going to miss her," Bella said wistfully. She'd gotten used to having her sister's company. It was going to seem quiet once she'd gone.

"A few of us are going fishing tomorrow. To that same spot I took you. My cousin Andrea and Marco, who also works at the concierge desk. Why don't you join us? It's supposed to be a gorgeous day."

Bella smiled. "I'd love to. I was wondering what I was going to do with myself tomorrow."

"Perfect. Meet us out front at noon tomorrow and bring your lucky lure!"

CHAPTER 21

"I think you should go out with him at least one more time." Lucy had stopped by Paula's cottage Sunday afternoon before they went to family dinner at their mother's house. Neither one of them wanted to have their dating lives dissected over the dinner table, especially if Aunt Vivian was there. She could be relentless with the questions.

"I don't know if that's a good idea." It wasn't that Paula didn't like Jason. He was a nice enough guy. But she hadn't felt a single spark on their date the night before. He took her to The Gaslight, which was a great date spot, with good food and live music. It was a fun night. She felt like she was having dinner with a friend, though, so she wasn't sure if it was fair to him to waste his time with another date.

"So, I've dated a lot of guys that I didn't feel attracted to on the first date, but I still give them at least another chance or two, because sometimes the attraction does come. Not always, but sometimes. Remember Bill?" Lucy dated him for over a year and they somehow managed to remain friendly after the breakup.

"You weren't attracted to him at first?" Paula didn't remember that.

Lucy laughed. "Not even remotely. But he was so nice and funny, and we had a great time together. By the third date, he was much cuter, because I knew him better and bam, the attraction was there. It might have also had something to do with the fact that I overheard someone else say they thought he was hot."

Paula laughed, too. "Funny how that works. How did your date with Ben go?"

"We had fun! He's not my typical type at all, but he's a nice guy and really outgoing. We went to The Club Car for dinner and drinks, and I think he knew a half dozen or so people there. I like him enough to go out with him again."

"Well, that's good."

"You know, I have an idea. He mentioned going to see some blues bands next Saturday afternoon. It's at Cisco Brewers and will go all afternoon with five or six different bands playing sets. It's an outside thing and there will be beer, of course, but wine, too, and all kinds of snack stuff, like hot dogs. Very casual. Why don't you and Jason come with us? It might be more fun with a small group."

"That's actually not a bad idea. If he calls this week, I'll suggest it to him."

BELLA WAS SAD TO SEE JULIA LEAVE SUNDAY MORNING. SHE WAS more alarmed, though, by the text message her sister sent from the airport. While waiting to board her plane, Julia was checking Facebook and there was a picture of Bella and Julia in the Sweet Inspirations shop and the caption, "Is Cami Carmichael vacationing on Nantucket? If not, she's a dead ringer except for the hair."

Panic swept over Bella. She wasn't ready to deal with the media yet. Not on Nantucket, which until now had felt like her safe place. She thought about what to do and then she walked down to the lobby and went to the hotel's luxurious spa, which also had a hair salon.

She made sure not to smile when the hostess greeted her—and that was hard, but necessary. She didn't want anyone else to put two and two together.

"Can I help you?"

"I'd like to get a cut and color please."

"Let me check and see who is available." She took a look through her schedule. "Stephanie can help you. Please follow me."

She led Bella to a chair facing a mirror in the back of the salon, which was perfect. No one was likely to notice her there. A moment later, a stylist walked over.

"Hi, I'm Stephanie. What are we looking to do?" Stephanie didn't seem to recognize Bella, and she relaxed a little. No one other than the girl in the store had come close to recognizing her but now that her picture was on social media, Bella knew she had to change her look immediately.

"Nice to meet you. I'm Bella. I'd like to get some layers and go to a rich auburn with beachy loose curls all over. Kind of the Meg Ryan look if that makes sense?"

"Got it. Huge Meg Ryan fan." Bella wasn't surprised. Stephanie was about fifty so probably saw all of Meg Ryan's romantic comedies. Bella's natural hair color was a dark strawberry-blond, but she'd been strongly encouraged to bleach it blond when she got her first big break. The thinking was that redheads weren't as popular. Bella didn't agree or like it, but she wanted to work then, so she bleached it a sun-kissed blonde for her first role and it became her signature look.

Stephanie chatted away while she stripped off Bella's existing color and then applied the lighter shade. Bella learned Stephanie was a Nantucket native, married with two children, and one just had their first child.

"So, I'm a grandmother, finally. It took them long enough. They've been married for almost ten years."

"Congratulations, that's exciting."

Once the color was applied, Bella relaxed even more. No one was likely to recognize her now. She looked quite ridiculous with her hair going in all different directions and half of it covered in foils. Stephanie explained that she wanted a layered natural highlights effect, which sounded good to Bella.

An hour later, when her hair was rinsed, cut, dried and curled, Bella opened her eyes and was amazed at the transformation. The Meg Ryan bouncy curl look was cuter than she'd expected and the rich, red color matched her skin better and made her eyes pop. She was still a little nervous about people recognizing her, but no one had seen her as a redhead before and they wouldn't be expecting the hairstyle, either. She knew she had to take additional precautions, though. She wouldn't be going anywhere, not even to the beach with Nick and his friends, without her dark aviator sunglasses and a floppy beach hat.

She also knew that it was time to have a conversation with Nick, before he heard the truth from someone else or, God forbid, the media.

"WHAT'S GOING ON AT THE HOTEL? IS THAT SOMEONE FROM TMZ?" As Nick pulled up to the entrance to pick up Bella, he noticed several vehicles that seemed to be sitting and waiting for something or someone. He glanced in his rearview mirror. "Do we have anyone famous with us right now?"

"Not that I'm aware of," Andrea said from the backseat where she and Marco were sitting with Nick's packed cooler in between them.

"I haven't heard anything, either," Marco added.

"I don't see Bella yet. I thought she'd be out front by now." Nick was running a few minutes late and it was five past noon. He noticed a woman with striking red curls walking towards them. He couldn't see her face as she was wearing sunglasses and a huge floppy sun hat hid her face. She was also dressed in dark, baggy sweats. But when she reached the car, she looked up and he realized it was Bella and she wore a panicky expression. He unlocked the door and she jumped in and immediately locked it behind her.

"Is everything okay? You look great. Love the hair."

"Thank you. I'll explain when we get to the beach, if that's okay."

"Of course. That's my cousin Andrea in the back and Marco. They both work at the concierge desk."

"Nice to meet you both," Bella said politely.

Something was definitely off about Bella today. She sounded stressed and a little scared. Nick wondered what was going on and he hoped he could help—at least to get her to relax and take her mind off whatever was bothering her.

"I hope you're hungry? We have a ridiculous amount of food. Marco made Brazilian steak tips to cook on the grill and Andrea made a pasta salad. I also made a caramelized onion dip, spicy tuna tartare and, of course, cheese and crackers."

"I am and that sounds wonderful. I brought some wine and chocolate from Sweet Inspirations. My sister and I were just there yesterday."

Once they reached the Eel Point beach, they unloaded everything, and found a good spot near the water to set up their chairs and the grill.

Bella peeled off her huge sweatshirt and baggy sweatpants and had on a cute pair of shorts and a short-sleeved Nantucket red t-shirt. It was warm out, so Nick wondered what was up with the dark baggy sweats but didn't feel it was appropriate to ask.

Once everything was settled and Andrea and Marco had thrown their lines in the water, Bella turned to Nick. "Can we take a quick walk?"

"Of course." He realized she didn't want the others to hear what she had to say.

They walked down the beach until they were out of earshot.

Finally, Nick asked, "Is everything okay? You seemed a little frazzled when I picked you up. Is there anything I can do to help?"

Bella sighed. "This is incredibly awkward. I probably should have told you sooner, but it's just been so nice being Bella on vacation and totally anonymous."

Nick had no idea what she was talking about. "Okay."

"I love that you have no idea who I am. That's such a gift, to be able to totally be myself and just have fun."

"What do you mean?"

"So, remember when we met and I told you that I was out of work?"

He nodded.

"Well, that was true. But I didn't explain what that meant or what I do. I live in L.A. and am an actress. I just finished up a movie and am taking a much-needed break. I get recognized and hounded by the media, so it's been wonderful to have a break from that."

As Bella was talking Nick's mind began processing what she was saying and connecting the dots. He'd thought she looked a little familiar when they first met, but he didn't think much of it.

"So, who are you? Someone that I might know?"

She laughed lightly and then turned the full force of her smile on him and he felt it again, the smile that was so familiar and so attractive to him.

"Maybe. Do you know who Cami Carmichael is?"

His jaw dropped. "Of course, and now I feel like an idiot. How could I have not noticed that?" He was blown away by her revelation and shocked that he never saw it.

"The shorter dark hair really made a huge difference. And when I went out anywhere, I usually wore my sunglasses, and no one gave me a second look. But I got a little too comfortable yesterday when I was shopping with my sister. I wasn't wearing the glasses and a young girl, a cashier in a shop—she noticed. And someone behind her snapped a picture and posted it on social media. So, word is out, and they know about the short dark brown hair."

"So that's why you got the new do. I really like it. The color suits you."

She smiled again. "Thanks. This is actually close to my natural color."

He shook his head in disbelief. "I can't believe you're Cami Carmichael. I did not see that coming."

"I'm sorry I didn't tell you sooner. But it was really nice when you just thought of me as Bella, someone on vacation."

Nick could see the worry in her eyes that now things might change. Beyond his initial shock, he didn't see why they had to.

"You're still Bella on vacation to me. Is Bella your real name?"

She nodded. "Yes. My manager thought for privacy reasons, I should use something different. I am glad I agreed to that."

"Yeah, Cami doesn't fit you as well. You're Bella to me."

"Should I tell the others? I always worry about too many people knowing, but it sounds like it's already out there."

Nick glanced at Andrea and Marco, who were deep in conversation.

"I don't think you have to worry about those two. Andrea is a Whitley and she used to be our GM. She knows that it's important to keep secrets like this to protect your privacy. That's why we get so many celebrity guests here."

ANDREA AND MARCO WERE SEATED WHEN THEY RETURNED, WITH their poles in hand and Marco was in the middle of an animated story that had Andrea laughing. Nick and Bella got their rods ready and cast the lines into the water and then they sat, too. Bella took a deep breath and told Andrea and Marco what was going on and who she really was. After their initial shock, they were both very cool about it.

"We get a lot of celebrities at The Whitley and it's often a problem for them. You don't have to worry about either of us saying anything. We know how difficult that must be," Andrea sympathized. A moment later she grinned and said, "I do have one question, though. Is it true what they say about Grayson George being a jerk?"

Bella laughed. Grayson was her co-star in the last project she worked on. "You didn't hear it from me, but he's awful. I won't work with him again if I can avoid it."

"I knew it! I was never a fan of his."

"Have you had a good vacation so far?" Marco asked.

"Yes. It's been incredible and fun having my sister here this past week. She went home today."

"Well, you're always welcome to join us if we're doing anything. Sometimes we'll grab a drink after work at the outside bar," Andrea said. Bella appreciated the invitation.

"Thank you. I will probably take you up on that. Do you think I have to worry about the media coming onto the property?"

Nick shook his head. "No. We have a security team and if someone does come onsite, they'll be swiftly escorted away. But we can't stop them from waiting outside the main entrance, unfortunately."

"Maybe I'll lay low for a bit and hit the beach instead of going into town. I do have lots of beach reading to catch up on."

"That sounds like a good plan," Andrea agreed.

Bella was so relieved that Nick didn't seem to be too weirded out by her news. Too many times, that had happened. Once people realized who she was, they acted differently toward her. But Nick, his cousin and Marco were just fun, normal people and she relaxed and enjoyed the rest of the afternoon.

They caught a few fish—well, Marco and Nick did. Andrea and Bella didn't have any luck, but they didn't care. It was fun having a glass of wine and eating all the delicious food everyone brought.

"How did you make your steak tips, Marco? They're so good," Bella asked.

He grinned. "It's just garlic, a little olive oil, salt, pepper and fresh parsley. Lots of garlic!"

They stayed at the beach until almost six, when the temperature dropped a bit and they reluctantly decided to head home. No one was hungry enough to cook their fish because they'd been snacking all day, but Nick suggested coming for dinner the next night.

"I'm off tomorrow, too, and have some leftover fish from when Bella and I went a week or so ago. I can cook it all up. If that sounds good?"

"I'm in. I'm off around five," Andrea said.

"And tomorrow is a day off for me, so count me in."

Nick glanced her way and Bella nodded. "Definitely."

"Perfect, why don't you all come by around six."

When they got back to The Whitley, Bella was thrilled to see that the cars that had been waiting out front earlier were gone. Still, she pulled on her baggy sweatshirt, big sunglasses and floppy hat just in case.

"Thanks for coming with us, Bella," Nick said.

"Thanks for including me." She waved to Andrea and Marco in the backseat. "Great to meet you both. I'll see you all tomorrow."

WHEN BELLA WALKED THROUGH THE LOBBY, SHE THOUGHT SHE sensed a few people looking at her more than usual but wondered if she was just imagining it and was paranoid that she was going to be recognized. When she got to her room, she took a hot shower, wrapped herself in one of the comfy bathrobes and made a cup of hot tea. And then she opened her laptop and went online.

She saw the media had done some digging and recognized her sister from old family photos and that confirmed for them that the cashier was right, and Cami Carmichael was on Nantucket. Someone saw them get into the white Whitley Range Rover for their ride home, so that's how they knew where she was staying. She tried not to feel stressed about it by reminding herself that it was inevitable at some point that she'd be found out. And at least at The Whitley she was more protected as the hotel was on private and secluded grounds, and the beach was totally secure. The only way to access it was to walk across the property and there was good security.

So, she drifted off to sleep planning to spend the next day relaxing on the beach and doing some binge reading. And she was looking forward to dinner at Nick's. She was thrilled that her big news didn't seem to faze him, or Andrea or Marco, either. She enjoyed meeting the other two and thought they made a cute couple —although, she realized that she didn't know if they actually were a couple or not. They just seemed to fit together, from what she saw.

CHAPTER 22

Bella had the perfect beach day on Monday. The skies were clear, the air was warm, and no one bothered her. She walked the beach, swam a little and read a lot. She didn't see any paparazzi in front of the hotel and hoped that meant they'd given up and were onto something else.

She showered, dressed in her oldest, most comfy jeans and a thin white cotton sweater and was drying her hair when the phone in her room rang. It startled her because it was the first time the phone had rung since she'd been there. Everyone she knew just called her cell phone.

"Hello?"

"Bella? It's Andrea down at the concierge desk. I'm getting off in a few minutes and didn't know if you wanted to meet me in the lobby and we can walk over to Nick's together?"

"Oh, sure! I'll be down in a few minutes."

She hung up, ran a brush through her hair and grabbed a bottle of wine she'd bought earlier that week. She didn't want to show up empty-handed.

She donned her dark glasses, grabbed a light jacket and headed down to the lobby to meet Andrea.

They walked the short distance to Nick's place in less than ten minutes.

"I'll meet you there in a few minutes. I'm just going to run home and grab a salad I told Nick I'd bring."

Andrea walked toward the house next door, while Bella knocked on Nick's front door.

He opened the door a moment later and she tried not to stare. Nick looked amazing. He was just wearing a t-shirt and jeans, but his arms were lean and muscled and Bella had noticed on the beach that he had some impressive abs. His hair was slightly damp, and she guessed he'd recently showered. He grinned when he saw her.

"Come on in."

"Andrea ran home to get a salad she'd made." She handed him the bottle of wine.

"Great, thanks. Everything is just about done, so once they get here, we can eat." He opened the wine, poured her a glass and got a bottle of beer for himself. Marco arrived a few minutes later and Andrea was right behind him. They ate on the back patio and the fish was just as good as she remembered.

Bella mostly listened as the other three told stories that had them all laughing. Nick and Andrea were obviously great friends as well as cousins, and Marco was so full of energy and funny. They were entertaining, and Bella was surprised at how fast the hours flew by as they laughed and talked and had a few drinks. She was envious of the three of them, that this was just a typical night and they could do this whenever they wanted.

Finally, a little after ten, Marco yawned and a moment later Nick did, too. Andrea saw it and laughed.

"I think that might be a sign that it's time to call it a night."

"Yeah, I have the early shift tomorrow," Marco added.

"I'm in early as well to do our weekly orders," Nick said.

"This was a lot of fun. Thanks for cooking, Nick," Bella said.

He smiled the big slow smile that lit up his whole face.

"Anytime. I'll walk you back when you're ready."

She was about to protest and say she could go herself, but then she looked outside. It was dark, and she knew he'd insist anyway.

"Thanks. I'm ready."

They all said their goodbyes and Nick walked Bella back to the hotel. They walked slowly, chatting all the while.

When there was a lull in the conversation, Bella impulsively asked what had been on her mind more than once since she'd met Nick. "Nick, you're a great guy. How is it that you're still single?"

He laughed. "It's been a while since I've been in a serious relationship. It's hard sometimes with my job and the hours, all the nights that I work. Mary, the girl I was serious about, had a normal nine-to-five job and she just got sick of it eventually. Since then, I've kept it light and just dated here and there."

"If it was the right person, that wouldn't be an issue," Bella said.

"You really think so?" He sounded surprised.

She nodded. "I do. You could find a way to make it work, somehow. It's similar with me, maybe even worse as I'm often gone for weeks or months at a time on location. That means a long-distance relationship at times and that can be challenging."

"Yeah, I'd miss you if we were together and then you left for a few months," Nick admitted.

"It's not ideal, I know. There's something I've been thinking about a lot, though, since I've been here. I've had a lot of time to think. And I may be looking to put my own production company together. To build a team and make the kind of movies I want to see. And that would give me some flexibility on where things are shot and with scheduling."

"That sounds awesome. But wouldn't you have to be in L.A. for that?"

"Not all the time. The company could be based there, but so much these days can be done virtually. It's just something I'm thinking about."

"Well, it sounds exciting. I hope it works out for you. Though I have to admit, I'm going to miss you when your time here is up."

"I'm going to miss you, too, and this place. You're so lucky to be able to live and work here. I wish I could figure out a way to do that, but it seems impossible right now."

"Yeah, I guess that wouldn't work. You'll just have to take more vacations and come back in between movies."

She laughed. "Oh, I'm already thinking about that. I hear the fall is great here and there's a Christmas Stroll in early December."

"The Stroll is a busy weekend and a good time. If you can make it for that, I think you'd really enjoy it. It's like the last hurrah before the slow winter season."

They reached the hotel entrance, and both paused outside the front door. Bella wasn't in a hurry to go inside just yet. She impulsively leaned over and kissed Nick on the cheek. "I really had a great time, yesterday and tonight. Thank you."

Nick smiled and took hold of her hands. He pulled her close to him and every so lightly brushed his lips against hers. It was a quick kiss, whisper-soft, and it gave Bella the shivers.

When it ended, he looked her in the eyes and said, "I thought about doing that all night. Goodnight, Bella."

"Night, Nick."

CHAPTER 23

Tuesday morning at eleven thirty, Grandfather popped his head into Paula's office, David right behind him.

"Do you have a minute?"

"Of course." Paula wondered what the two of them were up to.

"So, David and I were just talking, and he mentioned seeing that a new restaurant just opened near the Wharf. The Portside or maybe Starboard?" He glanced at David.

"It's Portside. I noticed it when I was downtown the other day and asked your grandfather if he'd been there yet. He suggested we go for lunch and if we like the food, invite them to join the Taste of the Town event."

"Oh, that's a good idea. Grandfather, you'll come with us?"

But he shook his head. "No, you kids go ahead and go. I have an important meeting at noon." He grinned. "The boys are coming for lunch and a quick card game."

"That's right. It's already that time of the month." Once a month, Grandfather had some of his oldest friends in for lunch, cards and gossip. "We could go a different day, so you could join us?"

"No, we need to get this nailed down. I trust your opinion. Go and have fun."

"Want to leave in about fifteen minutes?" David asked.

"That's perfect. I'm just finishing up some paperwork."

DAVID DROVE AND THEY REACHED THE PORTSIDE A FEW MINUTES before noon. It was near the waterfront but on a quieter side street, so it wasn't as busy as the more visible restaurants. Which was a good thing as they didn't have to wait for a table and were seated immediately. The blue and white nautical decor and big glass windows overlooking the water almost gave the feeling of being on a boat. And the menu was mostly focused on seafood. Paula decided to treat herself to something she only got once or twice a season— fried Nantucket scallops. David went with broiled scrod and an appetizer of fried clams for them to share.

They chatted easily about everything from work to David's mother, who he said was doing great now that she had an afternoon companion. Everything was delicious and when they finished, Paula asked their server for the check and also if the manager was available for a quick question.

"Sure, I'll get Missy. She'll be right out."

Two minutes later, a familiar face walked toward them.

"David Connolly! It's been a long time." David stood and gave his high school girlfriend a big hug.

"It has been. How are you, Missy? I didn't realize you were working here."

Paula watched their interaction with interest. They both looked pleased to see each other. Missy still had long, very blond hair, which she had pulled back into an elegant, low ponytail. Lots of mascara and eyeliner accented her baby blue eyes and her lips shone with bright pink gloss. She was also as slim as ever and tall. Paula felt somewhat short and frumpy next to her.

"I just started here. The owners are good friends and we just opened a week ago. Are you just visiting? Or back for good?"

"I'm on a consulting assignment here for a few months, at The Whitley."

"Oh, nice! And your parents, are they good?"

He hesitated for a moment and then simply said, "They're both great. How about yours?"

"Dad just retired this year, so they're going on a cruise soon."

"It's great to see you. Part of the reason Paula and I stopped in here was to check out the restaurant and to invite you to participate in an event we're doing in July—a Taste of the Town. It might be good PR for you."

"Oh, it might be. Can you email me some details I can share with the owners?"

"Sure thing. I'll send it as soon as we get back. This is Paula Whitley, by the way. She's the new general manager at The Whitley."

"Paula. You were in school with us, too, a few years behind?"

Paula nodded. "That's right. It's nice to see you, Missy."

She turned her attention back to David. "I got divorced a year or so ago. Are you seeing anyone these days?"

"No. I'm still single."

Her eyes lit up. "We should get together soon and catch up over a drink."

"That sounds great. Let me know what works for you."

"I'll watch for your email and we can make a plan."

PAULA COULDN'T HELP NOTICING THAT AS THEY DID IN HIGH SCHOOL, that Missy and David looked good together. For some reason, the thought depressed her. Which was silly. She reasoned that it was just that she wasn't overly fond of Missy. She'd come into The Whitley for various ladies' group functions over the years and had never so much as said hello to Paula when she saw her. And it wasn't like she didn't know who she was, she clearly remembered as she said so today. No, she just always acted as though Paula, and many others, were beneath her.

That was while she was married, though. Missy didn't work then, and her husband was wealthy. They belonged to one of the swankier country clubs and she was involved in various charity organizations. Paula had no idea why they divorced, but she guessed that her financial situation wasn't as rosy as it used to be if she was helping to manage a new restaurant. Maybe the experience had humbled her. But Paula still didn't think she was worthy of David.

He was quiet as they drove back to the hotel. They were halfway there when his phone rang.

"Hi, Dad. What's up?"

Paula noticed a muscle in his jaw clench as he listened to his father. "You have no idea where she might have gone? I'll be right there to help you look. Don't worry, Dad. We'll find her." He hung up the phone and looked at Paula. "My mother disappeared. In the middle of the day, with her companion in the house. My father is on his way home from the office to help look for her. I need to go there, too."

"Take me with you. It will save time from having to drop me off. And I can help look, too."

"Are you sure?"

"Yes, turn the car around."

He did, and ten minutes later they pulled up to his parents' house. An older woman who looked to be in her sixties was on the front porch dabbing her eyes with a tissue. His father was talking to her and as they walked up they could hear him saying, "It's not your fault, Meg. Who would have thought she'd disappear while you were putting a load of laundry in?"

"Hi, Dad. Paula and I were just out to lunch, so we're both here to help look for Mom."

"Thank you both for coming. I'm going to head east, down the street and to the park. Do you want to head the opposite way and check by the pond, too? Meg, why don't you stay here in case she comes back?"

David led the way down the street, calling his mother's name.

"Has she ever done anything like this before?"

"No. But her doctors warned us this could happen. It just didn't seem real, though."

They walked the length of the street and then down to the neighborhood pond, going through the woods as it led back to his parents' house. Paula could tell David was getting more stressed as they walked and there was still no sign of his mother.

Finally, as they were close to the house, they heard a sneeze and walked toward the sound. They saw his mother, sitting on the ground, leaning against a huge tree, with her eyes closed. The sun was bearing down on her and a slight breeze rustled the leaves.

"Mom? Are you okay?" David asked gently as they reached her.

She looked up and blinked. Her gaze at first was confused, but then seemed to sharpen and she smiled. "David, it's so good to see you. What are you doing here?"

He chuckled. "Looking for you. You gave us a bit of a scare."

Her lower lip trembled as she looked around her. "I'm sorry. I didn't mean to scare anyone."

He held out his hand to help her up. "It's fine, Mom. I'm just glad we found you. Let's get you back to the house."

As they walked back, he asked her, "What made you decide to walk out to the pond?"

"I'd stepped outside for just a minute, to feel the sun on my face and then I heard the distinctive sound of a cardinal and I just wanted to see it. So, I kept following the sound and ended up by the pond. I never did find the cardinal."

They led his mother back to the house, and as soon as Meg saw her she rushed over and gave her a hug. His mother's eyes welled up again.

"I didn't mean to scare you. I'm sorry."

"Don't be silly. I'm just glad you're okay. What do you say we go in and have a nice cup of tea?"

"Do we have the vanilla one?" His mother sounded excited.

"Yes, I know that's your favorite."

David gave his mother a hug, too. "Mom, I have to head back to work. I'll see you soon, okay?"

"Okay, honey. Nice to see you." She glanced at Paula. "Who is your friend? She's pretty."

"Mom, this is Paula Whitley. We work together at the hotel."

"Okay. I'll see you soon, honey." His mother followed Meg inside, and they turned to leave and saw his father walking toward him.

"She's inside. We found her sitting by a tree down at the pond. She heard a cardinal and was following the sound," David said.

His father's face softened. "She's always loved cardinals."

"Dad, you should talk to Meg. I don't think she can take her eyes off Mom at all while she's here."

His father nodded. "I agree. It's not her fault. She was just trying to help, but now we know. I'll talk to her before she leaves today."

Once they were in the car again and heading back to the hotel,

David glanced her way. "Thank you for coming. That was the first time she's wandered off like that. Hopefully, it will be the last time."

"I'm sorry. I know that was scary for all of you. I don't think Meg will let it happen again. I felt bad for her."

"I did, too. And for my father. It's stressful for all of them."

"And for you, too," Paula added.

He smiled. "Thanks. It's just the strangest thing. I was there last night for our weekly pizza dinner and she was so good. Better than she's been since I first got back. But it seems that it comes and goes."

"You've had quite the day. Have you and Missy kept in touch at all over the years?"

He shook his head. "No. I haven't run into her at all when I've been home before. I knew she was married ages ago. I didn't realize she got divorced."

"I was surprised to see her working in a restaurant. I've seen her a few times over the years. She's come in for various events at the hotel and I don't think she worked then."

"She used to work as a hostess at one of the waterfront restaurants when we were in high school. I don't know what else she has or hasn't done over the years."

Paula smiled. "Well, she wants to catch up, so you'll probably find out soon enough."

"Right. I have to email her the details on the Taste of the Town event when we get back, too."

"I bet they'll do it. It's a great opportunity for a new restaurant."

"I agree. They'd be crazy not to."

WHEN THEY GOT BACK TO THE HOTEL, DAVID DISAPPEARED INTO HIS office and Paula was about to go check her email, too, when she saw her grandfather and Aunt Vivian coming down the hall.

"How was it?" her grandfather asked.

"Good! Cute place, mostly seafood. We invited them to participate and David is emailing the details to the manager to send to the present to the owners."

"Excellent!"

Aunt Vivian glanced pointedly at her watch. "That was a nice long lunch."

They had been gone a long time. Not that it was any of her aunt's business.

"Actually, our lunch wasn't long at all. But David had a family emergency, so we stopped by his parents' house on the way home." She didn't go into any more details than that.

"Oh, that's a shame," her aunt said.

"I'm sorry to hear it," her grandfather added.

"Everything's fine now," Paula assured him. She glanced at her nosy aunt. "If you'll excuse me, I need to get back to work."

CHAPTER 24

Paula headed to Lucy's cottage around two on Saturday afternoon. They were meeting Ben and Jason in a half hour at the Cisco Brewery for the Blues Band event. She knocked on Lucy's door, but there was no answer. Her sister rarely locked the door, so Paula checked it and then let herself in.

She guessed that Lucy was in her back studio and maybe lost track of the time. The blues music she loved was playing loudly so she probably didn't hear Paula knocking. She walked to the back and poked her head in the studio. Lucy was all dressed and looked adorable in a tie-dyed tank top and flowing white linen pants. Her hair was twisted up in a messy knot and she had a paint brush in one hand and was intently focused on dabbing pink paint onto a vivid blue sky.

"Hey, there. I knocked but it looks like you are in another world."

Lucy laughed and put the paintbrush down. "I was working on this earlier. Then went to change and while I was waiting for you, I started playing around again." She stood up, shook her hair loose and grabbed a brush and ran it through her hair a few times.

"Okay, I'm ready when you are."

Paula drove and there was already a good crowd in the parking lot when they arrived. Lucy saw Ben waiting at the entrance and waved. By the time they parked and walked over, Jason had arrived, too, and they all went in together.

It was a fun afternoon. It wasn't too hot of a day, but sunny and warm and the bands were excellent. Lucy and Paula had white wine while the guys tried a few of the different draft beers. They had hot dogs and fried bread dough and later on, Lucy and Jason had ice cream cones.

Ben kept them entertained and Jason was just as nice as Paula remembered from their first date. She wished she could feel some kind of attraction, but it just wasn't there. And as much as she thought Ben was interesting and funny, she was surprised that he and Lucy were a match. Maybe she was broadening her scope, which could be a good thing. But Paula also wondered if she was considering that Ben wasn't a year-rounder. When the fall came, he'd be heading back to Manhattan. And never in a million years could she see Lucy following him there. She loved Nantucket and being close to her family.

Maybe for both of them it was just a nice summer diversion.

"So, what do you think of the bands so far?" Jason asked her after they'd listened to several sets.

"I thought they were all pretty good," Paula said. She couldn't really differentiate between them. She liked blues music but didn't listen to it often enough to have a preference.

"I thought the second band was amazing," Lucy said.

Jason looked pleased to hear it. "I did, too. I think they are the best so far. I saw that they're coming to The Gaslight soon."

"Oh, that's good to know. They get some great bands there. I saw one a few weeks ago, Blue Soul, that was excellent."

"No kidding? I saw them last year, they're great."

Ben laughed. "I thought they were all good, too. I don't know a whole lot about blues, though. I like it all."

"Oh, I have some news," Lucy said. "Paula, I forgot to tell you. Some of my pieces are going to be at an art show next weekend."

"Really? That's great. Which ones?" Lucy had done a few art shows and her work always sold quickly.

"A couple of small tables, a few paintings, some mirrored wall hangings, and a few mailboxes."

Jason looked confused. "You make all that?"

"No. I find stuff at estate sales and then refurbish and paint my designs on them. The mailboxes are something new."

"That sounds really cool. I'll have to be sure to check it out," he said.

"I will, too." Ben grinned. "Have to support our local artists."

By the end of the afternoon, Paula noticed that Lucy seemed to be getting along really well with Jason. The two of them knew a lot of the same people and shared similar taste in music and art. She laughed and chatted with Ben just as much, but her connection with Jason seemed different.

When they all said their goodbyes, much to Paula's relief, Jason didn't mention getting together again. When they were in the car and on their way home, Paula thought about what she'd noticed and decided to say something.

"I think maybe you should go out with Jason."

Lucy looked at her in surprise. "What are you talking about? I'm dating Ben and you're with Jason."

"But I'm not. Not really. You talked me into this date. There's no spark there for either of us. But it looked to me like there might be a connection with the two of you. Unless you prefer Ben, of course."

Lucy sighed. "Ben's really nice, but he didn't mention anything about going out again this time. I'll wait and see. Are you sure you don't like Jason? He seems like such a great guy."

"He is. But he's not for me. I think maybe he's better for you. Maybe he'll come to your art show and you can see what happens from there."

"Maybe. I think Ben might still be dating Andrea, anyway. So, I will give this some thought."

Andrea was pleasantly surprised when Ben called on Sunday to see if she wanted to play her first round of golf with him the next day.

"I thought I remembered you saying you sometimes have Monday off?"

"I do and I'd love to. Are you sure it's okay for me to play on an actual course already, though?"

He laughed. "Yes, you'll be with me and I'll be helping you. It's the best way to learn—to just get out there and do it. It will be fun."

They agreed to meet at his country club the next day at two in the afternoon. Andrea wondered if he was still dating Paula. She felt a little guilty about that, but at the same time also had a sense of satisfaction that maybe she was taking something away that Paula had wanted. It seemed fitting, somehow. It still bothered her that she'd been forced to leave the role she thought she'd be in forever and by Paula, of all people.

She just didn't see how Paula was a better option. She didn't seem entirely comfortable in the role. Andrea couldn't help but notice that she often seemed nervous and quiet in her interactions with groups of staff. She was better at one-on-ones. Andrea had loved talking to groups of people. But truth be told, there were aspects of the job that she didn't enjoy. All the details and follow up needed and all the meetings and putting out fires. So many fires, all the time.

For the time being, she was actually having fun in the concierge role. It felt a bit like a vacation after the demand and stress of being the general manager. Until she landed a new GM role somewhere, it was a good way to pass the time. She was still hoping that something might turn up in Boston, but Elaine said there was nothing yet. Andrea also had the feeling that Elaine wanted to focus on the Manhattan job and close her on that one since she was a final candidate.

That interview was still two weeks away, though. She'd hoped to have something else in the works as well so she could have more than one option to choose from. But it didn't look like that was likely at this point. So, if her final interview with the board went well, she would have a big decision to make. One that she wasn't quite ready for. But she'd cross that bridge when she got there.

In the meantime, she was having fun, enjoying her job and had fallen into the habit of going out several times a week after work with her co-workers. She'd done that when she was the GM, too, but not as often as her schedule was more demanding. Now she had more time to play and her usual partner in crime was Marco, as well as a few of the others like her cousin Nick whenever he had the night off. Bella had also joined them a few times lately.

She enjoyed Bella's company. She was more down to earth than

Andrea would have imagined for a movie star, and it was fun seeing Nantucket through her eyes. Bella had a sense of wonder about everything and Andrea could tell she loved Nantucket. It deepened Andrea's appreciation for the island she'd grown up on. It was a beautiful place and when she thought about it, the idea of moving off-island was too sad to really deal with. But eventually she would have to. Just like Bella, who would have to end her extended vacation and head back to L.A. She also worried a bit about her cousin Nick. She could see that he was growing closer to Bella and was likely dreading when she'd have to leave as well.

Andrea decided to head to the driving range and hit a basket of balls, so she wouldn't be as rusty when she saw Ben the next day. She wasn't due to her parents' house for Sunday dinner until five. It was only three and she felt too restless to sit around, even though there were plenty of things she could do, like laundry or cleaning.

She went and practiced her golf swing for about an hour. The first half hour was frustrating as it felt like she was starting over and her balls were going all over the place. But after a while, it got better. Her balls went higher, longer and straighter. By the time she left, she felt as though she might not totally embarrass herself the next day, and she'd gotten a little bit of a workout and burned off some nervous energy.

She made it home and to her parents' house with minutes to spare. And she'd worked up an appetite as well.

"What are we having? Something smells great," Andrea said as she walked in the house.

Her mother looked up from the stove where she was stirring a big pot of red sauce.

"Just meatballs and sauce. Oh, and your sister made garlic bread."

"Yum. I brought a bottle of merlot. Shall I open it?"

"Yes. I'll take a glass and your sister and Aunt Vivian probably will, too, but check with them."

Andrea could hear her aunt laughing in the living room. She poked her head in the other room and saw Hallie and her aunt deep in conversation.

"So, your Uncle Freddy said he's ready to come home now. I asked him where he planned to stay, and he got mad. He flies in tomorrow, evidently. I told him there might be room at The Whitley."

"You're terrible," Hallie said. "You wouldn't really make him stay in a hotel, would you?"

Her aunt chuckled. "No, probably not. It is fun torturing him a little, though. He has some apologizing to do when he gets home."

"Do you two want some merlot? I'm about to open a bottle."

They both said yes at the same time, so Andrea went and poured wine for all of them.

"Do you need help with anything?" Her mother was chopping cucumbers for a salad.

"No, go ahead in the other room and relax. We're still waiting for your father to get home. Everything else is done."

Andrea handed glasses of wine to her sister and aunt and settled on a comfy chair opposite from the sofa where they were sitting.

"So, what's new with you?" Aunt Vivian asked.

"Not too much. I was just out at the driving range, hitting some balls."

"You've taken up golf?" Her aunt was surprised.

"Well, I needed to practice because I have a golf date tomorrow. I met a cute guy, Ben, at a cookout, and he gave me a golf lesson and tomorrow we're playing a round at his country club."

Hallie frowned. "Is that the same Ben that Lucy's been dating?"

Now it was Andrea's turn to be confused. "I thought he was dating Paula?"

"Not as far as I know. Lucy met him at the cookout, too, and they've gone out a few times. Paula told me that she gave him Lucy's number when they were chatting, and he expressed interest."

"Oh, I didn't realize that. Are they still dating?" Andrea didn't want to screw things up for Lucy if she was interested in Ben. She'd never had an issue with Lucy.

"I haven't heard otherwise." Hallie looked at her sister carefully. "You didn't seem concerned when you thought he was dating Paula. Is it different now that you know it's Lucy?"

Andrea sighed. "Yes. Lucy didn't steal my job." Both her sister and aunt looked at her with disapproval.

"That's not how I heard it went," her aunt finally said.

"Well. You haven't been around until recently. I still think Paula manipulated Grandfather into making this switch."

"You couldn't be more wrong," Hallie said. "Paula was even more shocked than you were. She never asked for this. Never wanted it."

"That didn't stop her from taking it, though, did it?" For the first time, though, Andrea felt a little niggling of doubt. Was she being too hard on her cousin?

"Okay, your father's home, come fix your plates," her mother called from the kitchen.

CHAPTER 25

Andrea had a blast playing golf with Ben the next day. It was just the two of them, so they weren't slowing down the foursome behind them and Ben was able to give her lots of pointers as they played.

"I can see why people get addicted to this game," she said after an unusually good shot.

Ben grinned. "It is fun. It can be frustrating at times, though. It's so much a mental game and sometimes you're in the zone and other times, not so much."

He made her laugh as they played. She liked his sense of humor and carefree attitude. When they finished, he suggested getting a bite to eat at the club. Because it was a Monday night, it wasn't as busy as usual, so the outside area wasn't crowded at all. They sat at the bar and ordered a round of drinks and a few appetizers to share. Neither one of them felt like a big meal.

Several times people stopped by to say hello and Andrea was impressed that he seemed to know so many people.

"You're like the mayor here," she teased him.

He grinned. "It's really because of my parents. They were one of the first members and a lot of the people I know here, I know through them and from being in Manhattan. There's a lot of us that go back and forth. Lots of families like mine where the husband is in the city during the week and flies to Nantucket on the weekends."

"Does your mother work?"

"No. My dad always worked long hours in the investment world, and she stayed home with us. She keeps busy, though, with lots of different groups and charity stuff."

Andrea thought back to his sister's wedding the prior year at The Whitley. It had been one the biggest she'd seen in her years of working there. It was amazing to her what some people spent on weddings. Ben came from a very wealthy family. Andrea wasn't normally impressed by that, but it was intriguing as he was also so normal and down-to-earth.

She liked that he split his time between Manhattan and Nantucket. If she did end up going to the Alexandria Hotel, it would be nice to know someone in the city. And like he said, his father regularly flew to the island on his days off. She could do the same. Especially in the summer months. For the first time, the idea of taking that job wasn't completely depressing.

"So, I have a secret. But you can't tell anyone," she began.

His eyes lit up. "I like a good secret."

"I'm a final candidate for a job at a hotel in Manhattan, The Alexandria. Do you know it?"

"Sure. They have a great restaurant/bar there. We go for drinks sometimes before seeing a show on Broadway. Are you seriously thinking about moving there?"

She nodded. "I haven't made any decisions yet and I still need to see if they even make an offer, but it's something I'm considering."

"You don't like Nantucket?"

"I love it here. But The Whitley is a family business and if I'm going to keep growing my career, I need to broaden my experience. Working at a Manhattan property could be very good for my resume."

"I suppose so. If you do decide to make the move, when I'm back in the city, I'd be happy to show you some of my favorite spots and introduce you to some people."

"I'd love that. I don't know a soul there."

He grinned. "Well, you know me. And like you said, I know a lot of people. It could be fun."

"It could be. I go back in two weeks for my final interview.. It's between me and one other person. No one else knows, though."

"Good luck. I won't tell anyone. In the meantime, any interest in going to dinner at The Gaslight this weekend? They always have good live music, too."

"I love The Gaslight." She was quiet for a moment, still feeling a little guilty about Lucy. "I have to ask. Are you still dating my cousin, Lucy? I don't want to step on anyone's toes, if you are."

"I appreciate that. No. Lucy's awesome. We went out a few times, but on our last date it was clear to both of us that the romantic connection isn't there. We don't really have much in common. She's a great girl, though."

Andrea smiled. "I would agree with that. You're not her usual type. And yes, I'd love to go to The Gaslight with you this weekend."

CHAPTER 26

David went to his parents' house for dinner Sunday night. They ordered his mother's favorite pizza as she wasn't cooking much these days and she'd never allowed her father in the kitchen, so his skills were minimal. But he had their favorite pizza place on speed dial. After they ate, David's mother wanted to watch TV and he and his father went out to the front porch to sit for a bit. They each had a can of beer and sat in the two rockers that faced the street. In the far distance, there was a sliver of an ocean view.

It was nice to just sit outside and enjoy the cooler night air. His mother was having a good day, but she grew tired after she ate, and her eyes were probably already heavy as she watched TV. She didn't have the energy to make conversation, so she'd suggested they go off and talk.

His father took a sip of beer and they were both quiet for a bit. Finally, his father spoke. "It's been good having you home. I know you have to head back soon, though. When does your assignment end?"

"It's been great being back. They actually just extended me a few more weeks. Alvin Whitley asked if I could stay on through the Taste of the Town event. So, I'll be here until mid-July."

His father nodded. "And then back to New York City?"

"Briefly, and then I'm on to a new engagement in Kansas City."

"Kansas City. Do you still enjoy all this traveling?"

Did he? "Most of the time I don't mind it so much. I wouldn't mind doing less. Sometimes there are assignments where I can do a lot of the work remotely and then I'm able to work out of the New York office."

His father smiled sadly. "Too bad they don't have a Nantucket office."

David laughed. "That would be awesome. It might be a hard sell for my boss, though."

"Oh, well. Too bad."

David was glad his time was extended as he wasn't ready to leave Nantucket yet. It had been a long time since he'd spent more than a few days there and now that he had, he knew it was going to be hard to leave. He thought about what his father said and wished there was a way he could spend more time there.

MONDAY NIGHT A LITTLE AFTER SIX, DAVID WALKED INTO THE CLUB Car restaurant and saw that Missy was already seated at the bar chatting with two older men sitting next to her. They seemed to be hanging on her every word. She was still beautiful with her long blonde hair, and those big blue eyes. Missy used to be into yoga, and it looked like she kept that up over the years. She was wearing a pink and blue sleeveless dress that showed off tanned and toned arms. She glanced toward the door and smiled when she saw David. When they'd exchanged emails about the Taste of the Town event, Missy had reminded him that they needed to have a drink to catch up and she suggested meeting at The Club Car, a popular spot for after work cocktails.

He made his way over to the bar and slid into the seat next to her. She leaned in to give him a hug hello.

"Don't you look handsome in your sharp suit." Missy smiled and batted her eyelashes, and for a moment David felt like he was back in high school. When they'd first met, she'd turned those blue eyes on him, and he'd been a goner. They'd dated for all of senior year and then a week before he left for college, she dumped him for a local boy. Missy never had any desire to go to college. She married that year and had two kids right away.

It had stung when she dumped him, but he knew a long-distance relationship would have been hard to keep up while he was at school. He saw her a few times over the years when he was home for summers. But once he moved off-island, he didn't run in to her again until just recently, when he was with Paula.

"You look very nice, too," he said. "What are you drinking?"

"I'll have a Cosmopolitan."

David ordered her drink and a draft beer for himself.

When the bartender set their drinks down, Missy lifted her glass and tapped it against his. "Cheers! To new beginnings." She smiled and held his gaze for a moment before taking a sip.

She was flirting with him. That was unexpected. He'd agreed to the drink because he thought it might be fun to catch up with an old friend. But he had no intention of rekindling things with Missy. He wondered if she thought he was staying on the island.

"I'm sorry about your divorce," he said.

"It happens. As my mother likes to say, 'everything happens for a reason'." Missy had married into one of the most prominent, wealthy families on the island. They developed and owned real estate and her ex, Bill Cooper, had inherited the business from his father.

David had never cared for Bill in high school. He was in their year, too, and thought he was better than everyone else. He'd rubbed it in David's face when he ran into him that he and Missy were engaged. At that point, David really didn't care, but Bill was eager to pour salt in the perceived wound. Just because he could.

"How are your kids?"

"Tommy goes off to college next year and Samantha is a year behind him. They're great kids. I'm lucky."

"Off to college, how did that happen?"

She laughed. "I know, right? The years went by so fast. I was only eighteen when I had Tommy. Another lifetime ago."

He nodded. It was hard for him to imagine having children that age. He hadn't even thought about marriage, let alone kids, yet. Though at thirty-six, he knew he probably should think about it at some point.

"He cheated with his secretary," Missy said bitterly. "Such a cliché, right?"

David wasn't sure what to say to that, so he just nodded again.

"And it's true what they say. If they do it once, they'll do it again. They married six months ago, and I've already heard some rumors that he's up to his old tricks again."

"That's too bad. Maybe you dodged a bullet, then. Better to find out sooner rather than later."

"That's true. And it's not like I've had any shortage of dates. There are quite a few eligible men on this island." She glanced at the man next to her who looked to be in his mid-fifties. He wasn't a bad looking guy for his age and if his Rolex was an indicator, he was well off, too.

"I'm surprised you're not off the market already," David said.

She looked pleased to hear it. "I could be, but I'm being really picky this time. I want to make sure I choose well."

"That's smart."

"Enough about me. Tell me everything about you. What you've been up to and how long you're here for. Are you moving back?"

He shook his head. "I wish. But it's just not possible with my job."

She leaned forward and looked fascinated. "And what is your job?"

He told her about it and explained what he was doing at The Whitley.

"So, you're there to train Paula. You're not dating her?"

"No, I'm not dating Paula."

"That's a relief. She's not good enough for you. She's always been so mousy. I'm surprised they made her general manager."

That irritated him. "You don't know Paula. I'm not surprised at all. She's doing a great job. She's smart and a hard worker." And she never would have talked about someone the way that Missy was. Paula was a kind person. She was easy to be around and he realized he was going to miss working with her.

"That's all well and good, but I'm just saying it makes sense that you're not dating her. She's not your type at all."

"Oh, and what is my type?"

She smiled and lightly ran her hand along his arm.

"Well, at one point, I was."

He pulled his arm away. "We're not kids anymore."

"No, we're adults." She grinned. "It could be much more fun now!"

He thought for a moment of how to nicely get it across that this wasn't going to happen. "Missy, I'm only here for a few more weeks. I'll be heading back to New York soon."

"Well, you have weekends off, right? Plenty of people fly back here on the weekends."

She was right. They did. But he'd never been one of those people. He tried a different tactic.

"Honestly, I'm not really looking for a relationship right now. It's too hard with all the traveling I do."

But she brushed that off, too. "Everyone wants a relationship. It just has to be the right one." She smiled and tried again. "Why don't you come with me to a charity thing at my country club? It's a fundraiser for the library and there's a silent auction with some great items up for bid. Philippe Gaston, the bestselling thriller writer, lives here on the island, and he's donated tickets to a private screening of his new film and a dinner at his house catered by his private chef. It should be amazing."

"When is it?" Hopefully on a date he was unavailable.

"It's the first Saturday in August."

He breathed a sigh of relief. "I won't be here then. My assignment ends in mid-July, right after the Taste of the Town event."

But Missy wasn't ready to give up. "Well, that's no problem. You can just fly back for it. It's on a weekend, after all."

"We'll see. That's a ways off."

"Just think about it."

Missy wanted a second drink, so David ordered another round and they chatted for another forty-five minutes or so until he said he had to get going.

"I have an early day tomorrow. It's been great seeing you, though. I'm glad we caught up."

"Me, too. And if you want to do anything, give me a shout."

He hugged her goodbye and promised to keep that in mind.

CHAPTER 27

"My father taught me how to make this when I was about eight. It's the one thing I've totally mastered. We used to make it all the time." Bella was at Nick's on his night off. They'd had pizza earlier and now she was making her signature snack. She poured the oil in the saucepan, added the popcorn and turned the heat on medium high. A few minutes later, it stopped popping and she emptied it into a big bowl and melted some butter to drizzle over the top. A few shakes of salt and it was done.

Nick grabbed a handful and gave her the thumbs up. "Perfect."

They resumed their spots on the sofa, side by side with the big plastic bowl of popcorn on Bella's lap. They were having a Netflix movie marathon and Nick couldn't be happier. Ever since the night she came for dinner with Andrea and Marco and shared a kiss afterward, they'd been inseparable. Whenever he had time off, they spent it together and since she was avoiding going downtown, they mostly enjoyed the beach, went fishing and relaxed at his place.

He'd never felt so comfortable with a girlfriend before. Bella was beautiful, but it wasn't just that. There was a sense of belonging that was new for him and he sensed it was for her, too. They hadn't really talked about their relationship yet. It was too new, and they were both aware of how limited their time together was. He didn't know what would happen when she had to go home to L.A. He was hoping that she could extend her vacation, but he didn't know if she would or if it was even possible.

"You're awfully quiet. What are you thinking about?" she asked softly.

He ran his hand though her hair, massaging her scalp gently.

"Just how much I'm enjoying this. Being with you. And wishing you could stay longer," he admitted.

She turned and gave him a quick kiss. "I'm working on that. I told my agent I'm not ready to come home yet and asked if she can delay my start date. I might be able to get an extra week or two, possibly."

He grinned. "I'll take what I can get."

"Maybe you can take some vacation time and come visit? I'd love to show you around the crazy town I live in."

Nick had never had any desire to go to Hollywood, until now. "I might be able to do that. I do have some vacation time coming."

"Keep it in mind. I'll have a better idea of my shooting schedule in a few weeks and we can plan it for a week where they don't need me much and we can do some sightseeing. Maybe take a drive to Malibu. It's gorgeous along the Pacific Coast Highway."

"Not as pretty as Nantucket, though," Nick teased her.

"Of course not! It could be fun, though."

"If you're there, it will be fun." He leaned over and kissed her, and she melted in his arms.

"Okay, what do you want to watch next?" she asked as she pulled away and reached for more popcorn.

"Surprise me." He didn't care what they watched. He was just happy being on his sofa, eating popcorn with Bella. He wished this was their normal, everyday life and not just her vacation. Once her time here was up, would she still feel the same way? He knew that he would. His feelings grew stronger every day and it had taken him totally by surprise, at first. He didn't know if she felt the same way, though.

"You're still spending time with Nick?" Bella's sister sounded concerned. Bella had kept her secret to herself until now, not wanting to jinx anything. And because she was afraid her sister would be the voice of reason and tell her she was making a mistake.

"We're not just spending time together. I really like him, and I think he feels the same way. If he was in L.A., I think we'd be an official item."

"You're not in L.A., though. You're on vacation—in fantasy land—not the real world. You only have a few more weeks until you have to leave. I just hate to see you get hurt when it ends."

"I know. I wish it didn't have to end. I mentioned having him come visit me. Nick has some vacation time he can use, and he liked the idea.

"Sure, but that would be his vacation. Still not real. What happens after that? I'm not trying to be a Debbie Downer, just thinking realistically. You live in two very different worlds. And do you really want to drag him into the craziness of the media in your world?"

Bella was silent for a moment. The media was the worst part of her job and she hated to inflict them and their lies on someone she cared about.

She sighed. "He'd hate that."

"I just don't want you to get your hopes up. Why not just enjoy the time you have left on Nantucket and don't expect anything more?"

"I know you're right. But I'm already pretty attached. I hate the thought of leaving here and saying goodbye."

"Well, the more attached you get, the harder it will be. Maybe try and slow things down a little?"

Bella laughed. "It's much too late for that. And I don't want to waste any of the time that I do have left. We're together constantly. It's pretty intense already. But in a good way. I think you'd really like him."

Julia was silent for a moment. "I do like him. He's charming and if there was any way for the two of you to actually be a couple, I'd totally support it. I just don't see how that's possible. Do you?"

"Not the way things have been, no. I keep trying to think of some way to make it work."

"Well, if you can find a way, then I'm all for it. I just want you to be happy."

"I know. And I love you for it."

Bella ended the call feeling sad and a bit anxious. Her time on Nantucket was winding down more quickly than she'd hoped. Her agent had tried to push the start date out two weeks and they balked at that, but agreed to give her one extra week before she had to report to the set. So, that was something. She hadn't told Nick the good news yet. But she knew she'd be seeing him later that night when he got off work.

On the nights he worked, she often met him at the outside bar for an after-work drink or they went to the beach during the day, or both. Nick was eager to spend as much time as he could with Bella and there was nothing she'd rather do than spend her time with him. She'd never actually been in love before, but she had a feeling this might be it. It exhilarated and terrified her at the same time, because she didn't know what the future held for them.

CHAPTER 28

At about three thirty in the afternoon, Paula stopped by the reception area to visit her sister, Lucy, and to help out if needed. Her job as the general manager wasn't as glamorous as some might think. She spent most of her time helping out wherever an extra pair of hands was needed. During the busy times of the day, she spent most of her time assisting at the front desk and welcoming guests to the hotel.

Their official check-in time was three and they often had a rush of guests in the late afternoon. Lucy had several people in line as did the other two front desk associates. Paula hopped behind an empty computer and waved the next person in line over. Twenty minutes later, the rush died down and she went to chat with her sister.

"How's it going?" she asked Lucy.

"Good. I just witnessed a top-secret affair."

"You did? Who?"

"The Cape and Islands Senator is here for two nights and look who is in his room." She pointed to the computer screen and Paula's jaw dropped.

"But she's married." It was a local woman—someone they knew as a total snob. Grace Peterson was married to an executive and was active in several women's groups and charity organizations.

"He's married, too," Lucy said.

"Well, isn't that something." It was one aspect of the job that never failed to surprise her. Quite a few people had affairs and booked rooms at The Whitley for the privacy.

"On a different note, I have some news," Lucy began. "I ran into Jason yesterday at Stop and Shop. I reminded him about the art show this weekend and he asked if I wanted to grab a drink after. I just wanted to double-check to make sure you're okay with that?"

Paula smiled. "It was my idea, remember? Yes, I am very much okay with that. I'm excited for you—and for the show. I'll stop by, too, at some point."

"Okay, good."

They both looked up as David walked across the lobby and waved as he saw them, before disappearing down the hall to the executive offices.

"He's an interesting one. Too bad he's not staying around. I thought he might be a good possibility for you," Lucy said.

"For me? David's great, but like you said, he's leaving soon. He also travels so much. He told me it's made it hard to have any kind of a serious relationship."

Lucy frowned. "I don't know how he can stand all that travel. Don't people eventually slow down on that and let other people take over?"

"I don't know. It didn't sound that way to me. He's a consultant and it's all travel. I agree, though, it sounds awful to me, too," Paula said.

"Speaking of people that would make a good couple..." Lucy glanced across the lobby to the concierge desk where Marco had just arrived for the evening shift, and he and Andrea were laughing. Andrea had another hour or so and then she'd be leaving for the day.

"Andrea and Marco? I don't know about that. I heard she just went out with Ben again."

"My Ben? Hm, you know I can see that, too. She definitely has more in common with him than I do," Lucy said.

"She looks happier than I've seen her in a long time. I know she was mad to lose the GM role, but it looks like she's having fun in concierge services."

"It's a much better fit for her," Lucy agreed.

"Oh, I have some huge news. We got a call this morning and the President is coming in a few weeks."

"The President? Like of the U.S.?"

"Yes, the one and only. Just for one night. He's being honored and giving a speech at some event downtown—a literacy thing, I think," Paula said.

"That's right, he has a memoir out now, doesn't he?"

"He does. It's crazy, though. They booked fifty rooms and he's only staying here for one night, but they booked the rooms for two nights."

"Fifty rooms?"

Paula nodded. "Yes, some of his secret service team are coming the day before to get the rooms ready. They're bringing bullet proof glass to install in the windows of the President's rooms."

"Wow."

"I know. It's an honor to have them here, though. I'm going to work closely with housekeeping to make sure the rooms are perfect for them."

"That's very cool." Lucy said and then her attention went to a new arrival in the lobby. "Hm, what is Aunt Vivian up to? She has a gleam in her eyes that usually means trouble."

Paula followed her gaze to where her aunt had paused to chat with Andrea at the concierge desk before heading toward her office.

"One never knows," Paula said. "It's still a mystery what she actually does here."

Paula chatted for a few more minutes with Lucy and was about to head back to her office when she noticed a somewhat familiar looking man in a sharp black suit walk into the lobby, look around and then head to the concierge desk, too. He spoke with Andrea and Marco for a moment then headed toward the executive offices. Paula still couldn't place who he was.

She walked over to the concierge desk on her way to her office. Andrea and Marco were chatting and looked up when she reached them, and she addressed them both. "Who was that? He looks so familiar, but I can't place him."

"Bill Cooper of Cooper Real Estate. Said he was here to see your Aunt Vivian," Marco said.

"She said she was expecting him and to send him on to see her. But she didn't say what he's here about," Andrea added.

"Okay, thanks. That's odd."

Andrea laughed. "Aunt Vivian is odd, so it fits."

ANDREA WATCHED PAULA HEAD BACK TO HER OFFICE AND REALIZED that was the first civil exchange they'd had since Paula started in her new job.

"What do you think your aunt is up to?" Marco asked.

"Who knows? She's still saying she wants to divorce Uncle Freddy, so maybe it has something to do with that. Maybe she's putting her house on the market. Your guess is as good as mine."

Andrea worked with Marco until almost five when she was due to head home. She was just thinking about what she was going to do for dinner when a businessman who'd just checked in came over to see them. He radiated frustration and panic. He was also soaking wet. The rain had started about an hour ago and it was blowing in all directions. The heavy rain was predicted but the wind was much stronger than anticipated.

"Lucy said you might be able to help me," he began.

Andrea smiled to put him at ease. "I'll do my best. What do you need?"

"I just flew in and my luggage apparently went in a different direction. All my clothes are on their way to the West Coast. And I have a business meeting first thing in the morning. Any suggestions?"

"You don't have anything else with you?" Andrea asked.

"Only what I'm wearing. This would be fine for the meeting, if it was clean."

Andrea thought for a moment.

"Why don't you come with me." She led him into their gift shop and to the clothing section where there was a selection of t-shirts, sweatshirts and shorts.

He shook his head. "I can't wear this to the meeting."

Andrea smiled. "No, that wouldn't be good. But you can change out of your clothes, find a t-shirt and pair of shorts here and give me your shirt and pants. I'll get them cleaned and pressed for you and deliver to your room first thing in the morning. Is eight o'clock early enough?"

He looked as though he wanted to kiss her. "You're an angel." He quickly picked out a long sleeve t-shirt with The Whitley Hotel logo on it and a pair of long tan shorts. He changed in the dressing room and then handed Andrea his shirt and pants. "I can't thank you enough. I need to pay for these clothes."

Andrea smiled. "It's all set. Don't worry about it. Just go and relax. Your clean clothes will be at your door in the morning." Andrea had a discretionary account where they could occasionally give out t-shirts or other items as advertising expenses. The goodwill they received from doing so more than made up for the cost.

"Thanks again. I really appreciate it." He went off to his room and Andrea wandered back to the lobby with the pile of folded clothes in her arms.

Marco raised his eyebrows. "I'm almost afraid to ask. What did you do with him?"

She laughed. "He's wearing a Whitley t-shirt and shorts and is relaxing in his room. I told him I'd get these cleaned and pressed for him and dropped off in the morning so he can make his meeting."

"What laundry is open now on Nantucket?"

She grinned. "The one at my house."

"Impressive!"

"I do what I can. And I should probably get going. Have a good night."

"You, too. Are we on for dinner and drinks tomorrow?" Marco had mentioned trying out the new restaurant, Portside, that had opened down by the waterfront.

"Sure, sounds good. See you tomorrow."

CHAPTER 29

At a few minutes before six, Paula finished her daily paperwork and closed down her computer. She was getting hungry and realized there wasn't much in her house, and the last thing she felt like doing was cooking. Maybe she'd feed Chester and order a pizza. It felt like a good night for that. She'd change into her sweats, crash on the sofa watching TV and go to bed early.

She stepped out into the hallway at the same time as David, who was also done for the day. Her aunt was long gone, and Paula had no idea how her meeting with the realtor went or what that was about. She wasn't sure she really wanted to know, either.

"Any exciting plans tonight?" David asked as they walked down the hall.

She laughed. "Nope. Beyond trying to decide what kind of pizza to order. What about you?"

"The same. I'm beat today. Probably going to head to bed early."

They walked across the lobby and Paula noticed the sky outside was darker than usual, the wind was howling, and the rain was coming down even heavier than before. She'd known they were getting a storm but didn't think it was expected to be this bad. She was glad that she'd remembered to bring an umbrella. Still, with the driving rain she knew she'd likely be soaked anyway by the time she reached her cottage.

They were just about at the door when a huge gust of wind rattled the windows and with a whoosh, the power flickered and then snuffed itself out. They both paused and waited for it to come back on. The power rarely went out for long on Nantucket, and it wasn't unusual for it to flicker and then come right back to life. The lobby was full of people trying to check in and the girls at the front desk looked a little frazzled.

"The power should come right back on, hopefully," Paula said.

David looked outside. "That storm doesn't look like it's slowing down any time soon. Do you lose power often here?"

"Almost never. When we do it's usually a horrible snowstorm, and it's back up the next day. Or an accident when the lines get knocked out."

"Wouldn't surprise me if a tree fell on the lines. That might mean it's out for a while."

"Looks like I'm not getting that pizza." Paula headed over to the reception desk and helped explain to the guests that until the power came back, they wouldn't be able to check them in. Those who already had their room keys could still access their rooms as the locks were battery operated and since there were only three levels, people could easily take the stairs to their rooms. The elevators were set to automatically go to the ground level during a power outage and the doors could be manually opened. She took a deep breath and looked around. David was at the concierge desk talking to Marco and several guests.

When the lights still didn't come on after a half hour, and it was getting darker, Paula went to the housekeeping room and found a bunch of candles which she placed all over the lobby, on all the counters. David saw what she was doing and came to help carry out more candles. They went to the bar area which was just off of the lobby and placed them all along the bar as well.

Frank was the bartender on duty, and he came over when Paula set the candles down. "Great idea." The bar wasn't overly busy but there were a few guests enjoying cocktails. The restaurant was emptying out as there was no way for the kitchen to cook. Paula realized the power might be out for some time, and they still had a lobby full of people that couldn't check into their rooms yet. They were starting to look restless and frustrated, and she didn't blame them.

David looked around the lobby, too. "No generator, huh?"

She shook her head. "Grandfather considered it at one point, but we so rarely lose power that he didn't think the expense was worth it."

"Might be worth reconsidering, if only to power the reception area so people can get checked into their rooms," David said.

"I agree. And possibly for the restaurant, too. We should look into that again. Actually, I have an idea. I'm getting hungry, and I bet some of our guests are, too."

"What are you thinking?"

"I'm going to head into the kitchen and see if there's anything we can offer them."

Nick was overseeing the kitchen that night and when Paula explained what she had in mind, he was all for it.

"We have cheese and crackers. Some nuts. I can whip up some guacamole and chips. And we can splurge a little and give them a platter of shrimp cocktail. People always like that. And some brownies and cookies. Sound good?"

"Yes. Sounds perfect."

"Give me ten minutes and I'll have it ready for you."

Paula headed back to the bar. "Frank, we're going to put some snacks out for people in a few minutes. I'd like to offer everyone a round or two of drinks, as well. That might be welcome about now."

He grinned. "I think that's a fabulous idea."

Paula took a deep breath and walked into the middle of the lobby.

"Could I get everyone's attention, please?" Her voice seemed to wobble and echo in the room with its high ceiling. But the chattering quieted and people looked her way.

"I'd like to apologize for the weather. Unfortunately, we can't control the power outage and we don't know what time it will be back up. Hopefully soon. In the meantime, I'd like to invite you all to have a cocktail or two on us. Please head to the bar, and Frank can take your order. We're going to have some snacks for you, as well, shortly."

"Nice job," David said when she walked back over to him.

"You really think so? I know it's a little extravagant."

He smiled. "And that's why they come to the most expensive hotel on the island. For its legendary service. They'll appreciate it and a drink or two will help to pass the time and take the edge off for them."

Paula was relieved that he approved. His opinion mattered to her. She grinned. "Good. Want to help me carry the food out?"

Marco had heard their exchange. "I'll help, too."

Nick had everything ready for them and they carried out platters of cheese and crackers, plump shrimp with cocktail sauce on the side, bowls of salted nuts, and sliced salami and other cold cuts, patés, crusty sliced baguettes and a big platter of cookies and brownies.

The food and drinks were a hit and for the next few hours it felt a bit like a party in the lobby. Paula, David and Marco enjoyed a drink as well and snacked a bit.

"Has this ever happened on any of your other assignments?" Paula asked David.

"A few times, actually. One time in New York City on a really hot July night, there was a brownout and all of Manhattan went dark. That was fun. Picture all those tall buildings and no one can use the elevator."

"What did they do?" Marco asked.

"They tried to do whatever they could, but it was limited. The lobby was dark, there were no candles because everything was all on a higher floor that they couldn't access. They handed out snacks and it was mostly stuff from a vending machine, chocolate and chips, junk food. But they gave out beer and wine, too, from the hotel bar and that made people happy. The power finally came on a few hours later."

He glanced at Paula. "You handled this about as well as you could. The food and drinks were a smart choice."

"Thank you."

Paula made the rounds of the room again, checking in with the girls at the front desk and making sure they had a chance to have some food and a drink if they wanted. The atmosphere in the room had changed from tense to almost fun. When the power came on an hour later, the lobby erupted in cheers. Paula jumped behind the front desk again and helped to get everyone checked in while David and Marco brought the empty platters back into the kitchen.

Once everyone was settled, Paula and David walked out together.

"Well, that was an adventure, huh?" David said as they stepped outside. The wind had died down and the rain completely stopped, which Paula was grateful for.

"Certainly unexpected. It turned out okay, I think, though. Maybe even a little bit fun."

David smiled. "I had fun. See you tomorrow, Paula."

"Goodnight." As she walked home, Paula smiled to herself. It had been a crazy and chaotic night, but it had been a good one, too.

CHAPTER 30

"Are you having fun?" Marco's deep, amused voice got her attention. He was looking at Andrea with such warmth in his eyes that it gave her goosebumps.

"I am. I love this place." They were at The Gaslight for dinner and Andrea was having the best night. The food, as usual, was great and now they were having a cocktail and listening to live music.

It would have made her top five list of dates except that it wasn't a date at all. She and Marco were just two friends and co-workers having dinner. She reminded herself that she was also his boss. So, when she felt the occasional hint of attraction, she tried to ignore it.

"I love this song. Want to dance?" He stood and held out his hand and she did want to dance.

It was a slow jazzy tune, and they wrapped their arms around each other and swayed to the music. Andrea leaned into him and caught a whiff of his cologne. She liked the feeling of being in his arms and was disappointed when the music ended, and the next song was a fast one. They stayed on the dance floor and danced several songs in a row before taking a break.

She'd heard from Elaine that morning, confirming the date for her final interview in Manhattan. It was coming up fast, a week from Monday. She still had very mixed feelings about the opportunity. The job itself sounded great. The property was lovely and elegant, and really the perfect size. It was just the location. Could she actually see herself living in Manhattan? Leaving Nantucket?

She'd talked to Ben right after Elaine called. He'd checked in to see if they were still on for an event he'd invited her to—a book launch party for a writer friend. It was a cocktail party held at the White Elephant and Andrea knew it would be fun. So that was tomorrow night. Her social life had never been so busy.

She had to admit, she really preferred the hours of the concierge desk.

One thing she didn't miss was the hours the general manager had to put in. She'd just missed the blackout at the hotel the night before. Marco had filled her in on how Paula and David stayed to make sure everyone was taken care of. She would have done the same if she'd been the GM. But she wasn't sure she would have thought to offer free drinks and put food out. She begrudgingly had to admit that had been smart of Paula.

"Good news. My mother will be here in a few weeks. I can't wait for you to meet her," Marco said.

"She will? That's great. I look forward to meeting her, too." Andrea knew Marco and his brother and sister were close to their mother and missed seeing her.

"We'll have a big cookout when she gets here and have all of our friends over to meet her. She'll love that," he said.

Andrea had met his brother a few times before and just met his sister a week or so ago when a small group of them went out to Mimi's Place for dinner after work. His sister reminded Andrea of Marco. They shared the same smile and infectious laugh. He said they got that from his mother.

When another slow song came on, Marco didn't even ask if she wanted to dance. He just stood and held out his hand and she followed. They didn't talk at all as they swayed to the music. Marco was tall, just over six feet, and even though Andrea was barely five-five, they seemed to fit together perfectly. There were two slow songs in a row, which made her very happy. When the beat picked up, they stayed out there until the set ended and they were both laughing as they went back to their seats. Both of them had danced up a bit of a sweat as the dance floor was packed.

"Looks like that was their last set," Marco said.

Andrea glanced at the time and it was already past midnight. The time had flown by.

"They were great. We'll have to watch for when they come again."

"Definitely."

The waitress came by with their check and Marco quickly handed her a card before Andrea could even open her purse.

"What are you doing? Let's split this."

He shook his head. "Not tonight. This is my treat."

"You don't have to do that."

"I know. I want to. Maybe I'll let you return the favor sometime."

She laughed. "Yes, you will. Thank you, then. Everything was great."

He drove her home and walked her to her door.

"Thanks again, Marco. It was a fun night."

He smiled and for a moment, those eyes locked into hers and he leaned toward her and she caught her breath, worried and at the same time eager for the kiss that might come. But he didn't kiss her. He pulled her in for a hug.

"See you tomorrow, Andrea. Sleep tight."

CHAPTER 31

"It's not a date!" Paula insisted.

Lucy laughed. "Have you ever heard the expression 'If it walks like a duck, quacks like a duck…'"

"It's really not like that."

"Really? What is it like, then?"

There was already a good crowd for Lucy's art show. It was Saturday night, a little after seven. Paula had arrived about ten minutes ago. And David was with her. Though not at the moment. He was off chatting with Nick and Bella by the cheese and crackers table.

"We all went for drinks after work yesterday. We were just chatting about what we were up to for the rest of the weekend. And I mentioned your art show. And Nick said he was going, so David said that sounded like fun and could he tag along? So here we are. Not a date."

"Mm-hm. And did you all ride together, then?"

"No, David drove. Nick and Bella met us here."

Lucy smiled. "Interesting. Yet Nick lives next door to you, and you could have all driven together."

"I mentioned it to Nick, but he said wanted to take his own car as he wasn't sure what he and Bella wanted to do after. They might walk around downtown or get a bite to eat or just get take-out and go home."

"Okay, I guess that makes sense. Those two have been inseparable. I worry a little about him when she leaves. It won't be much longer."

Paula agreed. "I know. He said something to me about going out there to visit."

"To Hollywood? That's interesting."

"Oh, honey, look at this. This would look perfect in the baby's room." A woman admiring one of Lucy's pieces called her husband over to see the turquoise rocking chair with hand-painted pink roses all over it.

"We'll be back," Paula said and left so Lucy could talk to her potential customers.

"Champagne?" A server strolled by holding a tray of flutes filled with the bubbly beverage.

"Yes, thank you." Paula took a glass and a sip as she joined the others.

"Your sister is so talented," Bella said.

Lucy had a crowd of people around her now, asking questions.

"She really is," Paula agreed.

"Does it run in the family? Do you paint, too?" Bella asked.

Nick and Paula both laughed at that. "No. She's the only one. Nick and I have no artistic skills."

"We just appreciate those who are talented," Nick said and gave Bella a quick kiss. Bella looked beautiful and a bit mysterious as she was still wearing dark sunglasses. She was afraid to go out in public without them. With her rich red curls and the glasses, no one seemed to recognize her, thankfully.

Another server came by with a tray of stuffed mushrooms and they all took one. Paula helped herself to some of the cheese and crackers that were on the table, too. They walked around and looked at the other artwork that was displayed. There were some beautiful pieces. When they made their way back over to Lucy, Paula was happy to see that Jason had arrived and the two of them were deep in conversation.

They all said a quick goodbye to Lucy and walked outside. Nick and Bella decided to order Thai take-out and just go home.

"I don't feel like going home yet, do you?" David asked. "Want to walk around a bit? I haven't really played tourist since I've been back."

"Sure." It was a warm night and lots of the shops were still open. They strolled around, looking in the display windows and popping into some of the shops. They were a few doors away from Oath Pizza on the wharf when David asked if she felt like going somewhere for dinner.

"I actually wouldn't mind just having some pizza. Do you like Oath?" As soon as she saw the sign her stomach rumbled, and she started to crave it.

"I forgot about Oath. Sure, that sounds good." They waited in line for their pizza and brought it to a nearby bench and ate watching the last ferry come in for the night. The ocean was still and calm and the night was clear. The moonlight glimmered on the water.

"Are you looking forward to heading home?" Paula asked. David only had a few weeks left. The time was going by fast and the Taste of the Town event was right around the corner.

"I'm actually not looking forward to it. It's been good being back here. I hope to get home more often to see my family."

"How's your mom doing?"

"About the same. But a little better because now we have a plan in place and know what to anticipate." He smiled. "No more running away to the pond."

They were both quiet for a moment, enjoying their pizza and then Paula asked, "What's it like living in the city? Are you right in Manhattan?"

"I am. I have an apartment close to the office. It's convenient. I'm on the twenty-third floor." He laughed. "Very different from Nantucket."

It sounded awful to Paula. But she knew some people loved being in the city.

"Do you think you'll stay there? Long-term, I mean?"

He hesitated. "I honestly don't know. I've never really thought that far ahead. I don't have any plans to move any time soon, though. It's where my work is. Well, it's the place I sleep when I'm not traveling, that is."

"So, when you're not traveling, what do you like to do for fun in the city?"

He smiled. "Anything you want. It's there. That's one thing I love about Manhattan. Great sports teams, restaurants, shows. I have some good friends there now so there's always something to do."

"I saw a Broadway show there a few years ago. A few of us went for a girls' weekend and had a blast. We stopped at the M and M store in Times Square after the show." Paula remembered being surprised by how crowded it was in Times Square, people so close together that it was almost claustrophobic.

David grinned. "I'm a big fan of that M and M store."

"Have you ever been in Times Square on New Year's Eve? I can't even imagine how crowded that must be."

"No, we stay far away. I don't like it that crowded."

"I bet it must be beautiful at Christmas, though, with all the lights?"

"It is. But it doesn't hold a candle to the Nantucket Stroll. I haven't made it back for that in a long time. Maybe this year."

"That's always a busy weekend for us at the hotel." They were already almost completely booked. Many people came every year and booked for the following year when they left.

When they finished their pizza, they walked back toward the art gallery where they were parked. When they passed by The Gaslight, they could hear the music from the band inside. David slowed his steps and they listened for a minute.

"Feel like going in and having a drink, maybe catching a set?" he asked.

"Sure, why not?"

They went inside and were seated at a small cocktail table not far from the band. Paula ordered a glass of chardonnay and David a gin and tonic, a departure from his usual draft beer.

"It's my summer cocktail," he explained.

The band came on and played a good variety of older rock songs and current favorites. It didn't take long before the dance floor filled up. It was too loud to talk easily so they just sipped their cocktails and people-watched. David was easy to be with. As they'd spent more time together, Paula had grown used to having him around and realized she was going to miss him when he left. He was a great sounding board to bounce ideas off of, but she also just liked talking to him, too.

She wondered how things were going with Missy, if they ever ended up going out. David didn't talk much about his personal life. She assumed he was single but for all she knew there was someone in New York he was eager to get back to. For some reason, that thought depressed her. She'd wondered when he first told her about the situation with his mother if he was planning on relocating back to Nantucket. But it didn't look like that was a possibility. She knew job opportunities, especially for the kind of consulting work that he did, were pretty much non-existent on Nantucket.

A slow song came on and the dance floor filled with couples swaying to the beat. It was an older song that Paula had always loved, "Wonderful Tonight."

She glanced at David and he smiled. "Great song," he said.

Paula felt a sense of anticipation and wondered what it would be like to dance with David. To feel his arms around her. She hadn't really thought about him that way before, but suddenly she was very aware of everything about him. How his lashes were so long it was downright unfair, how his arms were muscled and how the laugh lines around his mouth only made him more attractive. He leaned forward and she prepared to get up and head to the dance floor. But then he sighed instead and leaned back in his chair and crossed his arms over his chest. And the moment was gone. She felt a bit silly for even imagining he was about to ask her to dance. They were not on a date. They were just two co-workers.

So, when the set ended and David asked if she was ready to go, she nodded. He pulled into her driveway twenty minutes later.

"Thanks for letting me tag along tonight. That was fun," he said.

"It was. You're welcome to tag along anytime."

"Goodnight, Paula."

He waited until she opened her front door before driving off. Paula stepped inside and locked the door behind her. Chester came running and she scooped him up and gave him a hug. She shook her head, frustrated with herself. It was no wonder she was still single. Instead of falling for the perfectly nice, available local guy, Jason, she instead found herself more interested in someone who was completely unavailable and soon to be leaving Nantucket.

DAVID DROVE HOME FEELING A MIX OF EMOTIONS, AMONG THEM regret that he didn't ask Paula to dance. There was a moment when he sensed he could have and she would have said yes and it might have been magical. But he hesitated and considered it for too long and talked himself out of it. He'd reminded himself that it was inappropriate, given their working relationship and he didn't want to send the wrong message. Especially since he found himself fighting an attraction that took him by surprise.

When he'd first met Paula, he found her attractive but quickly dismissed the thought, given their working relationship. And at first, he wasn't even sure if she liked him as a co-worker. She was definitely uneasy about the move into the new role and in having someone there to watch over her. When he gave her the feedback that she was too nice, he felt her retreat and regretted having to tell her that. But it was true. And to her credit, she immediately tried to do something about it. Even if she didn't like hearing it.

But he'd enjoyed working closely with her and lately they'd been spending more time outside of work together, too, and he found himself wanting to be around her. But as much as he'd love to date her, he knew it was impossible and he didn't want to start something he couldn't finish. He only had a few weeks left, and then he'd be heading home to Manhattan and probably wouldn't see Paula again. So, no sense in making things any more difficult than they needed to be.

CHAPTER 32

"Are you up for fishing tomorrow with Nick and Bella, and then dinner at his place? Should be a fun time." Marco leaned against the concierge desk, waiting for Andrea's reply. He was finishing up a shift and she was taking over for the evening.

She smiled. "I can't tomorrow. I have plans," she said vaguely.

"Yeah? What are you doing that's more exciting than coming out with us?"

She laughed. "I'm heading to New York for the night. I have Sunday and Monday off. Meeting an old friend. We might see a show or something." It wasn't a total lie. She did have plans to meet up with a friend, but the friend was Ben. It turned out that he had to go home for a real estate closing and to see another property.

Marco looked disappointed. "Oh, okay. Well, have fun then. I'll see you when you get back."

———

ANDREA TOOK A TWO O'CLOCK FLIGHT TO NEW YORK ON SUNDAY and checked into her room at a quarter to four. The hotel was as elegant as she remembered and the woman who helped her at the front desk was really lovely. She welcomed Andrea and quickly got her settled with a spacious suite. Andrea wasn't meeting Ben until six, so she took a book into the bath and soaked in the tub until her skin felt wrinkly. It was nice to just relax and read for a while.

She was excited to go out in the city. Ben had mentioned possibly getting tickets to a Broadway show. She wore a cute new dress she found at Nantucket Threads earlier that week—it was a sleeveless, black cocktail-length dress and was very flattering on.

He texted her when he walked into the lobby and she went down to meet him. He looked handsome in a navy blazer, dark pants and a pale-yellow dress shirt. He smiled when he saw her.

"You look gorgeous."

"Thank you. You're looking pretty sharp yourself."

They went to one of his favorite restaurants, a small Italian bistro a few blocks from the theater. And he'd managed to get third row center seats for one of the hottest shows on Broadway. She was impressed.

"How did you manage that?"

He grinned. "I know a guy. Our real estate attorney gets good seats all the time. He hooked me up."

Dinner was great and the show was wonderful. When it finished, they joined the crowds pouring onto the streets in Times Square.

"Want to go for a quick drink?" Ben asked. "There's a really cool piano bar not far from here."

"Sure."

He led the way to a cozy bar that had a huge piano and lots of small cocktail tables. They each only had one drink, but they stayed for several hours, singing along to the music and chatting during the breaks. It was a fun night, and the time flew by. When it was past midnight, they reluctantly decided to leave as Andrea's interview was at nine the next day. They strolled back to the hotel and when they reached the front door, Ben pulled her to him for a hug and then a kiss. It was a nice kiss, but Andrea was a little disappointed that the expected spark wasn't there. She was so sure that it would be. Maybe she was just too tired.

He met her eye and smiled. "Goodnight. And good luck tomorrow."

ANDREA WOKE EARLY THE NEXT DAY, ORDERED A BIG ROOM SERVICE breakfast of scrambled eggs, home fries, toast and coffee and felt pretty good about her upcoming interview. She wasn't as nervous as she normally was before an interview and she had a feeling it might go well. She'd found that the more it mattered whether she got a job, the more nervous she tended to be. Whereas when she was less invested, she tended to be more confident, more relaxed and interviewed better.

And that's exactly what happened. She was led into a conference room and took a seat at a long table where three interviewers faced her. Normally that would be intimidating, but she just smiled and actually had fun with the interview. She knew she had the experience, and she gave lots of good examples for each question that she was asked. When the interview ended, she knew she'd done well.

They asked 'buying questions,' and the final one was, "Ms. Whitley, if this were to work out, how soon would you be able to begin?"

She smiled. "I would have to give several weeks' notice but could start right after that."

"Excellent. We'll be in touch with a decision by the end of the week."

———

BY THE TIME ANDREA CHECKED OUT AND BOARDED THE PLANE HOME to Nantucket, her high from the interview had faded. And she worried about actually getting an offer and having to make a decision that she still felt so unsure about. The flight was smooth and as her plane landed on Nantucket and she turned her phone back on, it pinged with a text message and she smiled when she saw that it was sent earlier from Marco.

"Hope you're having fun in the Big Apple. Missed you yesterday. Caught lots of fish. See you tomorrow."

She texted back. "Glad you had fun and caught lots of fish. Any leftovers?"

Sixty seconds later, her phone pinged. "Lots. Dinner tomorrow night, my place?"

"See you then."

ANDREA HEADED TO HER PARENTS' HOUSE FOR DINNER MONDAY night. They'd postponed their normal Sunday gathering as both Andrea and her father were out of town. She wondered what her father was up to, as he rarely went off-island. Her mother said their Aunt Vivian would also be joining them as well as Uncle Freddy. As Andrea had expected, those two had kissed and made-up. Aunt Vivian was just all bluster and drama. She loved the attention.

The mood around the dinner table was festive. Andrea hadn't seen her father in such a good mood in a long time. And her aunt and uncle were madly in love again.

"So, how did it go? Do you think you have a good shot at the job?" her mother asked.

Aunt Vivian leaned forward. It was the first she'd heard of Andrea's interview. "What job is this?"

She addressed her aunt first. "It's a GM role at a boutique hotel in Manhattan." And then her mother. "I think it went well. I wouldn't be surprised if they make an offer. I should know by the end of the week."

"Manhattan. That's exciting. I didn't know you wanted to go there," her aunt said.

Andrea laughed. "I'm not sure that I do. I'd prefer Boston as it's closer or ideally something here, but there don't seem to be any opportunities either place at the moment."

"Aside from the location, are you sure that's the job you want? To go back into a general manager role? I've honestly never seen you as happy and relaxed as you've been since moving to the concierge desk," her mother said.

"I agree. And selfishly, I don't want you to leave. But, if it's what you really want to do, of course we will all support that," Hallie said.

"I honestly don't know what I want to do. The job seems perfect other than the location. And you're right, I have been enjoying the concierge role. But I haven't thought of it as something long-term, just a fun temporary role until I land a GM spot."

"I don't see why it has to be temporary," her mother said. "Work doesn't feel like work when you enjoy what you do."

Hallie nodded. "I've said that before, too. Work is much less stressful and more enjoyable when it's fun."

"I have a lot to think about. I've never really considered concierge as a long-term place for me," Andrea said.

"Well, maybe you should. I agree with the others," her aunt chimed in.

That reminded Andrea of something she'd meant to ask her aunt.

"Aunt Vivian, you recently had a realtor in to see you at The Whitley. What was that all about?"

Her aunt smiled impishly. "I called him in to do a fair market evaluation of The Whitley, for your grandfather."

That shocked the table into silence. Finally, Andrea spoke. "He asked you to do that? Is he seriously thinking of selling?"

"Well, no he didn't exactly ask me to do it. But I thought I'd get the information and then share it with him in case he might want to consider selling."

Her mother frowned. "Vivian, why on earth would you want to encourage that?"

"Well, I don't think any of you realize what that hotel is worth. We could sell it, divide the proceeds and never have to worry about working again." She glanced at Uncle Freddy. "Some of us could really use that money."

"Are you having money issues again?" her mother asked.

Aunt Vivian glanced away. Uncle Freddy put his hand on hers and squeezed it. She met his gaze and then sighed.

"I may have gotten into a bit of a jam in Europe. The casinos there are fabulous."

"That's what we were actually arguing about," Uncle Freddy added. He usually stayed quiet, but Andrea sensed he wanted to clear the air and let them know he wasn't the bad guy in what happened.

"He's right. He insisted that I stop going to the casinos and that's when I got mad and came home."

"Well, that makes more sense. But I thought you stopped gambling years ago?" her mother asked.

"I did. But then I sort of started again. I thought I could handle it and the casinos there are so lovely. But I know now that it's still a problem. I found a local Gamblers Anonymous group on Nantucket and have been going regularly. I'm not even buying scratch tickets anymore."

"But she was until I got home. I found a box of scratched off tickets in the garage," Uncle Freddy added.

"Why do you keep the tickets?" Andrea's mother asked.

"Just in case they might be useful. There's fine print on the back about holding onto them," her aunt said.

"I put them in the trash," Uncle Freddy said.

"So, what has Grandfather said about all this?" Andrea asked.

"I haven't talked to him yet. We have a meeting set for Tuesday morning." Grandfather had been out of town for the past week on a cruise with some friends.

"What will you do if he says no?" her mother asked.

Aunt Vivian smiled. "We'll cross that bridge when we have to."

ANDREA WAS SURPRISED BY A PHONE CALL THE NEXT AFTERNOON from Elaine, the headhunter.

"Great news! They want to offer you the job!"

The news wasn't all that unexpected, but the timing was. "Already? I didn't expect to hear until the end of the week."

"They all loved you. It was close with the other candidate, but they met with her yesterday afternoon, then took a vote and you won." She mentioned a very generous figure, more than Andrea had anticipated. She was shocked into silence.

"So, shall I tell them you accept? When would you like to start? That's another reason they didn't wait until the end of the week. They want you there ASAP."

"Well, this is exciting news. But I need to think about it. When do they need an answer?"

"I could probably stall them a day or two, tops. They don't want to lose the other candidate if you're not in. You are taking it, though, right? This is an incredible opportunity, and they came in higher than we expected on the money."

"I know. It's a very generous offer. I just need to sleep on it and let it digest."

"Okay. Let me know as soon as possible. And congratulations."

"Thanks, Elaine."

Andrea ended the call and took a deep breath. Now that she actually had the offer, she didn't know what she wanted to do. She really did need to sleep on it. Especially after the conversation with her family the night before.

———

And she was due at Marco's house in an hour. She finished up at five, went home to freshen up and headed off to Marco's. She stopped at Bradford's Liquors on the way to pick up a six pack of the local Cisco Brewers' beer that Marco liked and her favorite wine, Bread and Butter chardonnay.

Marco was outside on the deck, firing up the grill, when she pulled into his driveway. His car was the only other one there. She parked and carried the beer and wine over to him.

"Hey, there," he said when he saw her. "The door is open if you want to set that in the kitchen." He grinned. "If you feel like pouring us a drink, even better."

"Will do. Where are your brother and sister tonight? Are they working?"

"Alana is. Sergio is out with friends. I don't expect either of them back 'til later. So, all the fish is ours!"

She laughed. "How can I help?"

"Everything's done. I just need to throw the fish and veggies on the grill. Rice and salad are already made. We can sit outside and relax until it's ready."

"Works for me." She went inside and put the beer in the refrigerator and poured one into a glass for Marco. She also opened the wine and poured a glass for herself and brought both drinks outside. Marco was just sliding two aluminum foil packets onto the grill. When he closed the cover, she handed him his beer.

They sat at the round table on his patio and chatted for a bit. She told him about her day. It was his day off and it had been a comical day at the concierge desk.

"I think there might be a full moon. I don't remember the last time I had so many odd requests in one day. The first one was actually kind of romantic. The groom of a honeymoon couple called and wanted us to scatter pink Nantucket rose petals all over the bed. Then the wife of an older couple that was coming to celebrate his

80th birthday asked us to get several boxes of those chocolate covered cranberries from Sweet Inspirations and leave them in the room with a bottle of champagne."

"That sounds like a good combo, actually," Marco said.

She laughed. "I thought so, too. But the funniest request of all was from Mrs. Davis. She's arriving tomorrow and asked us to get a baby blue doggie sweatshirt that says Nantucket on it for her newest addition to the family."

"She got another dog? Or did something happen to Pepper?"

Mrs. David was one of their favorite guests. She came every summer for a month, rented one of their biggest suites, had people in and out visiting every weekend and she always brought her gorgeous Pomeranian, Pepper.

"Pepper's fine. She thought Pepper might be lonely and needed a sibling, so she recently acquired Daisy."

Marco chuckled. "I'm glad Pepper is okay. That sounds like quite the day."

"It was. I had one of the front desk girls cover the concierge desk so I could run into town and get everything. It was a fun day, actually."

"Never a dull moment at the concierge desk," Marco said.

It was the perfect opening for Andrea to mention her New York offer. She wanted to talk to Marco about it and not just spring it on him if she did decide to accept. But it was hard for her to bring it up, too. If she decided to take the offer, it was going to be even harder to leave, and she knew she'd miss Marco, too.

She waited until after they'd eaten and were relaxing with a second cocktail. They were still outside watching the sun beginning to set. There was no water view from where Marco lived, but it was still a nice area. His house backed up to conservation land and there were lots of trees everywhere.

Usually, the two of them were never at a loss for conversation and often had to be careful not to talk over each other in their rush to get their thoughts out. But suddenly there were some quiet moments. The normal flow of conversation seemed to dry up as the weight of what Andrea needed to say hung over her. Marco finally noticed it, too, and said something.

"Is everything okay? You seem a little distracted, not your usual chatty self."

She smiled. "I do have something on my mind. So, I didn't exactly tell you the whole story about why I went to New York."

He took a sip of his beer and held her gaze, waiting for her to continue.

"I had a final interview, for a general manager role at an upscale hotel in Manhattan. It's a great opportunity. And they made me an offer this afternoon. A good offer."

"I see. You don't seem all that excited about such a great offer. Do you want the job? If you do, if you think it might be your dream job, then you should take it."

She didn't expect him to say that.

"I don't know what to do. There are pros and cons. It's a great opportunity, but it's in Manhattan. That has never been my first choice."

"I think you have to decide if that's what you really want to do, too. Were you happier as a general manager than you are working in concierge services?"

She bit her lower lip as she considered the question for what felt like the millionth time.

"I feel like I should want this job," she admitted.

"Why?"

"Well, because it's the highest level and what I always thought I should be doing and what I did do for so long here."

"Do what you love and the money will follow…that's an old saying my father used to say. When a man loves what he does, it's not work, it's living. I guess it depends how you want to live your life. Only you can decide that, Andrea."

She knew he was right. And she knew she had a lot to think about. She smiled. "How did you get so smart?"

He leaned over and brushed a wayward strand of hair off her face. "You're making it too hard. Sleep on it and go with your gut. Go with what is going to make you feel lighter, happier. Maybe it's the Manhattan job. Maybe it's not."

"That's a good suggestion. I'll do that."

"There's something else to consider, too," Marco said softly and leaned in closely.

"What?" she whispered.

He closed the distance and touched his lips lightly to hers. The kiss made her toes tingle. It didn't go on for long, but it was powerful. When it stopped, he smiled again as he met her eyes. "I've wanted to do that for a long time. I just wanted you to know how I feel. If you stay, it could be amazing with us. I think you feel it, too?"

She nodded. "I do."

"I'm not trying to change your mind. If New York is what you want, I still think you should go for it. But I just wanted you to have all the information."

"I don't know if this is a good idea. I am your boss, after all," she said softly.

But Marco shook his head. "I already looked into it. There are no rules about dating co-workers or supervisors at the hotel. We're adults, Andrea. If it doesn't work out, I think we'd still be able to work together. And if it does work out—well like I said already, it could be amazing."

"I have a lot to think about. I should probably get going."

"You do." Marco walked her to her car and kissed her again, more thoroughly this time, and left her breathless.

"Sleep well, Andrea."

CHAPTER 33

Something was brewing. Paula didn't know what was going on, but it involved her Aunt Vivian. Her grandfather and her aunt went into a meeting at eleven that lasted over an hour and by the way Aunt Vivian had stormed out of office, Paula guessed it hadn't gone in her aunt's favor. Her grandfather had back-to-back meetings the rest of the day and at two in the afternoon, she noticed that David went into a meeting with him that also lasted for over an hour.

Paula had an odd feeling that it may have been about her as she wasn't included in the meeting and David's time here was almost over. Technically it was over, but her grandfather had asked him to stay on for the Taste of the Town event which was coming up on Monday. He was due to leave after that. The time was going by too fast. Paula didn't feel like she needed his guidance for a longer period of time, but she enjoyed having him around.

She went down to the reception area at three to help with the check-in rush and when it slowed and she returned to her office an hour and a half later, her grandfather waved her into his office and a moment later, David joined them.

"You may have noticed it's been a busy day today. Lots of meetings. Some of them were just catching up after being away, but there was one with your aunt that we need to discuss and also I met with

David to discuss his overall assessment of your suitability for the role."

Paula nodded. There wasn't much for her to say at this point. She'd known the assessment was coming. She thought she was doing a good job. She hoped David and her grandfather agreed.

"So, first your aunt. Did you know she had a harebrained idea that I might want to sell The Whitley?"

Paula was shocked. "No. I knew nothing about that."

"She invited a realtor in, got an assessment and then tried to convince me it would be a good time to cash in. For her to cash in is really what it came down to." He explained about her aunt's gambling addiction. Paula knew she'd had a problem with gambling years ago but didn't know it was an issue again.

"I'm sorry to hear that. I didn't know."

"None of us did. Except Freddy who was there. That's the real reason she came home and was all upset with him. He put his foot down about the gambling. But not before she lost most of their life savings." He sighed.

"I talked to David about it and we came up with an idea. I didn't want to involve you on this because you are family, and I wanted an outside, objective opinion. I also wondered if he might have run into anything like this before in his consulting and he has."

"Twice, actually. Gambling addiction is more common than people realize."

Her grandfather nodded. "Your aunt is already addressing the problem. She's joined a local support group. What we've decided to do is to advance her a portion of her inheritance—enough to give her a cushion and get her back on her feet and so they won't have to lose their house."

Paula's jaw dropped.

Her grandfather nodded. "Yes, she's really got herself and Freddy into a pickle. And it's not his fault. She lied to him about what she was up to. He thought she was out with her friends—and she was—but at casinos. It's a mess."

"Your grandfather isn't just giving her money, though," David added.

"That's right. I told her I'm not a bank and I have no intention of selling The Whitley—ever. I did tell her we can give her a real job here, though, and put her on salary. David came up with the perfect role for her."

"We thought she'd make a good program director," David said. "She can work with Hallie on putting together some packages where guests come for a long weekend or a week and have an educational experience—like a Nantucket history week where we have talks on different aspects of Nantucket and tours of the local museums. Or a Nantucket foodie week, where we line up cooking demonstrations and luncheons at area restaurants. A knitting weekend or a literature week. She can target her own age demographic especially, as they have the time and money for vacations like that."

"And she's like your cousin Andrea in that she's very social so she can be the hostess for the guests that attend, like a cruise director," her grandfather said. "When David said that, it made sense to me as we had all kinds of similar things on our cruise. And it's another way we can market The Whitley."

"Well, that all sounds like a good plan to me," Paula said. "How can I help?"

"You can oversee Hallie and your Aunt Vivian, and make sure they have the support they need," her grandfather said.

"Now that that is settled, it brings me to our other business. When I first brought David in, I asked him to help you settle into your new role and to give me an honest assessment at the end as to if he thought you were a good fit. I told him it wouldn't change anything as I'd already made my mind up, so your job is safe. But I wanted to know what he thought as someone that has been to a lot of properties. I'll let him share what he told me."

David smiled. "I told your grandfather I was unsure about you at the beginning. When he first told me that he'd promoted his back-office accountant to the general manager role I questioned that decision, but he told me to reserve judgement and to meet you and then I'd understand. So, I did, and I do. I think the biggest obstacle you've had is yourself and if you believed you could do the job and if it would make you happier than being in the office with your numbers. I know you liked that role and resisted this one?"

Paula nodded. "I did. I also felt guilty since I was taking it away from Andrea."

Her grandfather interjected. "But you weren't. Not really. Even if you didn't take the job, I was still going to replace Andrea."

"I know. And that's why I decided to give it a try. And because I didn't want to disappoint you," Paula said.

He smiled. "I don't think you could ever do that, my dear. If you don't want this job, it's not the end of the world. I could just call Elaine and get someone in a New York minute. But of course, I'd rather not do that. But it's up to you."

"I also told your grandfather that I think you're doing an excellent job. And you take feedback well, even when it's not what you want to hear."

Paula knew he was talking about his comment that she was 'too nice.' That had stung.

"You weren't happy with me. I knew it. But you processed the feedback and you tried to do better, and you did. You've grown in the role and I think you could do a great job for a long time, if you choose to."

Her grandfather smiled. "So, it's entirely up to you, my dear. What do you think? Are you happy in the role? If you're not, you can go back to what you used to do."

Paula took a deep breath and looked at both of them. "I didn't think I was going to like the role. To be honest, parts of it scared me a little, being so visible and out there everywhere. But I don't think I could go back to my old role. I think I'd miss the variety in this position and the challenge. I didn't realize it at the time, Grandfather, but you were right. It is a good fit for me. I just had to discover that for myself. I'm happy to stay on as the GM."

Her grandfather beamed. "Well, that's most excellent news. And I think it calls for a toast. There might be a bottle of that bubbly stuff you like in the refrigerator. Want to get it and pour us a cup?"

Paula went to his small office refrigerator and saw the yellow cardboard box that held a bottle of her favorite champagne, Veuve Clicquot. She got it out and brought it over to them.

"You got this for me? You were that sure we'd be celebrating?"

He laughed. "I think I know my granddaughter. You've never backed away from a challenge before. I felt pretty confident that you'd want to stay. And now we can toast and make it official."

Paula poured champagne for each of them and they tapped their glasses together.

"To you, and to The Whitley and many more happy years together," her grandfather said proudly.

CHAPTER 34

Andrea had Tuesday off and was scheduled to work the evening shift at the concierge desk. She slept unusually well and woke feeling rested and lighter and she knew what her decision was. Once she decided, there was no going back and she knew in her heart that she'd made the right decision, for her.

She was about to call Elaine when her phone rang, and it was Ben.

"Hey, there, just calling to say hello and see what your plans are for the weekend. Didn't know if you wanted to do something Friday night?"

"Hi, Ben. Thanks again for showing me around New York. That was such a fun night."

"Of course, anytime. If you take that job, we can do that more often."

Andrea hesitated—she always hated conversations like this, and she really did like Ben. "I've actually decided not to take that job. I'm happier here, and there's also someone that I've recently grown closer to and, well, I think I need to see where that goes. I hope you understand."

"Oh. Yes, of course. I'm disappointed, but I understand. He's a lucky guy, whoever he is."

"Thank you, Ben. It's been great getting to know you."

"You, too. I'm sure I'll see you around."

"I'm sure you will."

Andrea ended the call feeling sad and relieved at the same time. Ben was a really great guy, a catch for the right girl. But that girl wasn't her. There was only one person she wanted to kiss, and she couldn't wait to see him.

She called Elaine next and felt bad after that call, too, as Elaine wasn't going to get a commission from placing her. Hopefully, she could still fill the role, though, as Elaine shared that she represented the other candidate, too. It was a great opportunity, but it just wasn't the right one for her.

Andrea took a little more care than usual with her hair and makeup before going in to work, curling the ends a bit and using a new lipstick in a deep rose shade that made her lips look fuller.

Marco was at the concierge desk when she arrived and he smiled when he saw her, but his expression was guarded as if he was bracing himself for bad news. She walked up to him, smiled big and simply said, "I'm staying."

The light came back into his eyes and his smile matched hers.

"Well, you've made my day. I can swing back by and we can celebrate after your shift, if you like?"

"I would like that very much."

HER SHIFT ENDED AT ELEVEN AND AT A FEW MINUTES OF, MARCO texted her that he was at the outside bar saving her a seat. Andrea practically danced out the door and as soon as she settled into her seat, before she said a word, she leaned over and kissed him. "I've been wanting to do that all day," she admitted.

He grinned. "Just the first of many, I hope."

Andrea ordered a glass of wine, and after it came, she turned to him and raised her glass. "To new beginnings."

"I like that." He clinked his glass against hers. "So, you actually turned down that other job?"

"I did. No regrets, either. I woke up this morning and the decision was made. When I thought about going to New York and taking that GM role, I felt tense and stressed. When I thought about staying here working the concierge desk and being with you—well I only felt happy and at peace."

He leaned over and kissed her, and she felt like she was overflowing with happiness.

"I'm so glad you made that choice. I wasn't looking forward to going to New York to visit you."

"You would have come to see me in New York?"

"Of course. I'm not that easy to get rid of," he teased.

"I don't want to get rid of you."

"Good, because I'm not going anywhere. We're going to have so much fun together."

She smiled. "I know we are."

CHAPTER 35

They got lucky with the weather for the Taste of the Town event. The forecast initially called for it to be overcast, with possible showers, but the winds shifted, and Monday brought nothing but sunshine and warm breezes. There were a few glitches when the electric outlets didn't work correctly in all the sections, but Paula called in an electrician that got it all sorted and working by noon.

The restaurants were all set up in their booths and ready to go by three. The event officially got underway at four and the turnout was even better than expected. Grandfather was thrilled as he strolled around with Paula and David, checking out the different restaurants and their offerings.

"Isn't this marvelous?" he said as they made the rounds to make sure everyone had everything they needed.

"It was a great idea, Grandfather," Paula agreed.

"I just had a feeling it would go over well. There's nothing like it here and what else are people going to do on a Monday night? It's the slowest night for the restaurants and this is a great opportunity for them to show off what they can do."

Peter Bradford was there overseeing all the wine vendors and they ran into him and his girlfriend Paige and her two best friends, Lisa, who owned the Beach Plum Cove Inn, and her friend Sue, who owned an insurance company downtown. They were all sipping wine and snacking on tiny crab cakes from one of the restaurants.

"What do the vendors think?" Paula asked him.

"They're loving it, and a few have already asked if this is going to be an annual thing. You could probably lock most of them in as well as the restaurants for next year if you wanted," Peter said.

Paula looked at her grandfather and at David. Her grandfather smiled. "What do you think about that, Paula?"

Paula looked around at the huge crowd and the busy booths.

"I think that's probably a very good idea. Let's do it."

Her grandfather winked at Peter. "Looks like it's a go for next year."

"I'll let them know."

"We can let the restaurants know, too," David said. "That will make it easier for next year if most of them are already committed."

"I think just about all of my guests at the inn are here," Lisa said. "I'll let them know as well, and maybe they'll want to book with me for next year, too, when they check out. It's a wonderful event. You have all done a great job."

"Thanks so much," Paula said.

They continued to walk around and stopped at Nick's booth, where he was handing out tiny tuna tacos and plating up sample-size portions of rosemary mashed potatoes and short ribs and small cups of seafood chowder. Bella was by his side, adding bags of crackers for the chowder. She looked cute in a Whitley hotel apron, and dark sunglasses. Nick had beads of sweat on his upper lip and was in constant motion, plating food and chatting with people as they came up to the booth.

They waited for a lull before stepping over to say hello.

"How's it going?" Paula asked.

"This is fantastic. People are loving everything. And they're saying good things about all of it, the wine tasting and all the different sampling. I think we might have to do this again next year."

Grandfather laughed. "I think you're right. Peter Bradford already suggested it and we agree. Looks like it's a hit."

He turned to Paula and David. "Why don't you kids go get in line and try all of this good stuff, too? There's nothing else you need to do at this point other than enjoy it. I see someone I need to go visit with."

He left and David turned to Paula. "Shall we?"

They got in line and received a small square tray that had a space for a wine glass to hook into it. It was a clever design that let you set your glass into the tray so you could nibble on the food more easily. They roamed around and tasted a bunch of different wines and lots of food samples. There were so many good options. Most of the restaurants had a soup of some kind or an appetizer and an entrée, and some had a dessert choice, too.

They ran into Andrea and Marco at one of the wine stations and Paula was pleasantly surprised when Andrea was actually friendly.

"You should really try this Charles Krug Cabernet. It's ridiculously good," Andrea said.

Paula noticed that Marco had one of his hands on the small of Andrea's back and they looked like two people in love, or madly in like. Paula was happy for them.

They wandered away, and David and Paula tasted the cabernet that Andrea had raved about.

"She's right, this is really good," David said.

"It is. Sweet and silky and jammy," Paula said.

David laughed. "You sound like a real wine connoisseur."

She smiled. "I just know I like it!"

They continued to walk around and tried everything. A number of the restaurants were ones that she either hadn't been to before or hadn't been to in a long time, and she made a note to go again.

When they finished tasting a bit of everything, they filled their glasses a final time and found a bench to sit on.

"I can't believe tomorrow's your last day," Paula said.

"I know. These weeks went by too fast. I'm heading to see my parents from here for our last pizza dinner and then I fly out in the morning."

"Well, if you come back to visit, stop in and say hello. We'd all love to see you," Paula said. What she really meant was that she'd love to see him, but there didn't seem to be a good reason to say that. He was leaving. There was no future for them—assuming he was even interested, which he'd given no indication of.

"Of course. I'll probably be back in a month or so, when my latest engagement finishes up."

"Kansas City, right?"

He laughed. "Good memory. Yes, Kansas City. It shouldn't take too long."

"Well, I just wanted to say thank you. I appreciate everything you've done for us, and for helping me to settle in."

"It was a fun assignment for me. I'm glad that you decided to stay in the position. I meant what I said. You've really done a good job."

"Thank you." She wanted to say more than that. To let him know she was going to miss him, but it didn't feel appropriate. Instead, she finished her glass and stood up.

"You should probably get to your parents'. They're probably anxious to see you."

He smiled. "You're probably right. Take good care, Paula. Let's keep in touch."

Her heart leaped at the suggestion, but she knew he was probably just being polite. He gave her a hug goodbye and she wanted to hold on tighter, liking the feeling of being in his arms.

"Goodbye, David."

CHAPTER 36

Bella had so much fun helping Nick at the tasting event. They even had a chance to try everything, too, as when it slowed a bit, one of the cooks took over for Nick so they could take a quick break. They raced around, sampling what they could and tasting a few wines before making their way back to the booth.

Once the event was over and everything was broken down and put away, they went to the outside bar and had one drink each. Bella was overly aware that her time there was slipping away. She only had a few more days left and then she'd be heading home to L.A. and would begin shooting for the new film. She was excited about the film. Her agent had Fedexed the script and it was very good—very close to the book—which was exceptional. The story gave Bella the shivers and she knew it was going to be an important film and possibly huge for her.

But she dreaded leaving Nick. To his credit, he'd been great about it and kept reassuring her that it would all work out somehow. Once she knew her schedule, she was going to let him know so he could put in for the time off and book his visit to see her. She was excited about that, for the chance to play tourist with him in her world. She just hoped that it didn't overwhelm him. He hadn't really experienced what the media could be like. It wasn't pretty.

Andrea and Marco were just leaving when they arrived at the

bar. Bella noticed that they were holding hands and she was happy for them.

"They're official now, I see," she said to Nick once they were seated at the bar.

"Yep. I think it's great. They seem to be good together."

"They look happy. That's all that matters, right?"

Nick leaned over and kissed her. "Yes, that's all that matters."

THREE DAYS LATER HE DROVE HER TO THE AIRPORT. THEY'D HAD A special, romantic evening the night before. Nick had cooked an amazing meal for her, and they'd just cuddled on his sofa and she never wanted to leave. But they both knew she had to go the next day. It was so hard to say goodbye—to kiss him knowing she wouldn't be able to see him or kiss him again for a long time.

"Text me when you land," Nick said.

"I will."

"Bella, there's something I want you to know, before you go…" There was a sudden urgency to Nick's voice that alarmed her.

"What is it?"

He grinned. "Just that I love you. I wanted you to know that."

She felt her eyes well up. "Nick. I love you, too. So much." She kissed him again and didn't want to let go. But eventually she had to. It was time to board her plane.

"I'll text you when I land."

THE FIRST THING THEY DID WHEN BELLA SHOWED UP ON SET WAS TO find a hairdresser to fix her hair. They got rid of the red and brought back the blond. And then the Bella they wanted was back. She threw herself into the work, lost herself in the character and focused on making the best film possible. By the time she got home each night, she was utterly exhausted and spent. But it helped because otherwise she was just missing Nick.

They spoke most nights, even if just for a few minutes. It was strange being back in L.A. It felt foreign to her and she realized it had never felt like home. It was just a place where she worked and slept. Her life, her real home, was with Nick on Nantucket. But that wasn't her reality, unfortunately. Nantucket was being on vacation. L.A. was back to work.

Once she knew her schedule and when there was going to be a light week, she let Nick know and he booked a flight out. Knowing he was coming got her through the next few weeks.

———————

NICK FLEW IN ON A FRIDAY AND BELLA MET HIM AT THE AIRPORT. She started crying happy tears when she saw him. It had been so long, and she'd missed him so much. He pulled her into his arms, and she wanted to stay there.

"It's so good to see you. I've missed you so much," she said.

"Not as much as I've missed you." He grinned. "So, let's see L.A.!"

She took him everywhere, showed him all the usual tourist spots. They had spicy chicken pizza at Spago and walked along the Hollywood Walk of Fame, the sidewalk where celebrities had stars embedded in the sidewalk. They drove along the Pacific Coast Highway to Malibu and Nick agreed that it was beautiful, but Nantucket was still prettier.

And it was in Malibu that Nick experienced the media for the first time. They'd gone to Nobu for sushi and had a wonderful dinner. But on the way out, paparazzi were waiting and as soon as they saw Bella and Nick, they pounced, snapping pictures and peppering Bella with questions.

"Who is he, Cami? Is this your new boyfriend? Is he an actor? What is he in? Talk to us, Cami!"

She ignored them and instead rushed Nick to her car and they drove off. Her nerves were on edge and she didn't begin to relax until they were a mile down the road. Nick was quiet beside her.

Finally, he spoke. "I didn't really get it when you always wore those glasses and didn't want anyone to recognize you. I get it now. That was intense. Is it always like that?"

"If they see me, yes. It's partly my fault, though. Nobu is a pretty visible place and the paparazzi are always on the lookout there. But the food is amazing, and I knew you'd love it."

"I'm glad we went there. It was a perfect night. I'm also glad that I experienced the craziness that you deal with all the time. It helps me understand it. And I'm sorry that it's a regular thing for you."

She sighed. "It goes along with what I do. I don't like it, but I can't really complain about it. Plenty of people would love to be in my shoes. I'm very lucky to be able to do this."

"I get what you're saying. Celebrities know that fame is a part of the package. And the more famous and successful you are, the worse it is. But still, it has to be annoying."

Bella laughed. "That's an understatement. But it's better now, since you're here with me."

NICK KEPT CALM BUT HE WAS SHAKEN UP BY WHAT HE'D JUST experienced. The level of intensity and entitlement toward Bella was astounding. He was frightened for her safety. He remembered when Princess Diana was killed when she was being chased by paparazzi and the driver of her car lost control.

"Do they ever chase you?" he asked.

"Yes, all the time. If I'm out walking somewhere. Not driving, though. I won't let that happen."

"Good. Just be careful. Those people are crazy."

He didn't realize how crazy until he saw the newspapers the next day and the entertainment shows on cable and the internet. Social media was blowing up with coverage of 'Cami's New Boy'. In an instant, his whole life had been investigated and displayed online. Where he worked, what he did, who he last dated. It was all there. And it freaked him out. And Bella knew it.

The worry on her face was evident. "Are you okay? This is awful, I know. It's bad enough that they do it to me. I'm used to it. You didn't sign up for this. I'm so sorry, Nick."

He tried to reassure her. "But I did sign up for this. I just didn't fully realize it." He grinned. "Coming out here to see you, loving you. It's all part of who you are and being in your world."

She looked a little relieved to hear it. "It's still so unfair to you, though."

"Well, I'm not going to lie. It was nicer when we were both on Nantucket and no one knew you were there or who I was."

She looked sad. "That was vacation, not reality unfortunately."

"It's okay. We'll be okay." Nick tried to reassure her, and himself.

His week with her seemed to go by in an instant. And when she drove him to the airport and they kissed goodbye, he felt a huge wave of sadness. Before, when she left, they both knew he'd be flying out to see her in a few weeks. Now, they didn't have a plan. She still had at least two months of filming and he didn't have any more time off to use. He didn't know when they'd see each other next. He only knew it was much too far off for his liking.

CHAPTER 37

The bomb-sniffing dogs came first with the secret service security team that arrived the day before the President was due. They were beautiful animals, but it seemed odd to see them roaming the halls and going from room to room along with their handlers.

Paula and the housekeeping team had gone above and beyond to make sure the President's rooms were perfect. Paula had taken it upon herself to add some extra comforts, such as some sweet-smelling candles, a box of chocolates and a few new releases from local authors. She knew the President was a big reader and thought maybe he'd enjoy them, if he had any downtime to read.

She was surprised and dismayed to see that the President's immaculately cleaned rooms were pulled apart by the security team as they looked for who knew what in every possible nook and cranny. Beds were stripped, drawers taken out of dressers as the room was thoroughly searched. Finally, she was given the word that they could go clean up again. She immediately apologized to the housekeeping team and pitched in to help them redo the rooms.

And it didn't help matters at all when later that day she ran into Missy, who was at the hotel for a chamber of commerce luncheon. Paula regularly tried to attend these gatherings as she knew it was good PR for The Whitley, even when they weren't held at the hotel. Typically, the meetings rotated locations.

This time, at least, Missy appeared to recognize her and at first, seemed sweet enough. "Oh, hello, Paula, nice to see you again. The food here was wonderful, as usual. I bet you're missing David? I'm sure he was a huge help to you. Have you heard from him since he's been gone?"

Paula shook her head. "No, not yet. I don't think he's expected back for at least another month—to see his parents."

"Of course. He might be coming back to see his family, but he's also going to be attending the literacy gala with me at the country club. I don't suppose you'll be there?"

"I wasn't planning on it," Paula said. She'd never been to it before. It was one of those snooty events held at the most expensive country club on the island and unless you were a member or good friend of a member, you didn't make the cut for that guest list.

"You really should go sometime. It's a fabulous event. Well, nice seeing you." She sauntered off and Paula was left feeling grumpy and out of sorts. She didn't care about not going to the event, but she was disappointed to learn that David might be attending it with Missy. He hadn't mentioned that they were seeing each other, but then again, why would he? And it made sense since they had shared history and were both single. She thought he had better taste than that, though.

After all the anticipation for the Taste of the Town event, the following week felt anti-climactic and oddly quiet. Paula supposed she was missing David's presence, too. She'd grown used to having him right down the hall and bouncing ideas off of him. But she was slowly getting used to doing that with her grandfather and Hallie and Nick instead. And surprisingly, even her Aunt Vivian. Now that she had a defined job, and the stress from her financial mess was resolved, her aunt had thrown herself into her work and was doing a good job. Better than anyone expected, and she seemed to be thriving and enjoying it.

Aunt Vivian also happened to overhear the exchange with Missy.

"She's a bit of a witch, isn't she? My guess is she hasn't heard boo from David, otherwise why would she be asking you if you'd heard from him?"

Paula laughed. "That's a good point." Though she wouldn't put it past Missy to ask just to see if she could get a rise out of Paula and to make sure she knew that Missy and David had plans. But, like her aunt said, if things were solid between them, she wouldn't care or be fishing for information. She hoped that was the case. Missy really didn't seem to be David's type. Or at least Paula didn't think she was right for him. Who knew what David actually thought?

DAVID WAS MISERABLE IN KANSAS CITY. HE FELT LIKE A FISH OUT OF water there, for one thing. It was just so different from New York and Boston. But, more than anything, it wasn't Nantucket, and he was surprised by how much he missed being at The Whitley. Well, more accurately how much he missed being around Paula. Even though there hadn't been anything romantic with them, he missed her presence, missed discussing business ideas with her, having lunch together, and chatting about nothing in particular.

And more than anything, he realized he was totally over traveling. He'd done it for so long that he never gave it much of a thought. It was just part of his job. But he'd put a big part of his life on hold to do that job. He hadn't had a serious relationship of any kind in too many years.

Spending several months at home on Nantucket and especially seeing his parents regularly was a gift. It made him realize that time was precious and for his mother, it was slipping away, and he didn't want to have regrets when she passed that he didn't see her enough. He wasn't sure how he was going to make it happen, but he knew his current work life wasn't sustainable.

It needed to change. He needed to change. The question was how? He decided to approach finding a solution the same way he would approach it for any of his clients. Assess his options, identify possibilities and put a plan into action. He just needed to figure out what that plan would be.

CHAPTER 38

"Cami and her co-star Cameron are inseparable, and sources say an engagement announcement could come any day!" The cover of Stars magazine showed a picture of Bella and some pretty blond actor sitting in a car at an In-and-Out Burger. Aunt Vivian pushed the copy of the magazine toward Nick and he shoved it away so hard that it slid off the table.

It was a Sunday afternoon, and they were all sitting around the dining room table. They'd already eaten dinner and moved on to drinking coffee and snacking on coffee cake for dessert.

"I just thought you'd want to know, honey," Aunt Vivian said.

"I appreciate that," Nick said slowly. "But the media lies. You can't believe anything. That's what Bella always says."

His mother sipped her coffee and then weighed in. "We just worry about you honey. This all happened so fast with Bella. She seems lovely, but you really don't know her well. Maybe she has moved on and it makes sense she'd pick someone in the industry who understands what she is going through. Maybe it's time for you to do the same thing."

"What are you saying?" Nick tried not to sound as angry as he felt at the suggestion. He knew his mother loved him and meant well. But she just didn't understand how he felt about Bella and how she felt about him. They were in love and it was real.

"Just that it might not be real, honey. She was here on vacation. For an escape from reality. And she met you and liked you a lot, but you might be part of that fantasy, a vacation fling. I just wouldn't put so much weight on it lasting. You have a lot of strikes against you. And many miles."

She was right about that. They were on opposite sides of the country—about as far apart as possible—and unless he were to move to LA, that wasn't likely to change anytime soon.

"The distance is hard," he agreed.

"I'm just thinking it might be a good idea for you to move on, too. Get out there and meet some new people, that actually live on Nantucket. There are plenty of eligible women," his mother said.

"She's right," Paula agreed. "Don't get me wrong, I love Bella, too. I just hate seeing you so sad."

Lucy nodded. "I just wouldn't put all your eggs in the Bella basket. Even if you don't date anyone else right away, you need to stop putting your life on hold, and start living again—go out and have fun with your friends, come out with us."

He had been hibernating too much. Rushing home to make sure he was there to chat with Bella when she called. He hadn't gone out with his friends or even his family in a few weeks and that wasn't like him.

He nodded. "You're all right. Not that things need to end with Bella, I don't know how that is going to go, but I agree that I need to start having fun again. So, where are we going after dinner?"

BELLA WORRIED THAT NICK MIGHT BE SLOWLY SLIPPING AWAY FROM her. And she didn't blame him one bit. She'd been furious when the pics of her and Cam hit the internet and at the predictions about an engagement. It was so untrue—they were simply sharing burgers together, getting off-set for lunch and talking about how they were going to approach their scenes later that afternoon. Cam had never even looked twice at her. Not romantically. She wasn't his type—no woman was.

And it was frustrating because she knew his publicist had sent the tip to the media. Cam was at the beginning of a booming career as a romantic comedy star and was deeply locked in the closet. He hated it and wanted to be truthful, but all of his advisors told him it would be career suicide and a huge financial loss if he came clean too soon in his career. She understood that, but she didn't like being used as part of his chess game.

The only good thing was that it got the media focus off of Nick. She'd called him the minute the story hit, to assure him it wasn't remotely true. He'd seemed to understand, but he also was a bit distant lately as if something had shifted. She'd never had trouble reaching him before—now her calls often went to voice mail and he called her back hours later. Each time, he said he'd been out with friends or family at a bar or restaurant where it was too loud to talk on the phone and he didn't want to be rude to his friends, either. She understood that, but she'd also gotten used to being his first priority, so it didn't feel so good to be shifted down the list. But, at the same time, she was glad he was getting out and having fun. She just wished she was there with him.

She still had another whole month of filming ahead of her. They were on a six day a week schedule to wrap as soon as possible, which was good, but it didn't leave enough time for even a quick trip to Nantucket. Once they wrapped, she planned to fly there immediately. She couldn't wait to see Nick. And in the meantime, she was trying to come up with a way to stay there longer. She had something in the works and was crossing her fingers and hoping that everything would fall the way it needed to. Then she could share her good news with Nick. And hopefully, it wouldn't be too late for them.

CHAPTER 39

Bella was being all mysterious and Nick was intrigued. Her plane was due in at a quarter to four and Nick was at the Nantucket airport at three thirty. She'd been hinting for a few weeks that she had something big brewing but didn't want to say anything until it was certain. She was afraid she'd jinx herself. He tried to get her to spill but she just told him to be patient and when she saw him, she'd explain everything and hopefully have some very good news to share. She was still waiting on a final phone call, which hadn't come before she left L.A.

He parked, went into the airport and got a cup of coffee while he waited. It was a Friday afternoon so there was a steady stream of private jets flying in and taking off. Right on time, he saw a Jet Blue plane landing and walked outside to wait for Bella.

His heart jumped when he saw her walk off the plane. She scanned the area and then smiled and waved when she saw him. She ran over to him and he pulled her into a bear hug before kissing her hello and then finally speaking. "I can't believe you're finally here," he said.

She smiled. "You said I can stay with you for as long as I want, right?"

Nick laughed. "Yes. Forever, if that works for you."

She laughed and he realized she probably thought he was

kidding. But he'd be happy if she stayed indefinitely. He knew that wasn't likely, though. He'd settle for a week or two but hoped for longer.

They walked over to where the luggage racks were being wheeled over from the plane. Bella looked for hers and he was a little surprised to see she had two giant suitcases, more than what she'd had when she stayed at The Whitley for several months. She laughed when she saw his expression.

"I warned you I might stay a while. Let's go home and I'll fill you in."

They chatted about inconsequential things on the ride to Nick's house. He told her about the latest goings on at The Whitley and she updated him on the gossip around her film and also the buzz was really good.

"I think it's the best thing I've ever done, and everyone felt it was their best work, too. We're all so excited to see how the movie does. It feels like it might be big."

"I'm really happy for you. I read the book, by the way. Just finished it yesterday and you're right. It's something special."

When they got to the house, he carried in her bags and she followed with her carry-on. Once they were inside, she pulled a bottle of champagne out of her bag and went into the kitchen and opened it over the sink, so it wouldn't spill.

He got two glasses out of a cupboard for her and she filled them both. She carried them into the living room and they settled on the sofa in their usual spots. She handed him one of the glasses, and then took off her sunglasses and, as always, he was mesmerized by those gorgeous eyes of hers.

"So, what are we celebrating?"

She took a sip and smiled. "I have some really big news, huge, life-changing. For both of us." She paused dramatically.

"What is it?" He couldn't take the suspense.

"It just closed. I got the final call when I landed. So now it's official. I started a production company—Nantucket Rose Films."

"Congratulations. Love the name. So, what does that actually mean?"

"Not a whole lot, until I have something in production, and now I do. That was the phone call I was waiting on. So, first I optioned a book series and put a team together—a director, screenwriter and actress, which is me, and pitched the project to Netflix as a limited TV series. And they just said yes."

"Bella, that's awesome!" Nick knew it was huge for her and he was proud of her, but he wasn't sure it solved their problem as filming was still likely to be in Hollywood. "Where is the show set?"

She smiled. "Well, that's the best part. It's a six-book women's fiction series, set on Nantucket. And we'll be filming most of it here."

Now he was well and truly stunned. "Here? Not in Hollywood?"

"Here. I'll still have to fly to Hollywood a few times, but just for a day or two. The majority of the work can be done here."

"Are you sure you want to give up film, though?" He loved the idea of her working on Nantucket, but not if it meant it could hurt her career-wise.

"I'm not giving it up. I'm just being pickier about what I do. This will keep me here for the next year or so and I'll look into other projects after that. I will look into producing my own films, too, which will give me more control over everything. If this series goes well, it will be easier for me to get other projects made."

"Well, this is the best news ever. I'm thrilled for you. For both of us."

"And you're sure you don't mind me staying longer than you expected?" she teased him. "I can always rent a place if it's inconvenient."

He leaned over and kissed her to stop the ridiculousness. "I meant what I said, you can stay here for as long as you like. Forever wouldn't be too long for me."

"I hoped you'd feel that way."

"Hold that thought. I'll be right back." Nick jumped up and ran upstairs to his bedroom, pulled open the top drawer of his dresser and rummaged around until he found what he was looking for. He went back downstairs and resumed his spot on the sofa.

Bella raised her eyebrows at him. "What was all that about?"

He grinned and held out the small chocolate brown velvet box and flipped open the top. "This."

Her jaw dropped at the sight of the antique diamond ring.

"Nick," she began.

"Bella, I spotted this not long after you first went back to Hollywood. I was downtown walking around and something made me walk into a jewelry store I'd never set foot in before and it drew me towards it. One look and I knew that I wanted to give it to you. I wasn't sure when that would be, but I bought it that day and I've kept it in a drawer upstairs ever since. And it feels like the right time now."

Nick stood, turned around to face Bella and got down on one knee. He held the ring up. "Bella, will you marry me? I meant what I said about forever. When I think of forever, I see it with you. If you'll have me."

Her eyes filled with tears that spilled over as she spoke. "Of course, I will. I love you, Nick."

CHAPTER 40

P aula was in her office Friday and was thinking about what to do for lunch when her phone rang, and it was her brother, Nick.

"Hi, Nick, what's up?"

"Just wanted to let you know Bella and I are having a cookout on Sunday to celebrate our engagement. Everyone is coming—the rest of the family, Andrea, Marco all our friends. And, hopefully you."

She laughed. Nick had told them the good news the day after he'd proposed to Bella and also let them know that she was going to be on Nantucket for at least the next year. They were all thrilled for both of them. "Of course. I'll be there. Let me know what I can bring."

"Whatever you feel like bringing, bottle of wine or a dip or something, it's all good. There will be tons of food."

"I have no doubt. Sounds like fun."

Paula hung up the phone and stared out the window, watching the surf crash on the shore. It was early October, but the weather on Nantucket was still beautiful. The fall was always her favorite time of year on the island. It was less crowded with tourists and still warm enough to go to the beach. She thought about Nick and Bella and was really happy for her brother. She'd never seen him like this with anyone before. And they all really liked Bella.

Everyone seemed settled and happy these days. Lucy was going strong with Jason and Andrea and Marco were pretty serious. She'd never seen Andrea so relaxed and downright pleasant. It was nice to see. And then there was Paula. She hadn't heard a word from David, but she hadn't really expected that she would. She was feeling pretty good overall, though, as she'd really settled into her new job and was enjoying it more than she'd ever imagined that she would. She was glad that she'd stepped out of the back office and her comfort zone to try something new.

She poured herself another cup of coffee and checked some emails while she tried to decide what to do about lunch. She could run home and make a sandwich or order something to be sent up from the restaurant. She was just about to look up the restaurant menu when there was a tap on her door. She turned and did a double take when she saw David standing there.

"Hey, there. Sorry to interrupt. I thought I might catch you before you went to lunch. I just dropped something off for your grandfather. Truthfully, I could have mailed it, but I wanted an excuse to say hello."

"Hi! How are you?"

He smiled. "I'm good. Really good. Any chance you might want to grab some lunch?"

"I'd love to…I was about to call the restaurant, actually. We can just go down there, if that works."

"Works for me."

A few minutes later they were seated by the window and once they put their orders in, David continued to surprise her.

"So, I have some news. I'm not just visiting. I've moved back to Nantucket."

"For good?" Paula couldn't believe it.

"Yes. I rented a condo downtown and I'm going to rent an office at my dad's law firm."

"What will you be doing?"

"Well, I was miserable in Kansas City, and I had a lot of time on my hands to research possible business ideas. I approached it like it was a consulting gig for one of my clients and I'm pretty excited about what I came up with. I'm going to do consulting still, but focus on Nantucket and Boston and New York clients, and I'm also going to develop a series of educational trainings that hotels can use for new employees. There's a real need for it and it lines up with my area of expertise. It's also something I can do from anywhere."

Paula was impressed. "David, that sounds really great. Your parents must be thrilled."

"They are. Especially my dad. He likes the idea of having me in the office and just having me around. My mother seems enthusiastic but I'm not sure she really understands it the same way. But that's okay. I'll still be able to see her more often and that's the main thing."

"I think that's wonderful."

When their meals came, they chatted as they ate, and Paula caught him up on everyone that they knew and on Bella and Nick's engagement.

"They seemed like a great couple. I'm glad they were able to find a way to be together."

When they finished, David insisted on paying the check and walked her back to her office.

"So, there's one more thing," he said as she was about to walk through her door.

"What's that?"

"Well, now that I'm back here and we're not working together, how would you feel like getting dinner, possibly tomorrow night?"

She smiled. "I'd love that."

"Good. Oh, and there's also this…" He leaned over and kissed her lightly. And it was every bit as good as she'd imagined it would be. He grinned. "I've kind of wanted to do that for a while."

"Me, too," she admitted. "Oh, about dinner tomorrow night. I forgot that I already have plans."

His face fell. "Oh, okay. Another night, then."

She grabbed his hand. "No, I have plans already but that's okay. Nick and Bella are having a party to celebrate their engagement, and everyone will be there. I'd love for you to come with me, if you'd like. It should be fun."

"That sounds perfect to me."

EPILOGUE

Paula held a holiday open house the Saturday of Nantucket's Christmas Stroll weekend in December. She was excited to host everyone for the first time and they were all in a festive mood. David had helped her decorate the outside of her cottage and surrounding bushes with white twinkling lights. She'd just finishing making a big bowl of Christmas Sangria, with sparkling wine, crushed fruit and a container of rainbow sherbet. It was her signature cocktail and the family demanded she make it every year.

She and David went downtown the night before so David could experience his first Christmas Stroll in years. They'd walked up and down Main Street and all the side streets, stopping into various shops and participating in a gingerbread cookie decorating event. After walking up an appetite, they'd had dinner at Mimi's Place. It was pretty much a perfect night.

And now, as Paula looked around the kitchen and living room of her cottage, she smiled with contentment. Everyone she cared about was there. Nick and Bella were still deliriously happy and she'd just started shooting on her new Netflix show. Andrea and Marco were mixing margaritas over by the sink and laughing as they argued about who made a better one. Paula was actually starting to enjoy Andrea's company and her cousin seemed to be making an effort to be less ornery, which was much appreciated. Marco seemed to have a good influence on her.

Her sister and Jason were doing well, too. And Lucy's Etsy store was very busy for the holidays. She was working nights and week-ends to keep up with the demand and seemed to be loving it.

Aunt Vivian and Uncle Freddy were chatting with Paula's and Andrea's parents. Andrea's father had recently started a new job as a rep with a food supply company in Hyannis and was handling all of the Nantucket accounts. Andrea and Hallie both said they'd never seen their father enjoying his work like this before. They'd all wondered what his mysterious trip off-island was about and he said he'd kept quiet until he knew he had the job, because he didn't want to get anyone's hopes up.

Mia and Izzy were there, too, with their neighbor, Ben. He was getting ready to head back to Manhattan for the winter and was still hoping to eventually spend more and more time on Nantucket. Paula noticed with interest that he and Hallie were engaged in a spirited conversation and seemed to be hitting it off.

"It really is good to be back," David said. He'd walked over to where Paula was opening a new bottle of wine. Everyone else was gathered around the food table in the living room. And there was so much food, everyone had brought an appetizer or dessert.

"It's too bad your mom and dad couldn't make it," Paula said.

"We'll see them tomorrow. I think this many people might be overwhelming for my mother, and stressful for my dad, worrying about her. They're really doing great, though."

David's mother was stable and her doctor was pleased that her disease seemed to be staying steady instead of getting progressively worse.

"Just think, this time next week, we'll be in Rome," Paula said.

David grinned. "We're going to eat our way through Italy, and then London and Paris, too."

They were leaving on Sunday for Paula's dream vacation, made even better because David was going with her. They were going for two weeks. She hadn't taken that much time off at once in years.

"It's perfect. We'll be home just in time for Christmas," she said

David laughed and looked up. "Speaking of Christmas..." They were standing under one of the several sprigs of mistletoe that Paula hung earlier.

"Merry Christmas, Paula," he said softly
And then he kissed her.

THANK YOU SO MUCH FOR READING! I HOPE YOU ENJOYED THIS story. If you'd like to keep in touch, please visit my website for updates on new releases.

Watch for Nantucket News, book 7 in my Nantucket Beach Plum Cove series. To receive a notification when that is available or the preorder goes live, join my mailing list.

If you haven't started that series, click here for The Nantucket Inn.

If you like a little mystery in your women's fiction, please check out my newest release, Plymouth Undercover, set in my hometown.

Have you read The Restaurant yet? That is my biggest seller so far.

Thanks so much!

Pam

ABOUT THE AUTHOR

Pamela M. Kelley is a USA Today and Wall Street Journal best-selling author of women's fiction, family sagas, and suspense. Readers often describe her books as feel-good reads with people you'd want as friends.

She lives in a historic seaside town near Cape Cod and just south of Boston. She has always been an avid reader of women's fiction, romance, mysteries, thrillers and cook books. There's also a good chance you might get hungry when you read her books as she is a foodie, and occasionally shares a recipe or two.

She also has a very friendly and fun reader group on Facebook, please join the Pamela Kelley Reader Group there.

CPSIA information can be obtained
at www.ICGtesting.com
Printed in the USA
BVHW080416111122
651666BV00019B/1100/J